About the Author

Kate Wyburn attended the Royal College of Music, London, for two years. She then played the oboe in theatre orchestras and a wind quintet (as well as holding down a full-time office job) before starting a family. While raising her two children, she taught oboe for a few years but then changed to yoga teaching, after obtaining a qualification in the subject. More recently she has earned a living as a bookkeeper.

She now lives with her husband in East Anglia, where she has played a major role in caring for her mother. In her leisure time she sings in choirs as well as playing the piano.

COUNTERPOINT

Kate Wyburn

COUNTERPOINT

Vanguard Press

A CIP catalogue record for this title is
available from the British Library.

ISBN 978 1 80016 417 8

Vanguard Press is an imprint of
Pegasus Elliot Mackenzie Publishers Ltd.
www.pegasuspublishers.com

First Published in 2023

Vanguard Press
Sheraton House Castle Park
Cambridge England

Printed & Bound in Great Britain

Dedication

For my parents,
who instilled a love of music into my life.

Acknowledgements

I would like to thank my husband and other family members and friends who have put up with my absent-mindedness while writing this book.

Special thanks go to my brother, Martyn, who read the first draft and drew on his drama experience to make many useful suggestions; also, to my daughter-in-law, Emily, who proofread at a later stage and sorted out numerous details. My friend, Janet Denniss, was very supportive throughout the publishing process and helped me to make some final amendments. Her husband, Trevor, very kindly took the author photo.

Finally, many thanks to Pegasus Publishing Ltd who offered clear guidance and made the book a reality.

2018

Chapter 1

Luke was enduring the annual visit to a Norfolk carol concert with his mother. As usual, they had arrived at the last minute so that the whole audience could witness Delia Braithwaite and her famous son making their way to the front of the church, where there was a space reserved for wheelchair users. They were accompanied by Jenny, Delia's current carer.

This annual outing was an ordeal for Luke for two reasons. Firstly, he was already sated with Christmas music, having conducted several carol concerts and similar events in London; and secondly, he normally worked with professional musicians, some of the best in the UK, and a provincial choir and orchestra usually fell short of the standard he was used to. The conductor was clearly a sensitive musician and the choir had obviously worked hard on the music but as the concert progressed, Luke couldn't help wincing when his sense of perfect pitch was assaulted by the singers sliding into flatness in an unaccompanied piece.

There were compensations, however. The church was beautiful with its wide window recesses adorned with holly, ivy, poinsettia, and the results of a competition for the best seasonal arrangement. The scent of pine filled the air, courtesy of an enormous Christmas tree and best of all, this was an opportunity for Luke to relax.

Smiling didn't come easily to him but at the end of the first choir piece, he turned to his mother and tried his best. She wore a contraption to keep herself upright because osteoporosis was crippling her spine, so the movement required to return his smile was not very successful. Luke knew that it was tiring and painful for her to be in a wheelchair for long periods and wished with all his heart that he could reduce her suffering, but he could never seem to find the right words to show that he sympathised. He wasn't very good at conversation with anyone — coming over as gruff and unfriendly, and preferring to communicate through music — but for some reason, he was at his worst with this mother. She was interested in people, so constantly sought personal information about well-known musicians who had crossed his path, whereas he was only interested in whether they performed the music well.

Despite this, they always made an effort at Christmas, because it was one of the few times they could go out together. In order to make this possible, Delia chose a concert as close to Christmas Day as possible and Luke had to avoid scheduling anything that would clash with it. This was their annual ritual and he knew that she would be bitterly disappointed if he ever failed to get there. This year it had worked out well because the concert venue was the Sheringham church that the Braithwaite family knew well, so Delia was especially happy to have Luke by her side. In the interval she would want to show him off to old friends, and he would be a 'Good Boy' and go along with this.

Luke amused himself in the audience participation carols by singing a beautifully executed bass line (attracting annoyed glances from the choir basses whose notes were taken from printed music in an edition which didn't always coincide with Luke's version!) In the choir items, he allowed his mind to wander. At one point, a boy of about eight sang a solo and this took him back to his own childhood, when he had stood on almost the same spot, nervously singing the first verse of *Once in Royal David's City* with his musical parents looking on and bursting with pride. His father had made him practise until he could sing it in his sleep. Eric Braithwaite was himself a pianist, a music critic for East Anglian newspapers and an adjudicator at music festivals. He never seemed very interested in what Luke was doing unless it was musical, and even if it was, it was hard to earn his praise. He had died of a stroke some years ago, but Luke still felt as though he was looking over his shoulder at every performance he undertook.

The interval was as expected, with Delia glowing with pride as she presented Luke to as many friends and acquaintances as she could possibly cram into the time. For someone in such a high-profile profession, Luke was not socially adept but he gamely did his best to say something intelligent and appropriate to each one, then sank back into his seat with relief when the bell sounded for the start of the second half of the concert. Jenny hadn't left her place in the interval and was wrapped up in her mobile phone. He hoped that she'd remember to switch it off when the singing recommenced because electronic 'music' was one of his pet hates. In rehearsal, anyone guilty of letting a phone make a noise would have to deal with his famously sharp tongue, so one going off right next to him in a concert would be embarrassing.

He was tired after several late nights and a tedious journey, so had to fight sleep as the concert progressed. (It would be even more embarrassing to be seen nodding off in the front row.) Towards the end he was losing the fight and sinking into a light doze, despite the threat of humiliation, when a solo soprano voice caught his attention. He quickly scanned the choir to locate the owner of the voice and identified a youngish woman with light brown hair that was swept into a chignon. Her voice was plaintive, desolate, almost unearthly, and it was perfect for a small but significant part he was struggling to fill in one of his own compositions that was due to be recorded in January. The solo passage was short, but Luke straightened up in his seat and watched the woman for the rest of the concert. Her face was unusually mobile with expressions that perfectly reflected the sentiments of whatever she was singing. He decided to speak with her at the end. It might upset his mother who, no doubt, hoped to include him in more conversations, but this was too important to miss. When the final applause died down and the choir filed out, he told Delia he'd be back shortly and before she could say anything, made a beeline for the room off the main church that the choir was using.

***

Mary was tired and didn't really want to speak to anyone after the concert but engaging in conversation with the audience was expected. So, when a good-looking, middle-aged man asked if he might have a word with her, she quickly replaced her worn-out expression with what she hoped was a welcoming smile. (Luke almost missed her because her pale, drawn, exhausted face was so very different to the one he'd witnessed during the concert, but as soon as she smiled, he was sure he had the right person.)

'I'm struggling to fill a part in a work that I'm recording after Christmas and I think you have the perfect voice for it,' he said, instead of the complimentary remarks she might have been expecting. 'Can we get together tomorrow so that I can show you what's involved?'

Mary gave a half laugh of surprise and disbelief, saying that he must have the wrong person. She pointed out the female soloist on the other side of the room.

'But you had a short solo, as well,' protested Luke. 'It's definitely your voice I'm interested in.'

Mary said that she was not a professional musician, had never recorded anything in her life and didn't think she could do anything like that.

Luke said that he could soon knock her voice into shape if they spent a little time together. He was in the area until Boxing Day, so could he call on her tomorrow?

'No!' exclaimed Mary in alarm, forgetting that she was supposed to be making polite conversation, 'Look, I don't know who you are but it's out of the question for me to do anything like that. I don't have time for one thing, and I don't want to be "knocked into shape".'

This was not going well for Luke. He reflected that she must be the only person in the room who didn't know who he was, and he was used to people being flattered rather than panicked if he asked them to work for him.

'I can see you're tired,' he said, fishing in his pocket and producing a card. 'Will you take this, think about it and ring me tomorrow?'

Mary was indeed exhausted, so she briefly nodded and took the card, just to get rid of him. Then she turned abruptly and headed for the cloakroom before he could say anything else.

As she was looking for her coat amid piles of others, her friend Fran came in and asked what Luke Braithwaite had been talking to her about.

'Everyone was really envious and we're all wondering why he picked you out.'

Mary glanced at the card that Luke had given her and realised that she had heard his name mentioned on Radio 3.

'I didn't know who he was while he was talking,' she informed Fran, with a sigh. 'But now I know his name I can place him. I've heard music that he's conducted but never actually seen him, so I didn't recognise him.' She recounted the conversation in as much detail as she could remember and added that she had probably insulted a Very Important Person and hoped that it wouldn't reflect badly on the choir.

'I wouldn't worry about that,' said Fran. 'He and the lady in the wheelchair — his mum, according to one of the basses — are talking to our conductor now and they all look perfectly happy, but I hope you're going to ring him tomorrow to say you'll do it. It could be the chance of a lifetime.'

Mary said she'd think about it but must get home before she became too tired to drive safely.

Home was a social-housing bungalow with special-needs adaptations, in Cromer. Mary and her son Sam had moved there following the departure of Adrian — Sam's father. It was designed to cope with the various items of equipment she had used to care for her son but was quite pleasant in many ways. There was a large central hallway, a sunny lounge, wet room and two bedrooms. The garden was paved but Mary had done her best to brighten it up with plants in tubs and shrubs trained against the fences. She was especially proud of the honeysuckle that had spread everywhere and blessed the air with its heady fragrance in the summer months. She liked gardening but there was never time to do much because of the long hours she worked in a care home for the elderly.

When Sam lived there, indoors had looked more like a hospital ward than a home because of the equipment that was in constant use, but now that had all gone, revealing many scuff marks and stains and the whole place looked shabby and in need of redecoration. In one corner of the lounge stood Mary's piano. Recently, she'd had it tuned in a fit of determination to revive her playing skills after many years of neglect, and some new music rested on top, but she hadn't done much with it yet, usually being too tired after work. She did keep the choir going, though. That had been the one thing she kept for herself through the long years of looking after her son, paying for a carer to sit with him so she could go to the practices and concerts. Now she was free to go out whenever she wanted to, without having to make arrangements well in advance. She was free to watch what *she* liked on television, free to enjoy a leisurely bath, and free to sleep without interruption. Unfortunately, she was usually too tired to enjoy any of these things and sound sleep eluded her, whatever she did.

On reaching home after the concert, she dumped her bag in the hall, threw her clothes over a chair, and cursorily brushed her teeth. She fell asleep instantly but woke up again after only a couple of hours. This was typical and, with a sigh she turned over, plumped the pillow, and began to go through a relaxation technique. Doing this sometimes resulted in nodding off and even when it didn't, concentrating on releasing tension gave some benefits. Tonight, however, she couldn't seem to stop herself from thinking about the invitation to sing that she had received after the concert, and she rehearsed several versions of what she might say if she rang Mr Braithwaite. The cautious side of her personality, which she thought of as "Mary Mouse" — a childhood nickname bestowed by her father — whispered that it would be very stressful to take part in anything organised by a famous conductor and listed all the pitfalls and potentially embarrassing and humiliating situations she could find herself in. Her reckless side — "Beryl the Peril" (taken from her father's treasured boyhood comic annuals, which he occasionally allowed her to read) — kept interrupting Mouse, stridently pointing out that it was high time that Mary spread her wings and this would be an exciting opportunity. These arguments were accompanied by endless repetitions of *Good King Wenceslas*, which was stuck in her brain — a carol that she didn't even like. In the end, she got up and made a milky drink, thinking that, for once, it didn't matter if she finally got back to sleep when it was nearly morning (the usual outcome) because tomorrow was Sunday, so she didn't have to go to work. Monday was a working day, but it was also

Christmas Eve so would be followed by two days off. She didn't have much planned — just Christmas dinner at her sister's house and the rest of the time she hoped to spend catching up on sleep. At about four a.m., Mary went back to bed and at last found the longed-for oblivion.

Chapter 2

Mary woke up around nine a.m., feeling better than she had done for a long time. She ate breakfast while still wearing her dressing gown, sitting with her feet up on the settee, continuing the inner debate about whether to accept the invitation to sing. Mary Mouse was still telling her to refuse and Beryl was saying 'go for it'. Suddenly, an image of Beryl delivering a hefty punch between Mouse's eyes flashed across Mary's mind's eye and bolstered by Fran's words of encouragement, she decided to go for it. She hated making phone calls to strangers so prayed for courage and inspiration for suitable words. (Mary was not religious in any formal way but believed there was some supreme power at the heart of creation and she found that asking whatever it was for personal qualities, usually meant that she could access them.) She did feel more courageous as she reached for her phone to make the call but was interrupted by the ringing of the doorbell. She scrambled to her feet, clutching the belt round her threadbare dressing gown, and stumbled barefoot to the door. When she opened it, she froze in amazement. Luke was standing on her doorstep.

'Oh' he said, glancing at her clothes. 'I thought I'd left it late enough.' There was an awkward pause, and then he thrust what looked like some music at her. 'I thought you might like to look through this. I've marked the bits I'd like you to sing.'

While Mary was still trying to decide how to respond, he added, 'Look, can I come in for a moment?' Prompted by Beryl, Mary thought, *Oh well, I don't have to think about what to say on the phone now,* and stepped aside to let him in. He quickly spied the piano through the open door into the lounge, entered the room, sat down on the piano stool, and played a few chords. 'In tune and up to pitch!' he observed with obvious pleasure, and began playing through some of the music he had brought. Defeated, Mary sank down on to the settee, thinking that she had let a madman into her house. She wondered how he had found out where she lived.

'This is your first entry,' he said, singing the part loudly in an impressive baritone voice. He paused to say that she would represent a dying blue whale in the section titled *Sea Creatures*, so obviously his voice wasn't suitable — he just wanted to give an idea of what was involved. Mary had never heard anything like it before, but she found the music strangely arresting so asked who the composer was. He looked a bit embarrassed and held up the book so she could see the cover, which said *Requiem of Life* by Luke Braithwaite.

'So, you're the composer, as well as the conductor?' He nodded. 'Well, it sounds beautiful and very interesting,' responded Mary, who was impressed, despite feeling cross. 'But I still don't see how I could possibly do justice to it! How much music does the whale have?'

He played through the rest, identifying her phrases, other soloists, choral and orchestral sections. The whale phrases were short but hauntingly beautiful. Eventually, he ground to a halt, stating that the rest would not involve her and asking if she would like to try singing a few bars.

'I'm not up to it!' replied Mary Mouse in a panic. 'You must know lots of professional singers who would make a lovely job of it, whereas I would have to practise it for weeks and would need lots of help before singing it to anyone, let alone...' Here she petered out, lost for suitable words to describe him. She wondered if she might still be asleep and dreaming this; it all seemed so unlikely. Then she remembered that she hadn't given him any contact details and bewilderment turned to anger. 'And anyway, you shouldn't even be here. Who told you where I lived?' He began to reply but she burst out, incongruously. 'And haven't you noticed I'm not even dressed?'

He half smiled at that and then looked crestfallen. 'I'm afraid I get a bit carried away sometimes. As for who told me, no one did directly; the names of soloists — even those like you with just a few bars — were on the programme. Your conductor mentioned your first name when I remarked that you had a striking voice, so I knew which one you were and found your postcode and phone number through the internet. A helpful neighbour of yours gave me your house number.'

That came as a bit of a shock to Mary, who didn't think she had ever done anything that would result in her details being in the public domain. And whichever neighbour had helped him out would surely spread the message about her handsome visitor far and wide. After a short silence, she remarked that he could have rung her or messaged before turning up on the doorstep.

'I tried,' he replied, 'but you didn't answer.'

Mary glanced at her phone and, sure enough, there were two missed calls and a text message. That took the wind out of her sails.

'The sound was switched off. I was exhausted and slept in,' she told him in a small voice.

Luke held out his right hand, suggesting that they start again and Mary moved to shake it by way of apology — after all, she was in the wrong for not picking up his messages — but before their hands connected, she felt a spark of electricity so violent that she jumped back with an exclamation. She felt embarrassed, thinking that, at the very least, he would think she was crazy, or, even worse, that he would interpret the shock as a sign of sexual attraction. In her confusion she collapsed back onto the settee without actually shaking his hand and he dropped it, looking a bit embarrassed himself.

'Static — I'm wearing synthetic clothes,' she said, hurriedly and then felt foolish because he might not have felt anything. 'I'm sorry but I don't feel I can just launch into singing. I'm barely awake, for one thing.'

'Okay,' he capitulated. 'I'll leave it with you and call back later this afternoon, when you've had a chance to look at it. I am staying in Norfolk until Boxing Day so I can help you with it and, trust me, you have the right voice. Professional singers often have preconceived ideas about how they should sound, whereas your natural voice is exactly what I'm looking for. How would four p.m. suit you?'

Mary Mouse tried to argue but Beryl elbowed her out of the way and just nodded. Luke took that for agreement and left, calling 'See you later', over his shoulder.

Mary sat staring into space for a moment or two but then, on an impulse, went through to the front of the bungalow and, standing well back, looked out to see what kind of car he drove. She thought it would be something flashy and expensive because a conductor might have a big ego and choice of vehicle was usually linked to personality. She was therefore amazed to see him riding an ancient bicycle, narrowly missing an elderly lady, who was struggling across the road with a huge bag of shopping.

***

Luke set off along the coast road towards Sheringham, looking out for icy patches, having encountered one outside Mary's bungalow, where he'd almost hit a pedestrian. He breathed deeply, enjoying the fresh salty air, and imagined that London was leaving his body with every exhalation. He had loved living there as a young man but now it just seemed too busy and too noisy. His flat was cramped, and he often dreamed of space, big Norfolk skies and the tall cliffs around Cromer. On a whim, he turned off towards one of the beaches and parked his bike. The sea reflected the leaden sky, so it appeared to be dark grey. He enjoyed the roar of the incoming waves, made louder still by large quantities of pebbles on the move, and ignoring the cold air, he simply immersed himself in the sights and sounds. He would have liked to stay there for a long time, allowing the exhilarating atmosphere to generate ideas for a new composition, but remembered that his mother would, by now, have eaten her breakfast and be wondering where he had got to. He really should have shared the meal with her but was keen to get some fresh air and track Mary down, so had gulped down some cornflakes and retrieved his bike from the garage, planning to make up for missing breakfast by pushing his mother to the sea front later. Unfortunately, the sky looked full of snow — or heavy rain at the very least — so he was probably facing a few hours in her sitting room, instead. There was an element of frustration in trips home because he longed for freedom to unwind in his own way, but his mother always wanted him to spend the whole time in her company, which he found, frankly, boring. She would want him to talk about everyone they had met at last night's event and give a detailed account of every concert he had conducted over the last few months. He knew that these were reasonable expectations but would prefer to be alternately composing and walking or cycling. In the evenings, the TV would be on and Luke, having little interest in it, usually occupied himself with a book while Delia enjoyed the latest drama. Every so often, she would make comments about the programme she was watching, fully expecting him to be as glued to the screen as she was. He knew she lived for his visits and tried to be the person she wanted him to be, but it was hard going for someone who was, by nature, a bit of a recluse. It was laughable that he had ended up in the highly prominent role of orchestral conductor.

As Luke completed the journey to Sheringham, his thoughts turned to Mary, and he briefly wondered if the unmistakeable spark of electricity between them might lead to a romantic liaison. He had found her tousled hair, ancient dressing gown and bare feet strangely appealing. However, he suspected that it would interfere with what he really wanted from her — her voice in the recording of his latest composition — so he reluctantly rejected the idea. A pity really, because he had not been with a woman for some months now.

His mother was frosty when he got home, and he apologised for his absence at breakfast and explained what he'd been doing. Unfortunately, she did not understand why Mary was more important than she was, and the icy atmosphere persisted. Luke asked Jenny if his mum could be wrapped up warmly and wear her waterproof cape so that they could go out, but Jenny was horrified at the idea of her charge being exposed to the elements on such a cold day, so the sitting room it had to be. Luke bore it well, hoping to build up some credit before he had to set off for Cromer again.

***

At 3.55 p.m. Mary saw him arrive in a Honda Civic. She had used the intervening hours to practise the marked parts until the notes and timing were secure, because she didn't want to look like a complete novice. She had also showered, washed her hair and taken some time to choose flattering but casual clean clothes (telling herself that this was to assist her self-esteem rather than to look nice for a physically attractive man). However, he made directly for the piano again, without even glancing at her. He took her through some vocal warm-up exercises, supported by the piano, but she kept running out of breath, so he turned and said they needed to work on that.

'No wonder you can't breathe properly,' he stated, looking at her properly for the first time. 'Your posture is dreadful; your shoulders are hunched forwards, and your chest is caved in. What has happened? You didn't hold yourself like that at the concert!'

The truth was that Mary felt extremely nervous to be singing before someone near the top of his profession and the defensive posture he had described was one that she unconsciously adopted whenever she felt threatened. On top of that, she was nervous about having a man in her bungalow. She knew this was ridiculous, but her life had been so restricted by caring for Sam that she had forgotten how to behave with men, apart from the very elderly ones in the care home where she worked. Furthermore, Luke was looking directly at her chest and that felt invasive.

'You're trying to hold your shoulders in place,' he snapped. 'Let them go! Forget about trying to put them anywhere and concentrate instead on gently contracting your pelvic floor muscles. Then lift your breastbone while keeping the back of your neck long. Relax your arms and your shoulders will fall naturally into place.'

Mary tried to follow his instructions, (how dare he mention her pelvic floor?) but her body kept reverting to defence mode.

Luke watched her struggling and wondered if he'd made a terrible mistake, as he'd never seen a worse case of nerves. After a lengthy pause, he asked if she could tell him why she didn't have problems with posture or breathing the previous evening, but she just backed away from him and shook her head.

'Well, you're like a different person now,' he observed. 'Last night you were relaxed and open and your face was a kaleidoscope of different expressions.'

Mary's dismay increased. Had he spent the whole concert watching her? In a panic, she muttered,

'I'm sorry but I can't do this,' and sat down on the sofa with her head down and hands clasped tightly together between her knees.

Something stopped Luke from letting her throw in the towel at this point.

'Look,' he said. 'Presumably you've found out who I am by now and are finding a one-to-one session a bit intimidating. Why don't you go over there (indicating the far side of the room), close your eyes, and try once more to follow my instructions?'

Beryl the Peril stepped in, suggesting that one more attempt wouldn't hurt, and Mary quickly got up and stood as far away from Luke as was possible, turning her face to the wall for good measure. After a few breaths, she was amazed to find that she could now do as he asked. There was still one problem, however, how could she see the music without standing next to him? She turned, her eyes scanning the space between them. Luke, reading her thoughts, held out his copy.

'I can manage without the music,' he informed her.

Mary took it and, after few more deep and uninhibited breaths, indicated that she was at last able to tackle the first phrase of the whale song. He stopped her after the very first note with instructions to think the note before singing it, so as to get it perfectly in tune with the accompaniment. When she did that, he stopped her again, describing how she could get a fuller tone. Then he criticised the leap between the first two notes because he said the interval wasn't perfectly clear and demonstrated how he could hear intervening slurred notes that shouldn't be there. Eventually, she got through the first few bars without interruption, and they moved on to the next entry. It took a long time to get through the whole part because of the rigorous attention to detail but then he surprised her by saying that it was getting there, technically. So, bolstered by his encouragement, she asked tentatively what would be involved in the recording session.

'Well, I'm not sure how·long the whole thing will take but I can arrange it so that we can spend as much time as necessary to get your section up to a satisfactory standard on the first day, so you only have to come once. It will be in London, Henry Wood Hall in Southwark on the 28th of January. Unfortunately, there tends to be a lot of hanging around with these things. If anything goes wrong, we have to repeat it until it goes right and even if it's perfect, the recording staff will want to go through their processes, so you might have to sing it several times. It will probably be a long day with an early start, so you'll need to book a hotel. Eventually you'll get paid but I'm afraid it won't be much.'

The sum he mentioned sounded more than adequate to Mary, who had been wondering where she would find the money for the train fare and a London hotel. He promised to have further details sent by email after Christmas.

'Won't I need to come to rehearsals?' she asked.

'Yes — but in view of the distance, we could manage if you just came to the final one. I can ask a choir member to fill in for the others. I don't know the date for that yet; my agent does all that. But, for now, we do need to meet again to consolidate what we've done — twice, ideally. Are you free tomorrow?'

Mary explained that she had to go to work and wouldn't be home until after five p.m. Actually, she was lying about the time, she finished at four but knew she would be too tired to launch straight into another singing marathon. Luke thought for a moment and then asked if she would mind going to his mother's house, which was in Sheringham. 'She likes to eat at six thirty, so we could do an hour before that and then you could have dinner with us. She would like that.'

Mary hesitated, dismayed at the prospect of prolonged social contact with him, and eventually said that she couldn't possibly intrude on a family meal on Christmas Eve and besides, she was vegetarian.

'So are we,' he responded. 'And my mother and I run out of things to say to each other so a visitor will be most welcome.' Then he paused and asked if she had a family, with his eyes on Sam's photo.

'No' she said, in a clipped voice.

'And the young man in the photo is...?'

'My son,' was the stony reply. 'He died.'

Clearly taken aback, Luke apologised. A silence hung in the air, during which he noticed that Mary's defensive expression and posture had reasserted themselves and he decided that it might be wise to avoid further questions. Instead, he asked for something to write his mother's address on. Mary recognised the street, but the house was simply called "Cadence", without a number, so he gave her further details about where to find it, saying, 'See you tomorrow evening then,' and left without giving her a chance to reply.[1]

Mary slowly looked around the room, which seemed alive with an unusual and vibrant energy, as though a whirlwind had been through it, leaving subtle and faintly disturbing traces behind. The piano seemed to have taken on a deep lustre and now dominated the room. The lamp and overhead light seemed brighter. The biggest stain on the elderly carpet seemed to resemble a whale!

Eventually, she pulled herself together and prepared a simple meal, but she felt jumpy and unsettled and found herself pushing food around the plate. She realised that a good night's sleep was essential if she were to cope with work, another singing lesson and a meal in a strange house with one unknown person and

---

[1] Cadence is a musical term meaning a progression of chords that comes at the end of a composition, section or phrase.

one obsessed person, who took it for granted that he could take over her life for the sake of getting a few bars of music right. As a long-term insomniac, Mary had a number of strategies that had helped in the past: a warm bath, a milky drink and an evening activity that did not involve too much thinking. She opted for wrapping presents for the family get-together on Christmas day, then wrote down several reminders, imagined putting various anxieties into boxes, and then meditated for a few minutes before slipping into bed.

Unfortunately, none of it worked and she slept only in short snatches. Around three a.m., she awoke fully after an erotic dream. There was no escaping where that had come from! She turned over with a sigh, telling herself that the person who had just infiltrated her life was definitely off limits for that sort of thing, as he must live in a very different world to hers. It was probably only lust, born of frustration anyway, arising as a consequence of having lived like a nun for many years. There were simply no opportunities for developing a sexual relationship while Sam was alive and, since he died, she'd been permanently exhausted by grief and insomnia. It was hardly surprising that she should feel attracted to the first man who crossed her path. Now Mr Braithwaite was out of the box, the question of her proposed part in a professional recording worried her more and more. After spending much of the night imagining various pitfalls, she realised that if she was stressed now, the level would be unmanageable by the time she went to London and, in the end, she decided that she would send an apologetic text the following day, explaining that having slept on it, she realised that it was out of the question for a number of practical reasons and extreme nervousness. She even put the light on and drafted out what she intended to say. After that, she slept fitfully again for a short time until the alarm went off.

***

Luke left the bungalow wondering if Mary might be too nervous to sing in the recording. He couldn't understand how she could be so different to the attractive and confident performer he had seen at the concert. Was she afraid of *him*? He didn't think he'd said or done anything particularly frightening; the musicians he regularly worked with had to take much worse than anything he'd dished out today — but then, they were professionals and hardened to his sniping and shouting. He still wanted Mary to sing the whale song because her voice was perfect and she had a very good sense of phrasing, but he decided to put her through her paces at the next practice, just to be sure she could cope.

Chapter 3

On Christmas Eve, Mary's shift at the care home was even more of a struggle than usual. Apart from tiredness, two carers were off sick and several residents, who were going home for Christmas, needed help with packing. Also, a lady with dementia became very upset and Mary, who was usually good at calming people, just could not come up with the right approach to defuse the situation and she ended up with an unspeakable mess in one of the bathrooms. The manager came to see what all the noise was about and crossly told Mary to take five minutes out, while she and another carer cleaned up. Mary went to the staff room and slumped into a chair, wondering if there would be consequences to what had just happened. Wearily, she took out her mobile phone and looked at the message she had prepared in the night — even more determined to end the stress of trying to sing alongside experienced professional musicians. Her finger hovered over the send icon, but something stopped her from connecting with the screen. Was she crazy to pass up the chance to be part of something so exciting? And the music — Requiem of Life — from what she had heard, was hauntingly beautiful. Wouldn't it lift her out of the rut she was in? Perhaps she could sleep a little after work before going to the Braithwaite house. After another session she would have a better idea of how manageable the part was. She decided to leave the text in abeyance for the time being.

Four o'clock came at last and Mary drove home as quickly as possible, switched off her phone and collapsed on to the settee. She fell asleep instantly, but a stray car horn woke her up again half an hour later. Despite this, she felt strangely refreshed, so quickly changed into the first decent clothes she could lay hands on, dragged a comb through her hair and drove the few miles to Sheringham.

The house was quite easy to locate, mainly because it was so large. It was old — probably Victorian — with two bay windows at the front and an impressive front door with a stained-glass panel. She had worried about where to park, but security lights came on, revealing a large, gravelled area in front of the building. As she reached towards the bell-push, she noticed that the door glass depicted musical instruments, a harp, a violin, a trumpet and a drum. She smiled, her hand fell away, and she studied the glass with interest. Then she heard Luke shouting inside and Mary Mouse cringed and pleaded for escape, but before she could run back to the car, the door was opened by a young black woman who introduced herself as Jenny, Mrs Braithwaite's carer. She said that she'd noticed the security lights were on and had come to investigate.

'Oh, hello — I'm a carer, too,' said Mary. Jenny looked very surprised and not too pleased at that, saying that they didn't need any more carers and she had been told to expect a musician. 'I'm that as well,' Mary informed her, noticing that this made Jenny look very confused. 'I work in a care home but sing in my spare time,' clarified Mary.

'Mr Braithwaite just said that a musician was coming to go through a part,' said Jenny, 'but, as you can hear, he's not in a good mood. Rather you than me!' It sounded as though Luke was very angry with someone on the phone and Mary dreaded to think what that might mean for her session. Jenny had moved to open a different door to the one from where the shouting came, saying that perhaps Mary would like to meet Mrs Braithwaite while waiting for the phone call to end. Mary took a deep breath to steady herself and followed Jenny into a pleasant but old-fashioned room where an elderly lady sat crookedly, with her feet up, in a reclining chair. She greeted Mary and invited her to sit down.

'Come and get warm by the fire and tell me a bit about yourself. Luke said you were going to join us for dinner and that will be lovely. We don't get many visitors here and my son isn't the best at conversation. I'm sorry that he's making such a noise, his first horn has resigned on the brink of launching the new work.'

'In that case, perhaps he won't want me here,' replied Mary, hopefully. 'He must have to find someone else urgently.'

'Well, I've told him he won't be able to do that at Christmas, so he might as well relax, but he never does that. He's trying to make one of his admin people ring round tonight and of course he doesn't want to! That's what all the shouting is about — as well as whose fault it was that the player resigned in a huff, but we'd better not get into that. Do you know anyone round here who could do it?'

'No — I don't really move in professional circles,' explained Mary. 'I'm not even sure why Mr Braithwaite wants me to sing in Requiem of Life, but he seems very determined.'

'Once his mind is made up about something musical, there's no changing it. He's been looking for a voice with a mournful, whining quality for some time and, when we heard you at the carol concert, he insisted that you were perfect. By the way, I enjoyed that concert very much.'

Mary was dismayed to hear that she'd been chosen on the strength of her whining voice but didn't have time to reply, because at that moment the door opened, and Luke walked in. He glanced at her briefly then marched straight out again, calling 'Come on, Mary,' so she smiled apologetically at Mrs Braithwaite, grabbed her bag, and hurried after him into the room opposite. Luke was already seated at a grand piano and he began playing the introduction to her first entry before she could even find a suitable place to stand. Unsurprisingly, she did not make a very good job of the opening notes and he stopped with a sigh, saying that he thought they were past all that.

'I'm sorry. I wasn't quite settled and ready,' gabbled Mary. 'One minute I was talking to your mother, and then you rushed me in here and started playing even before I'd stopped moving!'

'Well, if you can cope with that, you can cope with anything,' was the unsympathetic reply. 'Let's try it again and please put some expression into it. You're the last blue whale on the planet and you're dying. Just think about it, not only is it the end of you, it's the end of your species. No more of your kind ever again! What would that feel like?'

'Despairing?' Mary stammered, managing to get a couple of steadying breaths in before it was time to sing again. The first phrase was not very successful, but they kept going and, by the end, she felt she was getting inside the music. However, Luke said that it fell far short of the standard needed for a recording and proceeded to pull it apart, note by note, delivering each comment in a clipped voice, verging on rudeness. This went on for a long time until Mary Mouse was shaking and pleading for release. She opened her mouth in order to refuse to do any more but before she could speak, Luke told her to go through it without stopping, no matter what happened. Beryl reared up, saying *Right* —

this is it. Let's show him what we're made of! What have we got to lose? and before Mary knew what was happening, she had begun to sing again. Her posture straightened, her breath deepened, and she sang from the heart as she'd never sung before. Luke tried to put her off by introducing phrases from *We wish you a Merry Christmas* into the accompaniment, but Mary ignored it and made it through the whole section without any mistakes. Then she glared at him and asked if her tone was sufficiently 'whining'.

He looked up from the keyboard in surprise and regarded her with a smile playing round the edge of his lips.

'Why on earth do you think I'd want that?' he asked.

'Your mother said that's what you were looking for,' responded Mary, who had decided that she was never going to be good enough to satisfy him, so may as well say whatever came into her head.

'My mother's hearing isn't very good,' he pointed out. 'All I can remember saying is that I needed a plaintive, desolate voice and you have that.' After a moment's thought, he continued. 'I did tell her I needed a whinnying voice when I was looking for a horse.' An involuntary laugh escaped from Mary. 'She isn't very interested in my music so doesn't pay much attention to anything I say about it and may well have mixed you up with the tenor.' Then they both laughed and warning bells sounded inside Mary because he suddenly looked very attractive indeed and she wanted to forgive him for giving her such a rough ride. Should she really be so easily influenced by good looks?

As though reading her thoughts, Luke said, 'I'm sorry I put you through the mill just now. I had to be sure you wouldn't cave in under pressure. I hope you understand. My rehearsals can be quite challenging.'

Now Mary was thoroughly disarmed, and she felt herself blushing.

'Yes, it's fine,' she muttered, turning away.

He glanced at his watch and said, 'Let's go and see if there's any prospect of dinner', while walking out and clearly expecting her to follow.

Mrs Braithwaite and Jenny were not in the sitting room, dining room or kitchen but, in the latter, a pan containing vegetables was boiling over. Luke ignored it and went out again, sighing irritably, but Mary, who had detected bathroom noises behind one of the doors off the hall, ran to the hob and rescued the meal. She knew all too well how hard it was to be broken off from cooking that had reached a crucial stage in order to help a someone to the toilet, having done it countless times for her son. Jenny found her deftly managing everything but didn't look very pleased at the takeover. Mary apologised quickly, saying that she understood the problem of having to do two urgent things at once and hoped Jenny wouldn't mind an extra pair of hands.

'Thanks, but I can manage now,' Jenny said, tersely.

Mary gave up, saying, 'Of course. Just let me know if there's anything else I can do.'

She found Luke and his mother already seated at the dining table, so installed herself where another place was set. By way of conversation, she asked if Jenny would eat with them.

'She prefers to eat alone,' explained Mrs Braithwaite. 'Chris, my regular carer, always keeps me company and we have some good conversation over meals, but Jenny is a temporary replacement over Christmas and is quite different. I try to treat her as a friend rather than an employee, but she disappears back to the kitchen or her room at every opportunity. She's a very efficient carer though and a good cook.'

The disappointment and loneliness in her voice were unmistakable and they made Mary determined to make this meal a pleasant social occasion, even if it was unlikely that the son would join in because he was frowning intently at his phone and texting.

Jenny served an unfamiliar but tasty concoction with rice and the rescued vegetables, and Mrs Braithwaite asked Mary a lot of questions about her family, work and musical background. Mary found her easy to talk to, so told her about her sister, the time looking after Sam and her work at the care home.

Luke suddenly looked up from his phone and asked why she didn't care for children, as that was where her experience lay. This took Mary by surprise. She had almost forgotten that he was there, because he seemed to be too preoccupied with his phone to be listening but before she could say anything, his mother rebuked him.

'I imagine that would be quite painful for someone who has recently lost a child, don't you think?' Then she sighed in a resigned way and muttered, 'Of course you don't.'

This interchange puzzled Mary because it seemed unfair to slap Luke down when he had tried at last to join in. She decided to make an effort, so turned to him with a smile.

'Of course, childcare seems to be the more obvious choice, but your mother is right. I just couldn't face being with children and teenagers who reminded me of Sam and there is a shortage of carers for the elderly.' She hesitated, wondering if that would offend Mrs Braithwaite, who was elderly herself, had a carer, and was clearly incapacitated.

However, Mrs Braithwaite said, with a rueful smile, 'Yes, we're a dreadful nuisance, aren't we?' and went back to asking Mary questions, with obvious enjoyment, while Luke went back to his messaging.

The meal progressed with Jenny appearing at appropriate times and Mrs Braithwaite questioning Mary about her education. After dessert, she summoned Jenny and asked to be taken to the bathroom again, which meant Mary was left alone with Luke. She wondered if she should initiate some conversation but couldn't think of anything to say, so decided to sit quietly until Mrs Braithwaite came back and then thank them and take her leave. However, instead of picking up his phone again, Luke sat drumming his fingers on the table and then suddenly asked why she hadn't gone to music college in view of all the piano, singing and theory examinations she had passed.

'I didn't want to be a teacher and I wasn't good enough to be a performer,' she stated simply.

He pressed on. 'So, why not university to study something different? Then you'd have had a degree and more options for a career.'

This was something Mary already had regrets about and his ability to pounce on one of her weakest points was unnerving. She took a deep breath and told him about starting sixth-form A' Level courses but leaving school before taking exams because she was very keen on Adrian (Sam's father) and he wanted her to get a job so that they could set up home straight away. She was aware that this made her sound weak and easily led but, not wanting to lapse into an uncomfortable silence again, she ploughed on.

'I got an admin job in the buyers' office of a department store and worked my way up to stock controller. Then Sam arrived and I gave up work completely because looking after him was a full-time job in itself. Adrian thought I should carry on working and put Sam in an institution, but I just couldn't bring myself to do that. He couldn't face having our home life dominated by a child with special needs and didn't want to give up the rather extravagant lifestyle that we had built up. He gave me an ultimatum. I dug my heels in and, to cut a long story short, he left, and I looked after Sam. It meant living in local-authority housing on benefits because the house Adrian and I had was heavily mortgaged.' *There*, she thought. *Now you know it all.* She was acutely aware that her life was a million miles from this rather gracious home and the glittering career that Luke was pursuing and realised that she had coloured up and was sitting with shoulders hunched forward, arms folded and a caved-in chest — all of which he must have noticed because he was now regarding her with a puzzled frown. He didn't comment, however, and Mary was wondering whether she had the courage to ask him how he had arrived at his enviable position in life, when Mrs Braithwaite reappeared.

When Jenny had made her comfortable at the table again, she beamed at Mary and asked if she would play Scrabble with her. Mary enjoyed the game and was actually rather good at it, having played in a club in times past, and she amused herself with a Scrabble app when she was tied to the house. As Mrs Braithwaite was looking very hopeful and, as her son would almost certainly not demean himself to play a board game, Mary agreed.

'And you Luke,' said his mother, in a tone that brooked no argument. 'Surely you can put that wretched horn player out of your mind, ditch the phone and indulge your mother in some family time now it's nearly Christmas Day!' Then, turning to Mary, 'I'm afraid he's not very nice to play with because he deliberately blocks other players from getting a decent word in anywhere. He always beats me but perhaps you'll be able to give him a run for his money.'

'Why not?' Mary found herself saying because it seemed unkind not to help a lonely old woman to enjoy her Christmas. Luke had left the table and she thought he was ignoring his mother and refusing to play, but he surprised her, reappearing with a Scrabble set.

'Prepare to be slaughtered,' he declared.

Mary believed that she stood a chance of putting up a good fight in this, so looked him in the eye and replied defiantly, 'I have no doubt that you're brilliant at it but I'm not bad myself.'

He looked sceptical and wordlessly handed her the bag of letters. She drew a low one, earning the right to go first and they prepared to play, but before she had a chance to put the first word together, Luke said, in a provocative voice and obviously referring to the bad start to the singing lesson,

'Are you sure you're quite settled and ready?'

'Quite ready, thank you,' replied Mary, demurely, as she looked down at her rack. A slow and secretive smile spread across her face as she spotted a seven-letter word that would earn a bonus of fifty points and give her a flying start. She placed it on the board triumphantly and looked up at Luke, her face breaking into a radiant smile. He was transfixed for a moment because it reminded him of a shaft of sunlight unexpectedly breaking through thick cloud to brighten up the sea when it was at its gloomiest, but then he pulled himself together and offhandedly remarked that Scrabble was a game of luck, as well as skill. His mother gleefully laughed out loud and congratulated Mary.

Delia was a good player but could not keep up with the others, who both played with a steely determination to win. Luke certainly had the edge on strategy, but Mary had developed an excellent vocabulary as a result of many lonely evenings with the Scrabble app and a dictionary. She didn't know where she found the energy — perhaps novelty overrode exhaustion — but she won the game by a narrow margin. Luke swore revenge in a future game and Delia couldn't stop laughing.

Well, at least I've made her day, thought Mary. She chuckled to herself on the way home and realised that, once over the ordeals of the practice and the meal, she'd had fun, something that had been missing from her life for a long time. Also, in the singing lesson, she had stood up to Luke's bullying and overcome nervousness well enough to give of her best. He had given her a rough ride only to be sure he could rely on her and had said that she had a plaintive, desolate voice. Wasn't that almost a compliment?

Chapter 4

Mary awoke on Christmas morning from a dream about an enormous Mary Mouse. She had her arms folded and was saying, 'I never thought I'd say this, because in all the years that I've known her, we've never agreed — but Beryl the Peril is right about that singing. Pour our grief into it.'

Both the image and the voice were incredibly clear and relevant to her current situation, so Mary sat up in bed and thought about what they might mean. She noticed with interest that the Mouse had said *our* grief rather than *your* grief, as though she were not a separate entity. Perhaps it was her own intuition telling her that the whale song really would help her to get over losing Sam. And Beryl had stopped her from throwing in the towel when Luke put her under sustained pressure; the reckless comment about her whining voice had paid off, resulting in laughter rather than offence. Overall, singing in Requiem of Life now felt right.

She got up and drank a glass of water — her usual way to begin the day. The only signs of Christmas in the bungalow were a few cards dotted about and a pile of presents in one corner. They looked rather incongruous in the plain and shabby surroundings, but Mary wasn't bothered by that, she just luxuriated in the fact that she didn't have to rush off anywhere. She put the radio on and found some Christmas music to put her in the right mood.

Dinner at her sister Deidre's house was scheduled for two p.m. and as it was only an hour and a half's drive away, Mary planned to leave around eleven, so that she'd have time to help in the kitchen or play with the children when she got there. She was a dutiful aunt, despite finding it difficult to be with children since Sam died. Even when he was alive it was quite hard, because she couldn't help comparing their progress with his, but today she felt ready to make a special effort to be cheerful and good company. Deidre and her partner Tom had stuck by her and helped when they could through the whole of Sam's life and had tolerated her being miserable and withdrawn since his death. Now she vowed to give them a break from all that. She and her sister had been close since childhood — especially so when their mother died — and Mary valued that closeness and wanted to preserve it.

Her positive attitude continued through the noisy and slightly chaotic celebrations and she found herself enjoying Christmas. After the meal, Tom said he'd keep the children amused so that the sisters could enjoy a chat while clearing up in the kitchen and they overlooked the fact that this left them with the chores, as uninterrupted time together was precious. Deidre asked her sister how her job was going, and Mary pulled a face and said she didn't really feel fulfilled in it, but it would do for now. She moved on to recounting the strange train of events that had started at the carol concert. Deidre looked alternately amazed, amused and sceptical and finally commented that the 'mad Maestro' must have been impressed with Mary's voice. Perhaps it would lead to greater things?

'No chance of that,' replied Mary. 'He just thinks I have the right tonal quality to represent a dying whale. I don't think I would ever find another part like that!'

'Still, it sounds as though he thinks you're good enough for the recording and that's one hell of a compliment!'

Mary considered this and decided she must have done quite well, so could perhaps allow her self-esteem to rise a little, even if she never sang another solo. However, there were still a few niggling doubts around, despite that morning's uplifting and encouraging dream. Luke hadn't fixed a time for another practice and tomorrow would be his last day in Norfolk, so her next run through might be in rehearsal, with a room full of professional musicians. What would they make of her? She mentioned this concern to Deidre, who turned from stacking the dishwasher.

'Look — you've suffered enormous stress for years. If you really think this would be the final straw, why don't you just tell this strange person to get lost?'

'I'm in love with his music' said Mary, simply.

Now Deidre was looking at her with sisterly perception and saying, 'And who wrote the music?'

'Well, he did of course,' and then hurriedly, 'but that doesn't mean I'm falling for him as a person. I hardly know him, and he lives in a completely different world to me — and he's very bossy! Downright rude at times.'

'And is he good looking?' Deidre pressed.

Mary paused. 'He's not bad — but he looks stressed most of the time.'

'But what does he look like, physically?' pressed Deidre, who had never shared Mary's interest in music so was unlikely to have ever seen him conducting.

Mary considered for a moment and then came up with, 'medium height, medium build, dark but greying wavy hair, a bit receding, piercing dark eyes — probably in his mid-forties,' and neglected to mention how she had liked the way his longish hair curled on to his collar when he was playing the piano and had his back towards her — or how expressive his hands were.

Deidre said that if Mary did go to London, she would love to offer moral support and go with her but— and here she indicated the three children who had escaped from Tom's supervision and were now rampaging around the kitchen, pretending to be monsters. She finished the sentence with a shrug, and then said how nice it must be to be free to do exciting things like that. She sounded genuinely regretful and Mary, who had envied Deidre's happy marriage and healthy children, was surprised to find that her sister actually envied *her*. She certainly was very tied with a full-time teaching job and a home and family to manage.

They went back into the lounge and exchanged presents, adding piles of wrapping paper to the toys covering the floor. The children had opened sacks from Santa very early that morning, but Mary had brought extra gifts, which were causing much excitement when her mobile pinged and she saw that she had a message from an unknown number.

'I have to leave tomorrow around eleven. Is there any chance of a short run through before that? Also, my mother would like a word with you, if possible. LB.'

Mary handed the phone to Deidre, who asked what his mother might want.

'I haven't a clue,' replied Mary. Then, after a moment's thought, 'She has carers — a temporary one at the moment — and she knows I'm a carer. It could be something to do with that.'

The conversation was interrupted by a noisy, childish squabble at this point and Tom shouted that everyone was getting too excited and they could all settled down and watch the new film or go to bed. Unsurprisingly, the film was chosen, and the children calmed down, apart from elbowing each other for more room on the settee. Mary kept looking at Luke's message, trying to decide how to reply. There was no doubt that she was afraid, but she wanted to be involved in that wonderful music. Even Mary Mouse thought it would enable her to vocalise her grief and move on. Also, there might be the possibility of improving on her care-home job. She'd taken that because her stock-control qualifications and experience were now out of date, whereas she did have plenty of recent caring experience, but she really did not enjoy working in the care home. That decided her. She quickly prepared a text saying that she'd be there at ten the next morning and Beryl tapped send.

Deidre was engrossed in her tablet. After a while, she handed it to Mary who was confronted with a full screen picture of Luke. She handed it back to Deidre with the comment that the photo was obviously taken years ago and from a very flattering angle.

'Still,' said her sister, 'I wouldn't mind a few one-to-one sessions with him!'

'What's that?' Tom chipped in, looking suspicious.

'Nothing' said Deidre, hurriedly. 'I'm just joking about Mary's new music teacher!'

'Shut up, everyone. We can't hear!' shouted Jack, their eldest.

A few minutes later, the tablet was handed to Mary again and this time there was a lot of text describing Luke's career to date, which Mary read with interest, her heart sinking as she realised that he was even better educated and musically experienced than she had thought. Why on earth had he spent so long over teaching her a few bars in Requiem of Life? Did eminent musicians really do things like that? And what was she thinking of to say she'd go back yet again? Wasn't she going to fall flat on her face when recording day came and what would the other musicians make of her? These thoughts preoccupied her for as long as the film lasted, by which time Jack and his sister Mai, who had already forgotten Christmas dinner and the sweets consumed since then, were whining about being hungry. Deidre took them into the kitchen along with Rohan, the youngest, and Tom put the news on television. It was full of flooding reports and the weather forecast predicted that the storm responsible would soon arrive in Norfolk, so Mary decided it was best to head for home as soon as possible. Deidre came out to the car to see her off, a coat held over her head against the rain that had already started, wished her luck for tomorrow, then continued speaking through Mary's open window.

'You've been very quiet since we googled LB. Are you okay?'

Mary Mouse was in charge again by now and she seemed to have forgotten her earlier encouragement, so Mary said, 'Not really. I wish I'd said no to tomorrow, now. In fact, I wish I'd said no to the whole thing — nipped it in the bud from the start. It's laughable that an amateur like me should be singing for a top professional.'

'Well,' said Deidre, 'you can still back out if tomorrow goes badly — but don't forget that you beat him at Scrabble. He can't be much cleverer than you are!'

'He drank wine at dinner, whereas I had a clear head and a dose of good luck,' said Mary, as she put the window up and drove off with a blown kiss and a wave, thinking that it was nice of her sister to offer encouragement but she didn't know as much about musicians as Mary did. Some of them could be critical and sarcastic about anyone not pulling their weight. It did make sense to have one last try though, if only because of the prospect of a better job.

Mary soon had to put it out of her mind because the wind and rain made driving difficult. She was relieved to get home and spent the evening reading, taking a leisurely bath and intermittently wondering what caring for Mrs Braithwaite might entail. In the end she put the matter into an imaginary drawer, along with Requiem of Life, before settling down to sleep.

***

Luke's Christmas day was very different. He had stayed up late the previous evening because a theme for a new composition was running through his head and he wanted to start work on it. Sometimes, the most promising ideas vanished by morning if he didn't get them down on paper quickly. On this occasion, the more he wrote, the more he was inspired to write, and it was two a.m. before he knew it. He therefore slept in and nearly missed sharing breakfast with his mother again.

'Oh, good,' said Delia when he entered the dining room. 'I was wondering if you'd gone out again. I've been thinking.'

'And Merry Christmas to you, too, Mother,' said Luke, plonking a kiss on her forehead. 'Go on then. What have you been thinking about?'

'Mary,' said Delia. 'I would like to ask her if she'd alternate with Chris as my permanent carer. Chris wants to go down to three weeks on, and three off.'

Luke couldn't see any reason why not. Mary was already working as a carer so was presumably qualified, so he promised to ask her if she'd come over again tomorrow. While eating breakfast, he wondered what it would be like to come home and find Mary there and quickly decided that he would like it very much. She had made him laugh. He couldn't remember when that last happened. However, he put off contacting her for a while, thinking that it would be best to let her enjoy most of Christmas Day in peace. He didn't want her to feel hounded.

Soon it was time to set off for church, another part of their Christmas ritual, and when they got back it was almost time for lunch, followed by opening each other's presents — a dress shirt for Luke because he needed a lot of those for concerts, and slippers for his mother. Then it was time for Delia's nap, so Luke was free to compose for an hour or so, which flew past because he was so absorbed in what he was doing.

The rest of the day was tedious. Delia expected him to spend it with her in the sitting room and he complied because it was Christmas Day and he wanted to keep in her good books, but melodies and harmonies for the new work were still running through his head as the television droned on. He left the room to fetch manuscript paper, but she looked at it suspiciously when he returned and announced that she was just about to suggest that they played Scrabble again. At least that was better than enforced television watching, Luke thought, and set it up, but the game wasn't very rewarding because he could beat his mother too easily. He found himself wishing Mary was there, she certainly gave him a run for his money. That reminded him that he hadn't asked her about tomorrow, so he quickly sent a text between moves and gave a satisfied smile when he got an answer in the affirmative.

Not for the first time, Mary wondered if she had slipped into 'Alice in Wonderland'. Everything that was said and done here seemed a bit weird and unexpected.

'You can't expect a mere slip of a girl to hammer the piano as you do!' exclaimed his mother.

'She's not as insubstantial as she looks,' he replied enigmatically, kissing his mother on the cheek and, as he hurried out of the door, calling out that he would ring her, and that Mary would hear from his agent.

She still had questions to ask about domestic arrangements and whether she would be expected to do housework, but Mrs Braithwaite quickly became tired and Mary soon gave up. She wrote her name and mobile number on the torn-out page of a notebook from her bag and put it on a nearby table under an ornament, suggesting that Chris be asked to give her a call when next she came, so that they could get together to decide if they were sufficiently suited to job-share. Chris could also show her round and give her a better idea of what would be involved, she thought. As she left, she heard a bell, presumably Mrs Braithwaite summoning Jenny.

***

Luke felt a familiar mixture of relief and guilt as he drove away from Cadence, relief at not having to struggle to make conversation with his mother any more and guilt for feeling relief. He had enormous sympathy for her condition but didn't know how to provide the affection and constant companionship that she craved. He'd really like to tell her about his strong drive to compose; how he felt 'on his beam' when concentrating his conducting efforts on getting his own work performed, and how he needed more time for it — but she loved to see him in evening dress, conducting classical music before large audiences in famous venues, and talking about anything else resulted in her disapproving look.

He was stuck in a vicious circle. He worked hard to maintain the standard that was now expected of him; that (and his appearance, much admired by a great number of female middle-aged concert goers) meant success; success meant that he was always in demand; that led to more work and the whole thing had become relentless and exhausting. He was forced to accept most of the work offered because he needed the money and because his friend and agent, Steve, understandably pushed him quite hard to accept engagements because his business was doing very well on it. He dreaded getting back on to that merry-go-round but couldn't see a way out of it — and he still had to find a horn player for Requiem of Life! At least he had the soloists sorted out.

***

As Mary returned home, she thought about Mrs Braithwaite's offer. She didn't really want to stick with caring for the rest of her working life but the position at Cadence would give her time to train for something else.

She phoned her sister, hoping to use her as a sounding board but Deidre was about to go out, so they didn't speak for long.

'Well, I would grab it with both hands!' she said. 'Nicer surroundings than the care home, only one person to look after, plenty of time off and occasional visits from a good-looking, intelligent, talented man who sounds as though he has your welfare at heart!'

Mary reflected that, when discussing her future, Deidre's main focal point was always about finding her a suitable partner and it sounded as though she had now decided that Luke might be a good candidate. If anything, he was the fly in the ointment as far as Mary was concerned, and she hoped he wouldn't come home very often. His thoughts about her taking the job seemed incongruous; she'd asked if she'd be suitable for his mother, but he'd replied with Mary's wellbeing in mind. On the one hand, it was quite gratifying to think that anyone had her welfare in mind, but on the other, shouldn't he be giving more thought to his mother's needs? He hadn't even asked Mary if she had any qualifications in care work. Furthermore, he was unpredictable and that made her uncomfortable. She liked to understand people; to know where she stood.

Then she worried that Mrs Braithwaite wouldn't remember to give Chris the note, and at that point decided she was being ridiculous. If she hadn't heard anything after a couple of weeks but still wanted the job, she could always ring them or call in. In the end, she firmly put the whole thing out of her mind, along with the recording session to which she now felt committed. Both could wait until the New Year.

and quiet in which to gather himself together was just too great.

He flung himself into a chair and quickly ate a bar of chocolate. The previous evening, he had conducted a well-known London orchestra in a concert in the Festival Hall. They had performed Beethoven's Ninth symphony and Mahler's Fifth — a demanding and lengthy programme. After that, he'd been persuaded to go out to dinner with some influential benefactors of the orchestra and arrived back at his flat, exhausted, at one a.m. He went straight to bed and fell asleep quickly, but that was a mistake because he woke up again an hour later with indigestion. He didn't get back to sleep for ages and when he did, he slept so deeply that he didn't hear the alarm that he'd set. Eventually rising, much later than he'd intended, he'd skipped breakfast and then negotiated the London traffic — arriving at the rehearsal hall with no time to spare. He knew that this set a bad example — indeed, he often berated other musicians for turning up at the last minute, emphasising the importance of leaving time to settle in. He closed his eyes and let himself drift for a few minutes before taking up the baton again.

***

After the break, Mary, who was now shaking with nerves, went to stand near the other soloists, ready to sing when needed. She was there for some time while

Luke continued to do detailed work with the other musicians — long enough to realise that she'd pass out before it was her turn if she didn't do something to calm herself. When looking after Sam, she had learned a lot about stress management and she now used every ounce of mental discipline that she could muster to ask for courage and calmness in order to get her posture and breathing right before her first entry. She was determined not to waste all the hard work she had put in and threw everything she had into remembering Luke's advice about good singing technique. Fortunately, the whale song was now so ingrained in her memory that she was able to produce it to order, without even looking at the music. She fixed her gaze on Luke and just let it happen. After the first few notes, she felt herself being carried along by the inspiring and evocative music. Very soon it was all over, and she waited for the stopping of the orchestra and the criticism that had been the lot of most of the others — but it didn't happen. Luke just continued to the next section and she was left standing there, wondering whether her performance was beneath contempt or actually good enough for her to escape unscathed. She became aware that her heart was hammering but stood her ground until Luke noticed that she was still there and, without missing a beat, indicated with a movement of his head that she could leave. He mouthed something that might have been 'okay', and that was it; or so she thought. When the other musicians finally reached the end of the work, Luke announced that they would conclude by going straight through it once without stopping. Mary's first reaction was pleasure because she would hear it properly at last — closely followed by dismay because her ordeal wasn't over. It was easier this time, however, with none of the drawn-out delay in which tension could build, and she was able to enjoy being part of such inspiring music.

She stayed near the front, through to the end, because that's what the other soloists did, and then went back to her seat at the side of the hall in time to see Chris turning Delia's wheelchair around and leaving the room, presumably in search of a disabled toilet. Mary followed them and offered to help but was told that she had done a great job and should relax and recover so she went back to the hall and sank gratefully into a chair. However, on looking up she was alarmed to see Luke heading her way. He collapsed into the seat next to hers and the close physical proximity caused her body to adopt its defensive posture. The exertion of the rehearsal had left him soaked in sweat and exuding testosterone, and Mary found that dealing with the effect that this had on her was every bit as challenging as singing her solo, and she immediately became hot and flustered.

Luke registered her discomfort but decided to ignore it and asked how she felt about her performance; a simple enough question, but Mary was stuck for words. He looked at her curiously and helped her out.

'I thought it was fine. Your first note sounded a bit wobbly the first time through, but if anything like that happens when we record, they'll just edit it out. A pity really, because slight imperfections make it sound more authentic.'

Mary managed to say 'thank you' but then dried up again, cursing herself for reacting like a silly teenager.

Luke decided to change tack and asked whether she was going to take up the position of live-in carer. This was easier and Mary told him that she had emailed the paperwork the previous day and would be starting next month. 'If that's all right with you,' she added, hurriedly.

'Yes of course,' he said, in some surprise. 'My mother really likes you and you have all the right experience. How are you getting on with Chris?'

Mary was relieved to have something easy to talk about and she praised Chris's cheerful approach and way of working. This topic kept her going until Chris and Delia came back and took over the conversation with much enthusing over Requiem of Life, which allowed Mary to gratefully retreat into the background. The hotel they were staying in was close to Luke's London flat and it was arranged that they would meet for dinner that evening.

Chapter 8

Delia needed a rest in the afternoon, so Chris and Mary
did likewise but, after that, they all took another taxi and
went shopping. Regent Street was like a different world
to Mary; noisy and crowded with many sights and
sounds competing for her attention. She much preferred
the relaxed pace of the North Norfolk market towns
with their small and intimate shops. She couldn't afford
to buy anything, but was fascinated by Delia's ability to
spend an alarming amount of money in a short space of
time. Chris darted about inspecting merchandise like a
butterfly, unable to choose between countless exquisite
flowers.

It was a scramble to get ready for dinner when they
got back, and Luke was already at the table when they
went down. The meal was not very congenial because
he was obviously unhappy about the Requiem of Life
rehearsal. He sounded off about orchestral players who
were practically sight reading and therefore not
confident enough to put much feeling into the music,
and a chorus master who had under-rehearsed the choir.
Chris tried saying that it sounded wonderful to her, but
she was not a musician and Luke did not hesitate to
point out that more knowledgeable people would find

faults that she was not even aware of. Mary also thought it was wonderful but decided to keep quiet rather than receive a similar put-down.

Delia said that she was very proud to have a son who could write music as well as conducting established music, but perhaps he was taking on too much. It crossed Luke's mind that now might be a good time to emphasise that composing was actually the most important thing to him and that he would rather let some of the popular concerts go, but he was feeling tense and disgruntled and didn't think he could do it tactfully. He didn't want to upset her because she had made the effort to come today. Perhaps, if Requiem of Life was successful, she might come to see him in a different light. As he remained silent, Delia tried again.

'That isn't to say it isn't lovely music.'

'Thank you, but it's meant to be disturbing rather than lovely!' he countered. 'It is designed to bring people face to face with the harsh reality of the loss of life on earth, but no one seems to get that!' Then as an afterthought, 'Except you, Mary, and you're the least trained of the lot!'

Mary was too stunned to come up with a reply to that and Delia jumped in again.

'Don't the orchestral players practise their parts before coming to rehearsal? If they were confident then they could concentrate on how it feels to be a dying creature.'

Luke sighed and leant back in his chair.

'I have covered all of it over the last few weeks, but I've had to draw players from all over the place and have never had a full orchestra because they all take on too much work in order to make ends meet. Most of them haven't practised enough to leave the mechanics of the music on autopilot and simply be expressive. I suppose it isn't their fault.'

'So why can Mary do it?' asked Chris.

At last, Mary found her voice and explained that she had only a few lines of music to work on and could therefore practise them thoroughly, and even though she was busy with a demanding job, she had made time out of sheer terror of getting it wrong.

'And I did find the music very moving, so it was easy for me to get inside it,' she added, after a short pause.

'Well, I'm pleased someone was moved,' said Luke. 'Obviously the answer is to tie each of them, in turn, to a chair and give them one-to-one tuition until they know it backwards. Then force them to live in my head for a week. Then they'd understand it.'

'Sarcasm isn't very becoming, dear,' put in Delia, and Chris asked if Mary had been tied to a chair and whether she had enjoyed being in Luke's head.

Mary started to laugh but quickly stifled it, noticing the glare that Chris was receiving. It was obviously no laughing matter to Luke and perhaps that was reasonable because he must have worked very hard on the music and understandably wanted it to be well performed and interpreted.

Then the thing that Mary dreaded happened — again. Delia asked Chris to take her to the toilet. While Delia was napping that afternoon, Mary had told Chris how difficult she found it to make conversation with Luke and asked if she could come with them if that situation arose again, so that she wasn't left alone with him. Chris had agreed but when Mary offered to help, Delia ruined the plan.

'Oh no, we can manage, can't we, Chris? You stay and talk to Luke,' she said, as if she were bestowing a lovely gift.

Surprisingly, he cheered up a bit as they left, remarking, 'Poor Mary, it seems as though you've drawn the short straw!'

She decided to ignore this and show him that she could be mature and sociable, even when faced with a provocative remark. After a moment, inspiration came.

'How do you go about composing a work like Requiem of Life?'

This was a masterstroke because it sent him into a long speech about having an idea that was powerful enough to be worth translating into music, then allowing musical themes to attach themselves to that idea. This stage often happened during a long walk — ideally somewhere quiet, which was difficult in London, but he had discovered a small, hidden park surrounded by quaint old buildings about two miles from his flat and he often ended up there. When he had the main themes in mind, he worked at the piano, trying out different ways to use them. This often seemed unproductive at first, but in the middle of the night, scraps of finished music sometimes came to mind, and they were so powerful that he scribbled them down immediately on manuscript paper that was always kept at the bedside. Then it was a case of putting in a lot of hard work to set that 'finished music' down in a way that others could understand. There was a lot more detail about the various stages and Mary was fascinated. When he paused for breath, she asked where he thought the gift for being so musical came from.

'There's probably a genetic tendency — my mother and father were both musical. Unfortunately, Mum has lost her singing voice now, but she was very talented as a younger woman. Because they loved music, they paid for me to have violin, piano and singing lessons. I did all the practical exams, plus keyboard harmony, theory and so on. I wasn't an easy child and their answer to my bad behaviour was to shut me in the music room, where the only amusement was to practise my instruments and scribble music. All my pent-up feelings ended up on pages of manuscript. It was probably terrible music, and no one ever did anything with it, but I suppose it flexed my muscles so that, when I got to music college, I found it easy to continue.'

'And why, after all that, did you become a conductor rather than a composer?' asked Mary, who was genuinely intrigued to know why he hadn't concentrated on composing, as it was obviously his greatest passion.

'I studied composition and violin at music college; no one took much interest in the music I wrote at that time, but I did well on the violin and was offered plenty of orchestral work when I finished my degree, so that's how I made a living for the first few years. Eventually, I got a leader's position but found it frustrating because my ideas frequently clashed with the conductor's. To cut a long story short, I ended up enrolling for a master's degree in conducting because I thought I could do it with more sympathy towards the music and performers than most of the conductors I played for. That probably sounds big-headed and maybe it was, but I was lucky, anyway. I got lots of engagements and I've been on a sort of international merry-go-round ever since!' He gave a hollow laugh. 'Here I am trying to promote a work about climate change yet I'm regularly clocking up countless air miles and probably destroying the ozone layer single-handedly!'

Mary was amazed to learn that he was an accomplished violinist because she was already impressed by his conducting, piano playing and singing. Also, she thought Requiem of Life was the most inspiring music she had ever heard, so he was clearly talented in many ways — perhaps a musical genius. She didn't know what to say about his concern about adding to pollution by international travel so changed direction slightly.

'I see your point about people not having enough time to practise your music but surely by the time you do the recording, they'll be *more* practised because of today and, another thing, some of them will care about maintaining the ecological systems that support life as much as you do and that will surely influence the way they play and sing. What you said on the subject today will slowly sink in.'

'And some of them will continue to laugh about the whole thing,' he quickly replied, with unmistakeable bitterness in his voice. 'I have overheard remarks, such as "Uh-oh. Here come the dying turtles again," when we start work on Requiem of Life. Come to think of it, I'm probably meant to hear it.'

Mary winced and said, 'Surely not!' in a shocked voice.

Luke shrugged and commented that anyone in the limelight was an easy target for ridicule.

'That aside,' he continued, 'I hope you're right about some of them caring about the environment and perhaps some will eventually see the possibility of music on the subject awakening interest and concern in the listener. Time will tell.' He paused. 'Anyway, thank you for coming all this way to sing and for helping my mother — and for listening to me droning on.'

He suddenly smiled as he said this, and Mary was startled into smiling back. She started to say that she had found singing in his composition enormously rewarding, but Chris and Delia reappeared, and Delia cut across her with apologies for taking so long,

'My fault as usual. Now, are we having dessert?'

'You've been ages, Mother. You go ahead,' said Luke. 'I need to get home because I have work to do in preparation for a concert in Paris tomorrow and I'm booked in for an early flight. I'll see you next week, Mary.'

Then, after a quick peck on his mother's cheek, he was gone. *Back on to the merry-go-round*, thought Mary. Some would enjoy his exciting lifestyle, but it was obvious that he did not.

By the time dessert came, Delia was noticeably flagging and couldn't eat much. She soon said she needed to go to bed and this time, allowed Mary to help Chris to get her ready. It was still quite early so, once again, both carers went to Mary's room.

'Thank goodness you're here!' exclaimed Chris, as soon as they were safely behind Mary's door. 'If you hadn't come, I'd have to have to lie there in the dark, listening to Delia snoring for two hours before it got to my usual bed-time!'

Mary wouldn't have minded an early night but enjoyed talking with Chris, so decided to try to keep going. She propped herself up on the bed and Chris curled her legs up on the easy chair and they chatted about Chris's love life. She had been spending her downtime at her boyfriend Phil's flat in Sheffield for some time now and he wanted them to buy a house together and make the relationship permanent. Now that Chris would only be working three weeks out of every six, this could work, but she wasn't sure she could put up with his untidiness. She described some of the messes that she'd encountered on returning to the flat after a spell at Cadence and the two women laughed about some of the things she'd found — such as parts of a car engine that he'd been working on, secreted under the bed.

Chris asked Mary if she had a serious boyfriend and Mary shook her head and described her recent circumstances.

'It sounds as though it's time you spread your wings a bit,' remarked Chris, 'but for goodness' sake don't get entangled with His Lordship. I'm sorry we left you alone with him again, but I didn't have a choice because Delia scuppered our plan. I was panicking a bit because she didn't make it to the loo and we had to get clean clothes, which took ages. I thought you'd kill me when we finally got back to the table, but I needn't have worried because you were obviously engaged in an intense conversation and grinning at each other like a pair of idiots! What were you talking about?'

'I asked him how he went about composing a piece of music and why he became a conductor and he seemed to really enjoy telling me. I hardly had to say anything because he went on and on,' explained Mary.

'Well — what I saw was two people leaning towards each other over the table, gazing into each other's eyes and smiling. That usually means a romantic encounter!'

Mary laughed and protested that it wasn't anything like that, but Chris looked sceptical.

'Well, I haven't seen him smile once in the three years I've looked after his mother and you managed to achieve it in ten minutes, and from a black-mood starting point, so you must have said something to bring that about.'

'I asked him about composing and conducting,' Mary reiterated, emphatically. 'After a long time on those subjects he thanked me for coming and that was all there was to it.'

It crossed her mind that he might have found her sympathetic response appealing when he mentioned the orchestra's mockery of Requiem of Life but thought it best not to tell Chris that part, so swiftly moved on to questions about Delia's care. Before long they were both yawning, so soon decided to turn in, but Chris stopped at the doorway.

'Remember what I said about His Lordship. He obviously likes you a lot but he's not a very nice person; he visits his mother occasionally but then hardly speaks to her. Also, he may be flattering you now, but that could be just because he thinks you'll be an easy conquest.' Mary looked shocked and said he'd done nothing to suggest that he may have that in mind. 'Well,

I suggest you look at his blog if you don't believe me,' continued Chris. 'He goes through women at a horrendous rate. I wouldn't want to see you get hurt. Be *very* careful!'

Mary went to bed after that, and fell asleep straight away but as so often happened, woke up again three hours later. Then she tossed and turned while the kaleidoscope of the day's events went round and round in her mind and Chris's parting remark began to bother her. She didn't think Luke was horrible — just unhappy and stressed and sometimes bad-tempered as a result, especially when the music that he'd written was not performed well. As for not smiling — he had actually laughed about his mother confusing whinnying with whining. Another thing she'd noticed at Christmas was that Delia sometimes spoke to him rather disparagingly, so if their relationship wasn't very good it could be partly her fault. However, it was probably best to steer clear of him as much as possible because, although she found him attractive in many ways, she sensed that he could easily break her heart.

Chapter 9

Chris had bought tickets for the London Eye, which took up most of the next morning and then they had lunch at a Chinese restaurant in Soho, Delia managing the chopsticks very well and the other two collapsing in giggles before requesting knives and forks. They had left the already-packed car in the hotel car park, so took one last taxi back there and then set off for Sheringham. Mary admired Chris's stamina; she seemed perfectly happy to do the lengthy drive home, as well as all the tasks she would have when they got there, and Mary hoped that she would be able to keep going at the same pace when it was her turn to take Delia on a trip.

It was only a few days before the recording session, but that journey would have to be made by train and tube and it would be very different to the relaxed time with Delia and Chris. She would travel the afternoon before, stay in the Southwark hotel recommended by Luke's agent, and would have to locate the recording studio the following morning alone and on foot. Driven by anxiety about not getting there on time — or worse, never finding it — Mary made careful plans and allowed plenty of time; too much as it turned out, because she arrived far too early.

It was, as predicted, a long and rather boring day with much repetition and it was quite cold in the redundant church. When they had a break, a couple of choir members tried to engage Mary in conversation, but she was reluctant to offer information about herself because her way into Requiem of Life was so odd. Everyone else had more to do than she did, so she sat alone, listening to the music and watching Luke alternate between conducting the various sections of the work and holding rather feverish conversations with the recording crew. He called for the Sea Creatures' section to be repeated in its entirety because of shortcomings and problems getting the balance between voices and instruments right.

'More pathos, please,' was the only comment addressed directly to Mary, so she did her very best to come up with that. The second attempt must have been more acceptable all round because he moved on to the next section, but Mary hung on to the end of the day, in case he went back.

It was well into evening by the time she got back to the hotel, feeling cold, tired and hungry. She couldn't face eating alone in the dining room, so asked room service to bring sandwiches. When she had almost finished them, the phone rang, and Luke's voice enquired why she had run away from the recording session so quickly.

'I was cold and hungry,' she replied, hesitantly. 'And I didn't think that you would need to speak to me.'

'I didn't,' he replied. 'There was nothing wrong with your contribution. I just wondered what you thought of the day in general.'

'Well — I don't really feel qualified to comment,' she replied, feeling somewhat at a loss. After all, she must have been the least musically informed person there and she couldn't think why he was ringing her at all. He must be exhausted after such an arduous day and surely needed food and recuperation himself, unless it was as Chris said, and he really did enjoy her company. His next words confirmed this because he asked her if she would have dinner with him.

Mary's tummy did a flip and she glanced down at her mostly eaten sandwich as she thought, *Thank goodness I have an excuse to say no.*

After an uncomfortable silence, she stammered that she had already eaten but that it was kind of him to ask.

'I thought you might be lonely after coming up on your own and sitting by yourself for most of the day,' he ploughed on.

'I didn't mind, and it was interesting,' she replied, not altogether honestly as the day had seemed very long. 'But thank you for asking me,' she repeated politely, hoping he would go away because she felt out of her depth.

'When are you going home?' he persisted.

'I'm hoping to catch the nine o'clock train in the morning,' she replied quickly. Surely, he wouldn't suggest breakfast!

It was Luke's turn to hesitate — presumably sensing that he wasn't getting anywhere. He muttered something about being rather tied up the next day, anyway, and moved on to asking when she would start at Cadence. With some relief at the change of subject, Mary said that she would take over from Chris the following Monday.

'Good,' he replied. 'Let me know if there are any problems.'

Mary said she would and started to say 'Thank you and goodbye,' but Luke continued.

'I'll send you a copy of Requiem of Life when I get one. It will be a while before the published version is available, but they said they'd send me an advance copy. I'll send it to you on a device that you can play through the sound equipment in the music room.'

'Oh, I don't think I could manage that!' said Mary, who had only an old-fashioned CD player at home.

'Don't worry — I'll tell you what to do. You can play it to my mother, if she's interested.'

Mary thanked him and said she couldn't wait to hear it. There was an awkward silence, finally broken by Luke.

'Well, I'll hang up then — goodbye' and at last the call ended.

She went over the conversation while soaking in the bath, aware of that feeling of incongruity that most of her conversations with Luke produced. Why on earth had he asked her out to dinner? He must have lots of musical friends to share an evening meal with, but he had definitely said 'Would you like to join me for dinner' rather than 'join us for dinner.' If she had agreed to go, it would have been very difficult to converse for the length of a meal, as they had little in common; neither of them was very good at social chat and they had probably exhausted the subject of composition.

It was kind of him to think that she might be lonely, but that didn't necessarily mean that he was kind by nature, he wasn't very nice to his mother, or at least not very good at keeping her company. Chris, who had known him for three years, thought that he was a 'horrible person'. Perhaps she was right, and he was just looking for an easy sexual conquest as relaxation after a hard day's work! As soon as this thought entered Mary's mind, she became acutely aware of her naked body and jumped out of the bath, grabbing the nearest towel. Then she felt ridiculous because there couldn't be anyone watching her. There was a full-length mirror in the bathroom so, after quickly rubbing herself dry, she let the towel drop and looked at herself properly for the first time in years. She was slim and her breasts were still nice. She thought that her hair would look better if it was artificially lightened to ash blonde instead of being left to its natural mousiness. Her complexion was fair, so she could easily get away with that. *All in all, I'm not bad looking,* she decided, *and it really is time I let myself think about sex again.* This was a can of worms for Mary because she hadn't had a proper relationship since Adrian left. Deidre was always telling her to register with an internet dating service and get something going before she ended up like a dried-out and wrinkled old prune. For a moment, she let herself consider Luke as a possible candidate, but she quickly quashed the idea and wrapped herself up in the towel again.

When she was in her night clothes, she took up her tablet and found his blog. For some reason, she felt guilty about reading it — as though she was sneaking a look at his personal journal. *Ridiculous,* she thought. *People write blogs because they want them to be read.* Strangely, the Requiem of Life recording wasn't mentioned at all in the latest entry, which had today's date on it — it was all about a recent concert in Paris and was full of smart remarks about the well-known musicians he'd worked with. Why wouldn't he want everyone to know about his own work? She frowned and read back over the last few weeks. There seemed to be a lot of after-concert dinners with glamorous people and there were broad hints that he knew some of the female celebrities *very* well. She could see what Chris meant but something about it didn't ring true. It didn't sound as though it had been written by the person who'd spoken about his composing aspirations at great length in the hotel the other night. Perhaps the blog was his public persona, and she'd glimpsed the real Luke in the hotel. Or — perhaps — the blog wasn't written by him at all? She decided that it would have to remain a mystery because she could hardly ask him.

Mary went to bed, still resolved to keep him at arm's length.

***

Luke felt a sharp pang of disappointment when Mary turned him down. He had been looking forward to more of the conversation that he'd enjoyed on the evening of the rehearsal and had taken it for granted that she would agree to meet him, because women usually bit his hand off if he suggested dinner. The thought of time alone with her had kept him going through the arduous period between rehearsal and recording, with that hectic dash to and from Paris in between the two. Now he felt thoroughly deflated and didn't know what to do with himself — and he was hungry. Resigned, he took a ready meal from the fridge and thrust it into the microwave. As he ate, he thought about his coming commitments and registered, despondently, that it would be weeks before he could get to Sheringham. Once there, Mary would have to talk to him. He looked at the schedule of forthcoming rehearsals and events on his tablet and contemplated moving or cancelling something. Then he wondered what on earth he was doing. He never changed things around to accommodate another person! In any case, he needed the money that all those things on his schedule generated. After the meal, he took out the manuscript of his latest composition and buried himself in that for a while. Composition was guaranteed to keep uncomfortable thoughts at bay but on this occasion, he was too tired to stick at it for long and soon headed for bed. Despite having eaten, he continued to feel hollow inside.

The period that followed was a blur of studying scores, meetings, travelling, rehearsing and performing. Shopping for food was rushed and haphazard, squeezed in between other things with little thought about the quality of what he was buying. Sundays offered the only free time in which to compose and he guarded them closely, only leaving the flat to walk and allow inspiration to come. On Sundays, Luke felt that he was truly himself.

The advance copy of Requiem of Life arrived, and he made time to listen to it late one night. He was nervous about this; so much effort, time and money had gone into it. What if he didn't like the result? But the technicians had done a good job — only occasionally trampling on his musical intentions — and he relaxed as he got further into it, even starting to feel quietly pleased. He stayed up later still to prepare a copy for Mary — and his mother, of course — although he doubted she'd be very interested. No one else received a copy. He looked for a response for a few days, but none came and the hollow feeling returned.

Towards the end of February, he learned of an unexpected respite in March, Steve, his agent and long-time friend rang to say that he was forced to re-schedule an orchestra meeting that had been planned for Saturday the 24th. That meant the whole weekend would be free. Luke brushed aside Steve's apologies and ended the call with a growing feeling of jubilation. He remembered Mary had said she would start work on the Monday following the recording of Requiem of Life and quickly worked out that she would be in her second spell of caring by the 24th. He could go to Cadence, renew their acquaintance and have time to compose, as well. He quickly sent an email about his intended visit.

Chapter 10

The last few days at the care home passed uneventfully for Mary and her final day was unremarkable. Carers came and went all the time, and no one did anything special to mark her leaving, but surprisingly, the manager said that she was sorry to see her go because the residents liked her. A few of the regular staff wished her luck in her new job and, before she knew it, Mary was out of the door for the last time and on her way home, where she spent the evening packing.

She arrived at Cadence early the next morning and Chris, sounding very lively and happy to have three weeks of free time before her, brought Mary up to date regarding everything going on in the household. She kindly said that she could be contacted by mobile if Mary was stumped about anything and then kissed Delia goodbye and left with a cheery wave. Mary felt rather nervous — not about care procedures, because she was experienced in that area — but about being responsible for the house, which was larger and grander than any that she had lived in. She prepared the lunch that Chris had suggested and ate it with Delia, who reiterated that she hated to eat alone and obviously enjoyed pumping Mary for details of her musical day in London.

Delia's condition, and the need to wear braces in order to remain upright, meant that she was in considerable pain by midday, so she always took a rest after lunch. Mary rested too for a while and then, taking the bell sounder, went to explore the garden. Chris didn't seem to be very interested in it, but Mary liked to be out of doors and was pleasantly surprised to find that it was quite big and obviously laid out with Delia's wheelchair in mind. Someone had apparently thought carefully about making it accessible and it was well maintained and attractive, with contrasting areas and plenty of places to find the best sun at different times of day. She couldn't see Luke taking on a project like this or the adaptations inside the house, so perhaps there were other relatives involved in helping Delia. Chris had mentioned that there was a regular gardener, which was fortunate because, much as Mary liked gardening, she couldn't see how such a large area could be managed alongside all the housework and care work. Chris had left the house clean and tidy so there wasn't too much to do at the moment, but it would be a different story as handover day approached.

There was still no sound from Delia and it was getting cold, so Mary went upstairs to look in on her. As she was sleeping soundly, she fetched some music from her room, thinking that the best opportunity for playing the Steinway would be at the beginning of her three weeks' work. The only piece that she had practised recently was one of Mendelssohn's 'Songs without words', which was hardly suitable for the 'piano bashing' that Luke had recommended but it was her preferred choice. She felt nervous to begin with as this instrument and these surroundings were associated with music lessons that had taken some courage on her part, but she soon settled down and began to enjoy playing an instrument that was far superior to her own. By the time Delia rang, Mary was well into her stride and didn't want to stop but duty called, and she ran upstairs.

The rest of the day went by smoothly and Delia was settled in bed for the night by nine thirty. Mary tidied up the kitchen and left things ready for breakfast in the morning then went to her own room, which was pleasant and comfortable. There was even a small desk so that she could work on whatever she decided to study. There hadn't been much time to think about it, but nutrition was one possibility. For years she had been learning, in an unstructured way, about food for health and for combating disease and had built up a large file of newspaper and magazine cuttings on the subject. She also had several books. Looking after Sam had required huge reserves of energy and eating wisely had helped to provide it. In addition, she reacted badly to most medication, both prescribed and 'over the counter' so had devised dietary changes that overcame many common ailments. It was a source of pride to Mary that she rarely went into a dispensary and she thought that this policy enabled her body's natural healing and balancing mechanisms to have free reign. She was also quite fit as a result of pushing Sam (who was quite heavy) around in a wheelchair and she hoped to continue this with Delia.

Over all, Mary was pleased with the first day in her new job and quickly fell into a contented sleep. When the bell rang at two a.m. she awoke with a start and couldn't think where she was or what she was supposed to be doing for a minute or two. Did Sam need her, was her first thought, closely followed by the sinking feeling that came with the knowledge that she had lost Sam. She grabbed a dressing gown and stumbled into Delia's room to help her to the commode. It took a while to sleep again after this but the next time she awoke it was daylight and she felt capable of dealing with whatever the day had to bring.

Delia and Mary soon fell into a comfortable routine and the days passed quickly, as there was plenty to do. They sometimes listened to music together and watched television in the evenings, but Mary felt that Delia, who was obviously intelligent and knowledgeable about all sorts of things, needed more stimulating activities. So she found the Scrabble set and a few other games that they could enjoy. Delia liked playing cards and taught Mary several games, promising to teach her the rules of bridge next time she was on duty. The problem with all this was that Mary didn't have enough spare time to keep Delia occupied as much as she needed and it all seemed too insular; in the whole three weeks, the only visitor was the hairdresser!

One day, at lunch, Mary asked if Delia ever went out socially or invited anyone round for a meal.

'My social life was all wrapped up with the choir I was in,' explained Delia. 'And when my singing voice went, it just wasn't the same. I went to a few concerts, but I wanted to be up there singing with them and I found it very frustrating not being able to do that, so I only go at Christmas now — and that's only because it's one of the few chances I get to go out with Luke. I don't know about you but, for me, the joy of belonging to a choir is twofold, there's the feeling of rapport and team spirit and the way that concentrating on reading the music and holding a part takes you out of yourself.'

Mary knew exactly what she meant. She was still attending choir practice as Delia had kindly suggested an agency carer for those evenings and she was enjoying the singing more than ever.

'Do people from the choir ever come to see you?' she asked Delia.

'They did to start with, but you know how it is. Conversation becomes strained when you're not sharing the same activity any more.'

It was obvious that Delia had become rather isolated, so Mary tried a different tack.

'Well, how about something different? You don't have any problems with card games so perhaps we could find a group for you to join.'

'I suppose it wouldn't matter that I'm stuck in this damned thing for playing cards,' Delia indicated the wheelchair, 'so it might be worth exploring — but you'd have to take me or entertain people here.' She added wistfully, after a pause, 'It would be nice to have more people to talk to.'

Mary started to say she didn't mind entertaining, but Delia cut across her.

'I know! I'll teach you to play bridge. Then we can join a local group and you can be my partner! I used to play in a group when I could get around by myself.'

'It might take me some time to learn enough to do that!' said Mary, in alarm. She was also thinking that this suggestion sounded time consuming and, although it might be interesting to learn a new skill, the housework would be neglected and there wouldn't be time to make the highly nutritious meals that she had taken the trouble to prepare, up until now.

'Well, that will be part of the fun,' responded Delia, who seemed delighted at the prospect of reviving an old interest.

Mary smiled at her, resigned to having to work longer hours as a result of agreeing to this plan. Perhaps it was more important to give a bored and lonely person something to look forward to than it was to worry about fitting in the housework. She did suggest, however, that they concentrated the lessons into the first two weeks of each spell of work so that she could prepare for Chris' return in the final week.

Delia's mind continued to work on the question of social activities so, over the evening meal, she told Mary that she knew quite a lot of people at church:

'Luke sometimes takes me to a service when he's home but that isn't very often. I don't feel I can ask Chris because she doesn't believe, but how do you feel about taking me?'

Mary was pleased that Delia had come up with another way to expand her social life so, although it meant adding even more to her workload, replied, 'I'm happy to take you and stay for the service but I don't really have conventional Christian beliefs.'

'Well — I'm not sure I do,' said Delia, 'but I miss the music and it would be nice to see some people I used to be friendly with again.'

They ate in silence for a moment or two but then Delia asked what Mary did believe. This was rather personal, but Mary enjoyed their conversations. She replied to Delia, cautiously.

'I know that Divinity exists because of experiences I have had in meditation and when listening to certain pieces of music, and I think there is a spark of that Divinity in all creatures, so all life is sacred. Some people, like Jesus, fully expressed that Divinity in their lives and we should try to live by their teachings, but I struggle to believe that he was the only one or that there is a person called God judging us or directing our lives. I mean, I do believe in God, but I think that it's something mysterious, beyond male and female —

something that is the source of all life — and I do pray to that, whatever it is, and my prayers are usually answered, but often in an unexpected way.' Then she added, anxiously, 'I hope none of that offends you.'

'Not in the least,' replied Delia. 'I pray as well, and I too think that other people can express Divinity. You and Chris for a start. It takes an angel to wipe someone else's bottom!'

'I don't mean that I'm in that category!' laughed Mary, but she was secretly pleased to be valued; there hadn't been enough of that in her life, to date.

In her third week at Cadence, the promised recording of Requiem of Life arrived with a handwritten note giving details of how to operate the sound system and where to plug in the memory device. The two women listened to it after one of Delia's afternoon naps.

'What do you think of it?' asked Delia, when it was over. Mary replied that she thought it had turned out very well after all. 'But do you really like this sort of music?' pressed Delia.

'It is different to anything I have heard before, but it gets under my skin,' replied Mary. 'I think he meant it to affect people like that — to impress people with the subject matter.'

'Well,' continued Delia, 'I know he's worked hard on it and it is impressive, but I'm afraid I still prefer baroque and classical music if I'm honest. But your part was very good, dear.'

Mary thanked her and asked if Luke had written much before.

'Oh yes — lots,' said Delia, quite dismissively. 'He was always scribbling music as a child. My husband Eric thought we should get someone professional to look at it, but he died when Luke was still in his teens and...' she shrugged, 'well — I went to pieces for a while and never got around to it. I thought someone would take notice at music college, where he wrote a lot more, but I don't think he pushed it hard enough — or perhaps it just wasn't very good. He clearly had a talent for conducting and that seemed to take over. He's paying to have this work recorded and published himself, you know. It's a huge gamble.'

Mary was shocked, as it must have cost a small fortune to pay all those musicians and sound technicians, not to mention a publisher. He had paid her, for heaven's sake! He also had a London flat, and presumably he paid his agent. Was conducting really that lucrative? Also, Delia's outgoings must be very high — running the house, maintaining the garden, paying her and Chris... The Braithwaites must either be very rich or verging on bankruptcy!

On the day before takeover, Delia went for her nap as usual after lunch, but Mary continued to work at getting the house as pristine as Chris had left it. She had already cleaned out the fridge and stocked it with suitable food for the next couple of days and dusted and vacuumed every room. All Delia's clothes were nicely in order and the litter bins had been emptied.

Delia's bathroom couldn't be cleaned until she had used it in the morning, but Mary still had two more to do. She worked quickly and energetically, so had time to check her emails before Delia woke up. There was one from Luke.

'Hello, Mary. I hope your first weeks went well and you fathomed out how to play that recording I sent. You must be looking forward to some unbroken nights. I thought I should give you advance warning that I am planning to visit my mother on Saturday 23rd March and will stay for two nights. I will eat with you and Mum but please don't go to a lot of trouble. Just serve whatever you would normally have. I hope you are both well. Luke.'

Mary glanced at her diary and saw that the 23rd March was the first weekend after she resumed work. It was all very well him saying that she shouldn't go to any trouble, but she would want it to be right for her own satisfaction — and there were the bridge lessons taking up a lot of time, as well! It looked as though the first week back would be busy. She started to type a polite but brief reply, but the bell rang before she could send it.

After dinner, she washed up and then watched a television drama with Delia, who went to bed soon afterwards. Mary went to her room to finish the email she had begun earlier. She read Luke's message again and felt guilty about not acknowledging the Requiem of Life recording, so amended the reply she had begun earlier.

Thank you for sending the Requiem of Life recording. We both enjoyed it very much. There are no problems or difficulties to report, and your mother is well and looking forward to your visit. Please let me know nearer the time what time of day you plan to arrive.

    Kind regards,
    Mary.'

Chapter 11

Mary's home felt cold and damp when she returned to it. Over the last three weeks, she had called in on choir nights to make sure everything was all right and to pick up the post, but could never stay for long enough to heat it properly. Now she turned up the heating and opened one of the letters that had arrived since her last visit. It was from the local authority, asking if she would consider giving up the bungalow so that they could offer it to someone with special needs. An alternative one-bedroomed maisonette in Cromer was available for immediate occupation, at a lower rent, if she was interested. It had already occurred to Mary that she had been given a two-bedroomed bungalow only because of Sam's disability and that she really ought to vacate it so that another person with similar needs could be helped. She decided to ring the housing office to discuss possibilities. Perhaps she could say that she would move if they found her somewhere in Sheringham, instead. It would be a lot easier to keep an eye on it when she was working, and Delia probably wouldn't mind if they stopped off there from time to time. But then there was the piano to consider. Maisonettes were usually quite small and often upstairs. Even if she could get a piano into one, the other tenants would probably complain about the noise. Could she manage without one in her own home? That would mean she could only play when in the Braithwaite house and, in view of Delia's time-consuming plans, there wouldn't be much opportunity for that. If she *could* find a property that would take a piano, perhaps she could just play very quietly, concentrating on learning notes, and then play at the proper volume when she had access to the Steinway.

After thinking it over, while sorting out her belongings, she decided to try for a Sheringham property and rang the housing office, explaining her job situation and the piano problem. The latter was dismissed with the words, 'I'm afraid we can't take hobbies into account,' but some sympathy was shown about the constraints of her job. The young man said that properties in Sheringham rarely came up but that he would put her on the waiting list and Mary left it at that, thinking that she had at least bought some time. She was now free to research the course possibilities and quickly found something she was interested in. The fees were a problem but, if she was careful, it wouldn't take too long to save up and, in the meantime, there was a lot of reading and internet research that she could do.

It was half-term and Deidre rang that evening, suggesting that they meet in Norwich for lunch the next day. Time alone together was a rare treat because Deidre was usually either teaching or looking after her own children in the school holidays, but Tom's parents were taking them out for the day, so Mary gladly arranged to meet in a tucked-away restaurant with cosy corners, where they could have a good chat in private. It was near the market, so Mary allowed time to browse the many and varied stalls. Good quality and unusual cheeses stood cheek by jowl with baskets and bags, and there were some affordable clothes. Mary loved the market and spent a pleasant hour stocking up on vegetarian food. By the time she met Deidre, her jute bags were bulging, and she struggled to fit them under the table.

Deidre wanted to talk about their father, Leonard, who was living in the south of France with Kathleen, whom he had married two years previously. After their mother died, he took care of his children's material needs but — badly affected by his wife's death — became emotionally distant. He was a doctor and, when the girls were old enough to support themselves, he had taken a job with a charity in the Third World. He was a poor correspondent and Deidre and Mary eventually gave up trying to keep in touch, both being very busy with their own lives. Leonard finally contacted them upon retirement, after he had moved to France, met Kathleen and set a date to marry her. Mary was unable to attend the wedding because Sam was a poor traveller and she couldn't leave him, but Deirdre and her family made several visits in the school holidays and got to know the couple well, while enjoying their swimming pool and the lovely weather. Kathleen was a lively and intelligent lady and Deidre liked her on the whole but complained that she never stopped talking. Now, it seemed that she had inherited some property in Suffolk, and they were thinking of living in it and keeping the French house for holidays. Mary had mixed feelings about seeing her estranged father and wasn't sure she wanted him back in her life. Before her mother died, they had been close, but she was hurt and angry when he neglected her afterwards. Part of her wanted to see him but another part thought he didn't deserve any attention at all. Deidre had obviously made her peace, but Mary wasn't sure she wanted to. They discussed this for a while and Deidre suggested asking the couple to stay at her house for a few days so that Mary could join them for a meal and ease her way back into a relationship in familiar surroundings. She pointed out that the children would make things easier because they always demanded attention, so would dilute any interaction between father and daughter. Mary was non-committal and moved on to telling her sister about her attempt to engineer a move to Sheringham, which led to questions about the first weeks at work there. Deidre thought that it sounded much better than the care-home job.

'And it means we might get together a bit more,' she continued. 'Is there any sign of LB paying a visit?'

'Funny you should mention that,' replied Mary. 'He's arriving a few days after I go back.'

'That should be interesting!' remarked Deidre, observing the rising colour in her sister's cheeks.

The rest of Mary's three weeks' down-time, seemed to pass very quickly. She tidied up the garden, cleaned the bungalow and gleaned plenty of new information about nutrition and health. She also learned the first movement of a Beethoven sonata and looked forward to playing it on the Steinway. Before she knew it, she was back at Cadence, hearing how Chris had fared. There were more tales about Phil's untidiness, but they were setting off for a holiday in Italy later that day, so Chris was eager to be off. Cadence was dauntingly clean and tidy and for the first time, Mary wondered if her job-share partner might be a little too focused on cleanliness at the cost of facilitating Delia's social life.

Chapter 12

Delia seemed pleased to welcome Mary back and, on the very first day, suggested a bridge session. Mary put it off until the evening, explaining that mornings were for fresh air, shopping and preparing lunch, and afternoons were best used for housework and cooking dinner. The first few days passed quietly in this way but, by Thursday, she was regretting agreeing to the bridge at all, as it seemed very complicated and not really her thing. Delia was full of enthusiasm and liked to go into strategic details, which left Mary going to bed with her brain in a knot.

On Thursday evening, she found an email from Luke saying that he had decided to travel on Friday. He would arrive too late for dinner, so not to worry about food. She sent a brief reply acknowledging this but made a mental note to have something simple in the fridge in case he hadn't stopped off to eat on the way. She also registered that he would be in the house for quite a long time and wasn't sure how she'd cope with that. She got butterflies whenever she thought about being in a domestic situation with him and was annoyed with herself for showing all the signs of having developed a silly crush more appropriate to a teenager.

He arrived when Delia was trying yet again to instil the rules of bridge into Mary's reluctant head. She hadn't been able to concentrate very well, was jumping at the sound of every passing car and was ridiculously wound up by the time she heard tyres crunching on gravel and the slam of a door. Mary knew this was stupid but years of isolation from normal social situations had left her anxious and ill-equipped to cope — especially when someone who sparked a physical attraction was involved. She knew she had survived several encounters with Luke without revealing her inner agitation — at least, she hoped it didn't show — but now it felt as though she was starting all over again.

She took a deep breath and got up to greet him. *Smile, ask him if he's had a good journey and offer refreshment. That's all there is to it,* she told herself. She carried that off well, adding that Delia was still up and in the lounge. Having got those opening remarks over, without making a fool of herself, she felt much better and went to make the sandwich that they had agreed upon, leaving Luke to greet his mother. She heard him go into the downstairs bathroom and waited until he was out again and back in the lounge, then took the food in and asked Delia if she needed anything.

'No, thank you,' she replied. 'I was just telling Luke how much you were enjoying learning about bridge.' Some hesitation must have shown in Mary's face, because he looked at her quizzically and read the situation well enough to admonish his mother for taking advantage of a captive audience to revive an old passion.

'You're much too good to play with a beginner and I'm sure Mary has other things to do,' he finished.

Mary took this as an exit cue and headed for the door again, saying that she did have some clearing up to do.

'I didn't mean you had to leave now!' said Luke, hastily.

'No — it's all right — I really do have things that I need to get on with. I'll be in the kitchen if you need me,' said Mary, making her escape before anyone could notice that she was colouring up.

She could always find work in the kitchen and used this to cool off until Delia rang to signal that she was ready to go to bed. Once engaged in familiar duties, she felt more secure and by the time she had her charge tucked up, Luke had moved to the music room. Mary knocked tentatively then put her head round the door, apologised for disturbing him and added that she was now going to bed herself and would just like to know what he'd like for breakfast in the morning. He was seated at the piano, writing on manuscript paper, and looked up with a smile.

'You sound just like a landlady in a guesthouse, Mary! I did mean it when I said you shouldn't go to any trouble for me. I can take care of myself in the morning thank you, but there is one thing you could do for me now, if you can spare a few minutes before you disappear again.'

'What's that?' she asked.

'Will you listen to a short piece of music I've sketched out?'

'Of course, but I don't think I know enough to say anything very intelligent about it.'

'I'm not asking for musical criticism — just any thoughts and feelings that come to mind when you hear it.'

This seemed an odd request to Mary, but she perched gingerly on the edge of the sofa to which he was pointing.

'It is safe to relax, I don't keep lions behind the sofa!' said Luke, sounding exasperated.

Mary smiled weakly, put a cushion behind her back and settled into it, willing herself to relax while he began to play.

It only lasted a couple of minutes and then he asked her what it made her think of.

After a moment, Mary replied. 'It sounds like someone tentative, wondering what to do next; gentle and rather sad.'

Luke looked pleasantly surprised and told her that was exactly what he was trying to portray.

'What are you writing?' asked Mary.

He hesitated and then said it was something in the early stages and he'd tell her more about it when it was nearing completion. Then he changed the subject and asked what she and his mother were planning to do the next day. Mary described their typical routine, adding that it could, of course, be changed if he and Delia wanted to do something different.

'I'd like to come with you when you go out for a walk, if that's okay. I could do with some sea air, myself. We could find somewhere in town for lunch after that,' suggested Luke.

'Well — I think Delia would like that. I'll ask her in the morning,' replied Mary, rising and heading for the door. They each said goodnight and Mary went to her room, trying to reconcile the pleasant and friendly person she had just left with the bad-tempered one who was more usually on display.

Delia was delighted at the idea of a walk and meal out with her son and took pleasure in choosing a suitable outfit. Mary was relieved to have one less meal to think about; lunch was always tricky as there was never much time to get it ready after returning from their morning outings and she usually found herself juggling the cooking with Delia's physical needs. Today, she could just enjoy the walk followed by a meal that didn't result in washing up. She didn't even have to think about making conversation as they walked, because Delia chattered constantly about the music that her son was currently conducting, and various musicians known to her from times past and still encountered by him on a regular basis. He didn't contribute much to this but, to be fair, she didn't give him much chance. Luke took over the wheelchair pushing, giving Mary a welcome break and chance to swing her arms freely and fill her lungs with sea air. It was warm for March and people were walking dogs on the beach. A few children, ignoring the prohibition signs, were clambering on the huge slabs of rock that protected the sea wall from the high tides that were constantly trying to erode this stretch of coast. Sheringham was a popular tourist venue and even this early in the year, the streets were thronged with weekend visitors making the most of the spring sunshine. Luke skilfully negotiated a way through the sightseers in search of a suitable place to eat and Mary noticed how careful he was to protect his mother from ice-cream-waving children and people whose attention was fixed on the scenery, rather than the wheelchair they were about to walk into. This all seemed to be at odds with Chris's assessment of his character.

Vegetarian restaurants with wheelchair access and facilities were in short supply but, as they all occasionally ate fish, they settled for a place that specialised in seafood. They were led to a table with a view of the main shopping street, but Luke looked doubtful and asked if they could go somewhere a bit more private.

'But this is perfect!' exclaimed Delia. An argument ensued with Luke saying that, if they could see out, then passers-by could see them, and he wanted a break from being in the public eye. Delia said that she loved being seen with him, so the more people who saw them, the better it would be. Mary could see both sides of this and hung back, biting her lip. Heads were now turning *inside* the restaurant, so Luke gave in and abruptly sat down. Delia wore a self-satisfied smirk and Mary registered that, although for the most part her employer was a friendly and charming lady, she was no saint and clearly enjoyed getting her own way and putting Luke in his place.

After making her choice from the menu, Delia kept her gaze fixed on the shopping street, eagerly watching out for people she recognised. Luke ignored this and, moved so that his back was angled away from the window.

'Have you decided on anything to study in your downtime?' he asked Mary.

Mary Mouse wasn't very happy about receiving his undivided attention but at least this was an easy question to answer, so she launched into a description of the course on nutrition that she had chosen.

'But why nutrition?' pursued Luke. 'I thought you might choose something musical.'

This was a bit more personal and Mary Mouse frowned. Then Beryl appeared and prodded The Mouse with a fork, pointing out that it was better than sitting in silence until their meals arrived, so Mary told him all about staying fit to look after Sam by working out which foods worked best for staying strong and healthy without the use of medication. Once she got into her stride with that, she found the courage to talk about the properties of food, according to the principles of yoga. She explained that the fresher the food, the more vibrancy it bestowed upon the consumer and that the type of food and preparation method could influence one's health. Now she was really warming to the topic, so continued, explaining that all forms of life were deemed sacred and the higher the nervous system in anything killed for food, the greater the damage to life itself. Eating plants was therefore thought to be less harmful than eating animals. It was also believed to be one of the ways to purify a person, both physically and spiritually.

'Stop!' screeched the Mouse. *He'll think you're crazy if you go on about that! It might even go against his religion!'*

'Of course, that's just a theory,' said Mary, quickly, but Luke merely asked if that was why she was a vegetarian.

'It's mainly for health reasons,' hedged Mary. 'I would have to be vegan to really take on board those principles.'

Without taking her eyes off the window, Delia piped up.

'Well, all I think about is whether the food tastes nice and arrives on my plate without harming any living creature.'

The fish turned up at this moment but fortunately she didn't seem to connect its demise with what she had just said. Mary caught Luke's eye, however, and it was obvious that he had spotted the irony.

As they ate, Luke confessed that his diet in London was dreadful, consisting mainly of ready meals and takeaway food. Mary made a few suggestions for quick and easy alternatives. Suddenly, Delia dropped her fork and waved frantically at a passer-by in the street.

'Luke, it's Mr Harrison. Why aren't you waving? You could at least smile at him!'

Luke looked out of the window and gave a half-hearted wave.

'Is that the best you can do?' asked his mother.

'I just feel as though I'm in a goldfish bowl,' said Luke.

'What was that?' said Delia, 'Speak up!'

'I don't want to shout,' he replied.

'Well, I can't hear you!' shouted Delia, attracting the attention of everyone in the restaurant. 'Oh, never mind. Mary, will you take me to the ladies, please?'

Luke had finished his meal so, aware that Delia would probably take a long time, asked if they would mind if he didn't accompany them back to Cadence as he wanted to walk a bit more. Trying to avoid looking too relieved, Mary said that she wouldn't mind at all. Delia threw him a disapproving look and shrugged. Luke gave Mary some cash for the bill and left.

***

Luke climbed Beeston Bump, an incongruous, rounded hill rising up from the low cliffs at the Eastern end of Sheringham. He planned to spend the afternoon composing and this was a good place for mentally developing musical themes. It was also a good place for gaining perspective on life, affording stunning views in all directions. To the north, endless sea with its ever-changing canopy of big Norfolk sky; to the west, the red roofs and chunky parish church of Sheringham; to the east — caravan parks strung out along the clifftops and the tall tower of Cromer church in the distance. When he turned to the south, he could see the village of Beeston on the wooded slopes of the hills known as Cromer Ridge. Luke surveyed the houses that nestled at the foot of the Bump and thought it would be nice to own one. Then he could climb the hill whenever he was working on a composition or facing challenging circumstances. On this occasion, he focused on 'Sunburst', his current composition, and was inspired with several ideas for progressing the work, so spent a good half hour pacing backwards and forwards at the top, attracting many a curious glance and indications that some of the passers-by recognised a local celebrity. A young woman had the temerity to ask him for an autograph and he replied brusquely that he was off duty and would appreciate being left in peace.

On his way back down, his thoughts turned to the intriguing conversation with Mary that had just taken place over lunch. He would like to know more about her life philosophy and considered various means of encouraging her to expand on it. He was aware that she might feel obliged to answer his questions just because he was her employer's son, or might consider him to be plain nosy and he would prefer to establish a more friendly basis for conversation. This wouldn't be easy because making friends had always been a problem for him. He remembered an episode at his boy's public school.

'Sissy Braithwaite likes music,' rang out a taunting voice, mockingly drawing out the syllables of 'music' so that it sounded despicable. Several other boys took up the refrain and followed him on to the playing fields, dragging him behind some bushes and challenging him to engage in some 'manly' sport. They wanted him to choose who to fight with and when he declined, they all had a go at him. 'Better keep his pretty face intact,' warned the ringleader. 'Can't have old Belton asking questions!' The pain and humiliation washed over him as if it had happened yesterday and he sank on to a nearby bench, rubbing his head with his hands as if to erase the memory. He knew it was ridiculous to let the bullying affect him after so many years and shifted his attention to the time spent at music college.

There, his aptitude for music and 'pretty face' had served him well, as many female students found him attractive and he could pick and choose which of them to spend time with. Unsurprisingly, for a young man in his late teens, he chose the best looking one —

Charlotte. Musically, it was an unbalanced relationship because he was far more talented than she but she was sexually more experienced and, if he was honest, he stuck with her mainly because of what she could teach him in that department. He went along with gatherings involving her friends but never made any of his own because he really only wanted to make the most of the musical opportunities at college. Participating in Charlotte's social life already took too much time away from that. They drifted apart in a good-natured way when they got their degrees and Luke went on to orchestral violin playing. He didn't socialise much with the other musicians however, preferring to spend his free time composing. Unfortunately, he couldn't get anything published but the violin playing took off and he rose up through the ranks of first violins in one of the more prestigious orchestras until, after several years, he attained the position of leader.

He shared the front desk with Lily and they quickly became an item. This was Luke's only serious relationship to date; they lived together for three years and it was the most sociable period of his life because Lily drew him into a circle of intelligent and interesting people — mostly musicians but not exclusively so.

'I thought we were happy!' he heard his bewildered younger self protest on finding out that she wanted to be with someone else.

'*You* were,' she snapped back. 'You took me for granted and expected me to play second fiddle in everything!'

He realised that she was right. He'd done exactly what he wanted to and had just expected her to go along with him. Any future long-term relationship would have to be more evenly balanced.

After splitting up with Lily, he left the orchestra and worked freelance for a short time before deciding to further his studies with a view to conducting. It was before his mother needed carers and she contributed to the cost of his MA, but he wanted to be as self-supporting as possible, so continued to play the violin while studying. This meant that he had little time to maintain friendships and, disillusioned with love, he avoided female company for quite a while.

It all changed when he became established as a conductor, because his growing popularity led to interest from many women keen to share the limelight. He found it all too easy to fall into a series of short-term relationships, doomed to failure because they were based on public perception of his character, rather than the real Luke. As soon as each partner discovered that he was reclusive, rather than the glamorous figure portrayed by the music commentators and critics, interest quickly waned. Because of the rapid change of partners, he gained a reputation for being a womaniser, but this was at odds with his natural reticence and it caused instability and emotional upheaval. Eventually, sickened by his own behaviour and the false picture it generated, he stopped reacting to feminine advances.

Now, his only real friend was Steve — his agent — with whom he shared the occasional drink or meal. Naturally, they often talked about work, but they also shared an interest in conservation and climate-change issues. Steve was happily married and despaired of Luke's haphazard love life, constantly reminding him that he would lose his looks, his much-admired hair (actually, this was already beginning to thin) and his ability to attract women easily. In other words, it was time to 'settle down' into a 'proper' relationship. Luke said that he was retiring from all relationships and focusing on music alone — which is what he did, but he had begun to feel lonely over the last few months. He missed sex, of course, but also craved stimulating conversation and the feeling that somebody cared about him.

By the time he arrived back at Cadence, thoughts about his life to date had displaced the music in his head. Annoyed with himself, he went straight into the music room and attempted to retrieve the ideas that Beeston Bump had generated.

***

Delia wanted her usual nap when she and Mary got back to Cadence, and Luke came in about an hour after she'd gone up. He went straight into the music room and Mary left the kitchen door open so that she could listen to the phrases that he was trying out on the piano, while she made a leek and cheese flan for the evening meal. She was fascinated to hear various treatments of a basic theme being tried, until eventually one was adopted and extended into a longer section of music. The Mouse was shocked by this eavesdropping, but Beryl insisted that it was a privilege to hear such inspiring music in the making.

Later, while eating the much-admired flan, Delia announced that Mary had taken her to church recently and they planned to go again tomorrow. Would Luke come with them? He surprised them both.

'Why not? We'll be able to talk to your old cronies and perhaps that will make up for my shortcomings in the restaurant.'

Delia looked at him suspiciously, not sure whether he was genuinely contrite or just being sarcastic. Mary suspected the latter but at least he was giving his mother plenty of attention. He even suggested another game of Scrabble after dinner.

'I sometimes have time to kill in hotel rooms when conducting away from London, so I acquired a Scrabble app. I'm hoping to get my own back for that humiliating defeat at Christmas, now I've had chance to practise.'

Mary couldn't conceal her amazement this time and wondered again why he didn't socialise with other musicians in his spare time. A Scrabble app in a hotel bedroom was a lonely occupation for someone who didn't have to be alone and it was at odds with his blog, which implied a scintillating social life. Whatever the truth about that, Mary was proud of her Scrabble skills and wanted to play again, so she replied that she was up for the challenge and hurriedly carried the dishes into the kitchen. The washing up would have to wait until Delia was in bed.

This time, he succeeded in confining the game to about one third of the board and Delia complained bitterly about there not being anywhere left to fit a word in. Mary did her best and managed quite a good score, regardless, but couldn't beat him and he went off into the music room looking decidedly smug. During the bedtime routine, Delia remarked that Luke obviously enjoyed Mary's company and said she hadn't seen him looking so relaxed for ages. Mary thought about that while washing up, it did seem as though he liked her, but she still felt that it would be a huge mistake to even think about becoming involved with him and firmly stifled her imagination, which had tripped her up in the past. A few years after Adrian's departure, she'd become attracted to someone in the choir and spent a lot of time fantasising about the romantic possibilities. Opportunities for developing a real relationship with him were severely limited by her carer's role. However, encouraged by her sister, she had eventually invited him to her home for a meal. Sadly, the evening was a disaster from start to finish. The food was badly cooked because she had trouble settling Sam and conversation during the meal limped along painfully, each realising they didn't actually have much in common. By the time they said goodnight, Mary felt foolish because he was nothing like the lover of her daydreams and she felt depressed for a long time afterwards, grieving for the mythical man who had occupied her thoughts for so long. She resolved to never let her mind dwell on someone in that way again.

The following morning dawned bright and clear with spring sunshine. Admiring the daffodils and aubretia, much in evidence now, Luke, Delia and Mary enjoyed the walk to church. They were greeted at the door by people who obviously knew the Braithwaites and a great fuss was made about moving chairs to make space near the front for Delia's wheelchair. She was placed at the end of a row in order to leave the aisle clear, which meant that Mary had to sit next to Luke, who would be able to hear her singing. She was self-conscious about this, but he had no such inhibitions and his voice rang out clear and strong in every hymn, with beautiful phrasing and breaths taken only where they would not disturb the flow of words. He took Delia up to the altar for communion and Mary noticed that he also participated. She was not confirmed so stayed in her seat.

At the end of the service, several people spoke with the Braithwaites and Mary hung back, noticing how happy Delia looked to have Luke with her. When the church was nearly empty, the organist hurried up the aisle towards Luke.

'Thank goodness I've only just seen you! If I'd noticed you were in here, I'd have fluffed everything. As it was, I only fluffed half!'

Luke seemed pleased to see him and they chatted for a while about church music and common acquaintances. Then he turned and beckoned Mary, saying that she would be a great asset to the church choir as she had done some very good work for him in Requiem of Life, could sing in tune and, most importantly, listened to instructions and watched the conductor. Matthew, the organist, said he'd be delighted to have her in the choir and, before Mary knew what was happening, it was all arranged that she should go to choir practice every Wednesday evening. When she pointed out that she couldn't leave Delia, Luke told her to book a sit-in carer for the weeks when she was working, as she did already for her other choir practices.

'I don't think I should do that!' said Mary, in alarm. 'Everything should be fair between me and Chris and I already get one evening a week off. Chris doesn't get any time off!'

Luke initially seemed rather taken aback at this challenge to his idea but, as her point sank in, said slowly, 'Okay, Matthew — I think we'll have to get back to you on this when we've had a chance to talk it over properly.'

Mary was distressed about refusing to sing in the choir and afraid that it might have seemed like a slap in the face after Luke had praised her singing in Requiem of Life. She had a feeling that it might not be easy to extract a positive comment about anything musical from him. She was quiet on the way home, thinking she may have offended him and wondering how to set things right.

After lunch, Luke went straight to the music room and Mary, not wanting to disturb the creative process, left him to it, abandoning the idea of further discussion about the choir while Delia rested. After dinner however, he suggested yet another game of Scrabble as a 'best of three' decider. This time, Delia said that she was too tired to concentrate and couldn't keep up with them at the best of times.

'Why don't you play in my sitting room?' she suggested. 'I can be in an easy chair and enjoy watching the battle of the Titans!'

So, once again, Mary quickly piled the dishes into the kitchen sink and sat down with Luke at a small table in Delia's room to play. This game took a long time because they both spent ages deliberating over every move, each reluctant to give the other the smallest chance of getting a good word in.

'Why don't you put a time limit on each turn?' suggested Delia, but this idea was unpopular because they were both enjoying the challenge. Well over an hour later, Delia said that she was falling asleep in her chair and would rather do it in bed, so Mary had to abandon the game and take her up. She apologised to Delia about the game taking so much time on Luke's last evening, but this was brushed aside with the observation that she had enjoyed the best weekend with her son that she could remember.

'You go and finish it, dear,' she said, 'and make sure you win. He could do with being taken down a peg or two!'

Mary was tiring but, reluctant to abandon the game, she went back to the sitting room, only to find it empty. Sighing, she turned towards the kitchen, but her disappointment quickly turned to astonishment as she recognised the unmistakable sounds of washing up. On entering, she was greeted by the incongruous sight of Luke with his sleeves rolled up and hands submerged in a generous quantity of bubbles.

'Thank you, but I don't mind doing that later!' she exclaimed.

'At the speed we're going, that will be after midnight!' replied Luke, turning to throw the tea towel resting on his shoulder at her. 'We can have this done in no time between us.'

Mary made a mental note to tell Delia that he had succeeded in taking himself "down a peg or two" by doing the washing up, and began to dry. Then she realised that this was an excellent opportunity to talk to him about the choir and the problem with managing her time in view of all the bridge tuition.

'I'm sorry about not welcoming your attempt to get me into the church choir. Do you understand why that would cause difficulties between me and Chris? We're meant to be job-share partners and inequalities can soon cause problems.'

'Yes — of course,' he replied. 'I just got carried away as usual and didn't think it through before suggesting it.' After a short pause, he continued. 'But you are a musician and it grieves me to see that stifled by the demands of a caring role. I hadn't realised just how tied you and Chris are when you're on duty here. How can you bear it?'

'I developed coping mechanisms while looking after Sam,' responded Mary. 'Spotting feelings of frustration before they can become deep-rooted and treating them simply as forms of energy that can be re-channelled into something else, ideally compassion for the person who is keeping you tied down.'

Understandably, Luke looked somewhat taken aback by this revelation about Mary's inner processes, so she hurriedly continued.

'Also, I find it useful to focus on making the most of what I do have, rather than what I don't have. In this case, thanks to you and Delia, I can continue with one choir so, if I throw myself whole-heartedly into that, I can make it enough.'

Mary felt embarrassed about giving away so much about her approach to life and changed the subject to the bridge problem.

'There is something else,' she said, tentatively. 'You did say that I could talk to you about any difficulties that cropped up while looking after Delia.'

'Yes, and I meant it, so there's no need to sound as if I'm about to shoot you for daring to speak! Just say what's on your mind.'

'Well,' Mary ploughed on, 'it's the bridge. Your mother is thoroughly enjoying teaching me to play and I want to do it with her because she is bored and lonely but it's taking a lot of time and I'm struggling to get all the domestic work done.'

He thought for a moment. 'How would you feel about a group of Mum's old bridge cronies coming here to play with her from time to time? It would mean you providing some refreshments, but you would be free to do other things while they were playing.'

'I was thinking along those lines myself, but the snag is, she might still want me to be her partner,' replied Mary.

'Not if I can find another one — someone who already knows the game well. Someone who can upstage you!' The last comment was delivered with a smile that gave her butterflies. 'Leave it with me and if Mum doesn't get a call about it within a week or so, let me know. Now, are you sure you feel up to finishing that game?'

Mary felt tired but agreed because it seemed unfair to refuse when he had done the washing up and was being so helpful about the bridge problem. They returned to the sitting room and play continued at a snail's pace with the scores remaining fairly equal until Luke got stuck and took so long trying to find a way forward that Mary closed her eyes while waiting to put her next planned move down.

'Mary, it's your turn,' said Luke, twice, before looking at her properly and realising that she was asleep with her head tucked into the wing of the chair. He studied her sleeping face with its clear complexion, apparently free of the heavy make-up favoured by many of the women he met these days, and considered various options for waking her up. He wanted to touch her; gently brush the hair back from her forehead; stroke her face; maybe even carry her upstairs. He wanted to make love to her — something that he couldn't possibly risk with his mother's carer. Imagine the fallout! Reluctantly, he settled for barking her name loudly, so that she awoke with a start.

'I think you've had enough. Shall we call it stalemate?' he suggested.

Mary hastily pulled herself together. 'Not yet. I have a good word already worked out,' as she put letters down that gave her a score taking her well above him. As she glanced up and registered his look of disbelief, she added, 'You can concede, if you like.'

He answered that by tipping the letters from his rack on to the board, remarking that he had a lot on tomorrow, including the drive back, so needed to get to bed.

'What have you got to do when you get back?' asked Mary, as they cleared the game away.

He described a ten-a.m. rehearsal with a well-known and prestigious orchestra in preparation for a concert at the Royal Festival Hall a few days later, followed by an evening meeting with his agent. It sounded like a lot of demanding work on top of the drive back to London and Mary wondered if he should have been preparing for the rehearsal instead of playing Scrabble. As if reading her thoughts, he responded.

'I should have spent the whole weekend looking at scores really, but my doctor tells me I'm digging myself into an early grave if I don't take time out to relax. So, thank you for helping me to do that and I'm sorry if I've worn you out in the process.'

'No,' said Mary quickly. 'I have enjoyed this weekend.' She realised that, over the last two days, her initial nervousness had faded, and she had indeed enjoyed herself.

However, overnight, Mary Mouse delivered a lecture about the pitfalls of letting Luke think he'd made another conquest.

He'll use you for entertainment whenever he visits, and it won't be long — judging by his blog — before that includes sex. You're worth more than that, my dear. Don't be so accommodating.

Beryl interjected.

*Haven't you noticed how much more alive you feel?
Are you really going to spend your whole life avoiding
men in case something goes wrong?*

Once again, Mary didn't sleep very well.

Chapter 13

The next morning, Luke left too early to phone anyone, so Mary didn't expect anything to come of his promise to re-unite Delia with her old bridge friends. However, a few days later, she heard the phone ring while upstairs tidying the bedrooms and it stopped before she could get to the extension. About ten minutes later, Delia rang her bell and, as Mary entered the sitting room, immediately exclaimed, 'You'll never guess who I've been speaking to. Edward, my old bridge partner!' Mary sat down and looked suitably impressed and interested. 'He had quite a serious heart attack a few years ago and, as he was the organiser, our little group folded up — but now he says he's feeling well enough to give it another try! There's just one problem though,' she continued, looking doubtfully at Mary. 'He wants to be my partner again and I'm afraid I was so pleased I said yes, and now I feel bad about leaving you in the lurch, you've put so much effort into learning the game!'

'Oh, don't worry about that,' said Mary, warmly, with a smile. 'I was struggling with the rules and a bit worried about letting you down if we got involved with a group. Now you can play with someone more experienced.'

'Thank you,' replied Delia. 'You're very understanding. He's going to ring round the other people we used to play with and see if any of them are still up to it. Unfortunately, people we used to know are dropping like flies. That's one disadvantage of living for a long time, you end up with fewer and fewer friends to do things with! Anyway, he will try to put at least one table together and he's very persuasive, so I'm sure he'll manage something. It's perfect because I was a bit worried about trying to join a new group of people who would probably be younger with sharper brains. Oh — there is one other thing though.' Mary encouraged her to continue. 'He asked if it might be possible to have it here. Are you still all right about that?' Mary suspected that Delia had already agreed to host the bridge group but gallantly said that it would be no problem at all and that she would be happy to arrange the furniture and provide refreshments.

Delia thanked her profusely and spent the rest of the day happily talking about old friends, which table and chairs would be suitable and what to feed her guests.

As Mary prepared the next meal, she wondered whether Luke made a habit of carrying his mother's friends' contact details around with him. Surely that was unlikely? Had he made a point of taking the relevant details with him? That would make him a man of his word and she liked that. She thought back to Adrian's infuriating habit of saying he would do something but then failing to carry it through. If she reminded him, he would answer crossly that he had already said he'd do it so why was she asking again? If she asked a third time, he would accuse her of nagging. If she waited a long time and then pointed out that he still hadn't done it, he usually said that he had forgotten! If she did the job herself, he would be scathing about the way she had done it. The longer they were together, the worse he became and even now, the memory of it made Mary feel tense. She reflected that it was possible that she had unconsciously absorbed the message that all men were tarred with the same brush and decided that it was time to keep a more open mind on the subject.

When Delia was in bed, Mary sent an email.

Dear Luke,

Your mother received a phone call from someone called Edward today and he invited her to partner him at bridge. Either you have contacted him as promised, or the strangest coincidence has happened! I'm inclined to believe the former, so thank you very much. Edward is ringing round in the hope of putting a table together and Delia is delighted. She is brighter than I have seen her since starting work here. Mary.

She was tempted to put 'Mary x' but thought that might prompt another lecture from Mouse, who was already unhappy about Mary initiating an email conversation.

She was in bed when her tablet pinged, and curiosity got the better of her, so she reached for it.

Dear Mary,

Yes — it was me and I'm glad I could help. I just hope he doesn't find too many friends for you to entertain!

I have attached a link to a Scrabble app that you might like to download. I have made the first move and we can play via the internet if you want to, but I know you are busy keeping Mum and Cadence up to scratch so won't be offended if you don't respond.

Luke x

Mary stared at the screen, mentally re-adjusting to this turn of events. The message was considerate and the tone friendly — and she was rather short of friends. She wanted to play the proposed game but couldn't help wondering what Chris would have to say about it. She was pretty sure that it would be something like, "You'll regret it. Don't encourage him. He'll amuse himself with you for a while and then drop you." Then there was the question of his temper. Did she really want to encourage contact with someone who might suddenly revert to the rude and impatient man she had witnessed on Christmas Eve and at the Requiem of Life rehearsal? Mary Mouse and Beryl the Peril had plenty to say about this, and it quickly escalated into the sort of argument that could last all night. Beryl thought that life was getting much more interesting but Mouse thought that it was getting much more dangerous. They both noticed how quickly he had produced the Scrabble app. Beryl thought this meant that Mary was on his mind so he must have feelings for her but Mouse argued that he simply wanted to continue a distraction activity that had helped him to relax over the weekend.

In the end, Mary became impatient with herself and decided that she may as well stop over-thinking the situation and simply do what she wanted to do; i.e., play the game, so Beryl got her way.

The next morning, she was busy as usual with Delia's washing and dressing routine, then breakfast and the usual walk, followed by lunch. She didn't get a moment to herself until her charge was settled for the afternoon nap but, as soon as she was, Mary set up the Scrabble board in her room and spent a pleasant half hour working out the best possible word to send back. This she did without a message, thinking that it should be possible to engage in the game without any chat.

It was two days before anything came back from Luke and his word came with an apology for the delay and a description of the work that he was engaged in. He also sent her a copy of his schedule for the next three months, commenting that it might be useful to know when there wasn't a 'hope in hell' of getting a reply from him for some time. This seemed a bit over the top and Mary wondered how long he thought they'd be playing for. Nevertheless, she thanked him in her next submission and remarked that the schedule seemed impossibly hectic. Obviously, chat could not be avoided! The correspondence went on in this fashion until he won — at which stage he immediately started another game.

In the meantime, Edward rang Delia again with the names of other bridge players and a proposed date and time. This had to be adjusted to fit in with Delia's routine, but the first session was fixed for the Friday before Mary finished her spell of work. She sent a text message to Chris, explaining what was happening, apologising for not telling her before and explaining that the whole thing had sprung up rather suddenly.

'Okay. Cool. See you soon,' came the reply and Mary breathed a sigh of relief. She was chronically anxious about upsetting people and didn't want anything to go wrong with her relationship with Chris.

The bridge session was a great success and soon after that it was handover day. Chris asked lots of questions about Luke's extended visit and soon winkled out of Mary that he had been much more involved with his mother's activities that had ever been the case when Chris was on duty.

'You've obviously worked some magic on him!' was her comment, followed by, 'I suppose I'll have to go to church from now on!'

Mary said that Delia wasn't expecting that and then raised the matter of a concert in Norwich, conducted by Luke, in about two weeks' time that she had noticed in his schedule. She hadn't said anything to Delia about it because she wanted to sound Chris out first, but now she suggested that they could all go together. Or if Chris didn't fancy it, she could have the evening off, and Mary would take Delia. 'Oh dear, you are keen!' remarked Chris. 'It's supposed to be your down time! Still, I suppose music is your thing.'

It turned out that Delia already knew about this concert from Luke himself but she refused to go on the grounds that she didn't want to sit in a wheelchair until late in the evening. Chris quickly resolved this difficulty by saying that she would bring her home after the interval and Delia readily agreed to this plan. Mary said that she would stay for the whole concert and go home by taxi, thinking that it would be expensive, but surely she deserved a treat once in a while.

***

Luke was taking tranquillisers, prescribed by his doctor shortly before his trip to Sheringham. They had worked well while he was there, because he wasn't under any pressure and could sleep whenever he liked but now, back at work, he was struggling. It was hard to get up in the mornings and even harder to come up with the zest needed to motivate others in rehearsal. His head felt thick and heavy and his legs were leaden. Whenever he settled down to look at music in preparation for the next session, he fell asleep.

What to do for the best? Stop taking the pills and go back to being a jangled, anxious insomniac, or carry on with them and let his career and reputation slip? A concert in Norwich was looming and his mother might decide to go to that. He couldn't bear the thought of letting her down with a sloppy performance; she set so much store by his success and she didn't have much in life to enjoy.

He tried doing without the pills and for a short time, was able to work more effectively, but soon relapsed into feeling jittery and unable to sleep properly. After a few days, the lack of sleep got to him and he started to feel like a zombie again, so he reasoned that he may as well take the tablets if he was going to feel continually tired with or without them. At least they controlled the anxiety that was threatening to overwhelm him. He'd just have to force himself to keep going when conducting. Will power, that was the answer.

Then he thought of recent conversations with Mary, who had devised ways of coping with the relentless stress of caring for a severely disabled child. Perhaps she could suggest ways of achieving calmness without the use of drugs. He drafted an email but, on reading it through, decided that it sounded clumsy and pathetic, so deleted it.

The Norwich concert was almost upon him now and he wondered if she might have noticed it on the schedule he'd sent or perhaps his mother would have mentioned it. Could he ask her if she was going, and if so, persuade her to meet him to talk things over? As if by Divine Providence, an incoming email from Chris chose that moment to arrive. It explained that Delia could only manage the first half but would like to see him in the interval if possible. Mary would be with them and could stay for the whole concert. Luke quickly typed an email asking Mary if she would meet him afterwards and he felt much better when she agreed. She was so resilient and capable. Sometimes she seemed nervous, but she was good at finding the courage to overcome that. It was as though she had a bottomless bag of personal resources and simply reached into it and fished out whatever quality was needed to meet life's challenges. He remembered the sympathy in her eyes when he'd told her about seeing a doctor; he had just woken her up and her normally guarded expression had given way to natural spontaneity. The thought of an imminent conversation with her kept him going for the next few days.

Chapter 14

Mary spent a lot of time researching and reading about nutrition when she got back to Cromer. She enjoyed long walks near the sea and the fresh air and exercise helped her to sleep more soundly. She went through all her belongings and re-homed or threw out those which were not being used, so if a Sheringham property came up, she could quickly pack up what was left. (If it happened during a work period, she would have a problem, but she decided that there was no point in crossing that bridge unless it actually appeared). While she worked through all the cupboards and drawers, she listened to Radio Three — surprised at how often works conducted by Luke were played. There was even a broadcast of an old interview, in which he sounded rather brusque but what he was saying was interesting. It was about the importance of a musician's sensitivity to the marriage between words and music in vocal works. This led her to wonder where the words for Requiem of Life had come from, because one of the things she loved about it was their close association with the musical phrases. Her download of the recording gave no clue but the work was now available on CD, so she bought one and saw that both words and music were attributed to Luke. Wasn't that unusual? Seemingly, his talent knew no bounds.

A few days before the Norwich concert, Luke sent a Scrabble word accompanied by a message saying that Chris had told him about bringing Delia for the first half. He was going to try to have a brief word with her before she left and would also like a longer word with Mary. Could she meet him after the concert? He wouldn't get up to Sheringham because he had a rehearsal in London at ten thirty the next morning, so had booked a room in a Norwich hotel in order to make an early start. Intrigued, she agreed, and he told her to wait in the foyer of the concert hall until he could join her.

**

The few days before the concert passed quickly and pleasantly and Mary felt quite relaxed as she accompanied Chris and Delia to Norwich. The programme included Rachmaninov's second piano concerto and Sibelius' seventh symphony; romantic music, which had been Mary's preference when younger, but her taste had lately widened. Still, she was interested to hear what Luke made of these well-known works. She registered that he looked stunning in evening dress but was determined not to be swayed by his appearance and listened to the Rachmaninov with her eyes closed so that she could give her full attention to the music. The pianist and the orchestra played very expressively, weaving their phrases together into a beautiful, yet stirring seamless whole that made Mary feel as though she was hearing the music for the very first time.

Luke did manage to make time for them in the interval and Mary thought he looked even more handsome at close quarters but also rather tired, considering that he was only halfway through the programme. There were dark shadows under his eyes. Afterwards, she helped Chris get Delia back into the car then ran back to the concert hall, getting there just in time for the second part of the concert. It took her a while to settle into the Sibelius but by the end of the first movement, she was back under the spell.

When the concert ended, she waited in the foyer until most of the audience had left and began to wonder if Luke had remembered their meeting. He emerged, at last, in the company of a genial-looking, middle-aged man who was talking enthusiastically about some future event. Luke glanced her way — obviously registering her presence — and then gave his attention back to whatever had to be settled before he could leave. He had changed into casual clothes and bereft of the glamour bestowed by evening dress, now looked older and totally exhausted. At last, his companion seemed satisfied and shook his hand with great vigour, before leaving. Mary stood and gave what she hoped was an encouraging smile but did not receive one in return.

'Let's get out of here,' said Luke, heading for the door. 'We'll go to my hotel, if that's all right with you, because it's the best chance of privacy. The bars and restaurants around here will be full of curious concert-goers.'

This would have triggered alarm bells in Mary had he not looked so ill, but she fell into step with him and ventured a complimentary remark about the performance. He brushed this aside and asked her to bear with him because he always felt wrung out after a concert and couldn't walk and talk. So they made their way to the hotel in silence, which felt odd. Mary used the time to employ one of her mindfulness techniques — focusing on the soles of her feet touching the ground, then movement, posture and breathing, in turn, so that by the time they reached the hotel she was calm and ready for whatever he wanted to talk about.

He stopped at the reception desk to order sandwiches and a bottle of red wine then led her to a small upstairs lounge that seemed to be deserted. In this private and quite intimate place, Mary wondered if he had seduction plans after all but on sitting opposite him, she could see that he really did look dreadful. She asked if there was anything the matter, besides exhaustion from conducting.

'No. Yes — everything,' he faltered. 'I'm not managing to hold things together properly. The doctor has put me on tranquillisers, and they make me so tired I can barely function. You once mentioned that you had developed coping mechanisms when looking after Sam. I'm wondering if you might be willing to share those so that I can ditch the blasted pills. Perhaps you could tell me a bit about how you managed the worst times — if that's not too personal?'

It was. Extremely personal. Dismayed at the extent of his belief in her abilities, she pointed out that his situation had nothing in common with caring, single-handedly, for a severely disabled child.

'I think you're wrong,' he replied. 'What was the worst psychological problem for you?'

'Lack of freedom,' said Mary, instantly.

'Exactly,' he replied, triumphantly. 'You had to keep going along with someone else's demands no matter how ill or tired you were. And you were short of money. I would say our situations had a great deal in common.'

The money problem came as no surprise to Mary.

'Your mother did let slip that you had funded the Requiem of Life recording,' she remarked. 'I didn't go fishing for information, but she likes to talk about you. Older people sometimes lose the ability to censor what they say.' She petered out, aware that she was going off at a tangent.

'My outgoings are enormous, Requiem of Life as you say; living in London; travel; not to mention Mum's care costs — which are staggering.'

Mary registered with a shock that he must be paying her and Chris. That made him her employer, didn't it?

'And I'm part of those enormous costs!' she reminded him, thinking that it wasn't appropriate for him to discuss his finances with an employee.

'Oh — I probably shouldn't have told you that. Anyway, it doesn't affect anything. For all practical purposes, Mum is your employer and how her care is managed is entirely between you and her — I wouldn't dream of interfering — but I would really appreciate it if you could tell me how you coped with Sam. Come to that, how you coped with singing in Requiem of Life with such composure. I watched you bring an extreme attack of nerves under control. How did you do that?'

'How did you register all that about me with so much else going on?' she asked, in amazement.

Luke collapsed back into his chair and sighed wearily.

'For goodness' sake — I'm struggling to keep my eyes open! Please stop trying to avoid the subject. How about showing me some of that compassion that you mentioned when we were washing up at Cadence?'

At this point a waiter appeared with a tray bearing wine, sandwiches, two plates and two glasses. Luke asked him to add it to his bill and poured Mary some wine.

'There,' he said. 'You don't have to drive, and it might help you to relax enough to tell me what you know about coping mechanisms.'

He appeared not to notice the irony of seeking advice from a person also in need of help to relax.

Mary took the wine out of politeness, but hardly ever drank alcohol so resolved to limit herself to a few sips, wanting to stay in control of this situation. She still felt reluctant to broach such a deeply personal, even spiritual, subject but recognised that he was pleading for help and guessed that pleading didn't come easily to him. So, after a lengthy pause, during which she closed her eyes and practised a visualisation that enabled her to focus on compassion rather than her own nervousness, she replied.

'Look, your faith in my abilities is very flattering but the truth is, I don't always cope. A lot of the time I just scrape by and I can only do that by clutching at a raft of spiritual support that I've built over the years. I'll do my best to describe that and hope you can get something useful out of it.'

Luke, who had kept quiet because he could see that Mary was wrestling with something, thanked her and settled down to listen. She began by describing Sam's condition, and some of the difficulties that she had experienced when looking after him — the need for infinite patience, being on call at all hours of the day and night, lack of freedom, disturbed sleep and, worst of all, grief and anxiety at constantly having to watch her own child suffer indignity, discomfort and pain. Luke looked sympathetic and she continued.

'Things became so difficult that I sought help from a carers' support group, and they suggested that I took up meditation to help me to stay on an even keel. The local authority put Sam into respite care for a few days, so I enrolled on a course about yoga and meditation. That was paid for by another organisation that helps carers to do something for their own wellbeing. I was involved in group meditations on the course and, in the last one of those, a wonderful sense of profound peace overcame me. I also had a sense of something awesome and bathed in light, hovering just out of reach. It was hard to come back from that, and when I did, I was amazed to find that almost an hour had passed; it only felt like a few minutes. I couldn't replicate the experience on my own at home, but I was very curious about it and read everything I could lay my hands on about meditation and related subjects. I ploughed through translations of the ancient writings on yoga and discovered that the postures that most people are keen on are only part of it. One of the early texts starts by saying that yoga is mainly about controlling one's own mind. That really grabbed me as I thought getting my mind under control would be the answer to everything! However, learning how to do it is far from simple. Some of the ancient instructions are quite bizarre! In fact, you're probably thinking this whole thing is quite weird.'

Here Mary looked doubtfully at Luke.

'It's certainly not what I expected,' he said. 'But it's also fascinating. Just keep talking, please.'

'Well, a book on enlightenment said that regular meditating usually results in something significant happening, so I tried to do it every day. Sam often interrupted me, so it didn't go very well, but I still found that it helped with insomnia. I was up two or three times every night and sometimes Sam stayed awake and in distress for hours. Even when he slept relatively well, I couldn't, because my natural sleep pattern was totally wrecked. However, if I was restless at night, I found that getting up and meditating for twenty minutes kept me calm and enabled me to get back to sleep more easily. Even if I was woken up again after that, I was able to cope with it better than before. I also had more patience with Sam during the day and he responded well to that. Then I started to dream vividly. Sometimes I woke up with a really strong image still in my mind and occasionally I heard a voice — usually telling me something relevant to what I was studying. Sometimes, words of encouragement. So, you see, I was getting voices and visions, which are generally regarded as a sign of mental-health problems.'

She looked at Luke nervously but his only comment was that she was the sanest person he knew, so she continued. 'I found a book on mysticism that said such things were only a problem if they instilled negative ideas into the mind and that they can be a sign of powers of intuition waking up. Then strange things began to happen in my everyday life — unlikely coincidences. For example, one day I was thinking about how to approach a problem with social care services. I was nervous because I had overlooked something I should have done and was casting around for inspiration, when a very kind and helpful social worker chose that moment to ring me about something else. She was very understanding when I owned up to what I'd forgotten and helped me to deal with all sorts of issues. I ended up with increased financial support. Things like that were happening all the time.

'One night, I had a startling vision of an angel and after that, whenever I had a problem, it just seemed natural to think of that figure and ask for help. It always seemed as though nothing was happening, but then I'd go and do some routine task and a perfect idea would pop into my head. And I could ask for qualities as well — patience, strength, courage, perseverance — whatever I needed to get me through. I had an idea about holding difficult people or suffering people in the light and found that dissolved feelings of anger or anguish. I was able to feel compassion for those people instead.'

Here Mary petered out, worried that he would write her off as thoroughly deranged and possibly feel that her spirituality was at odds with his religion. She took a sip of wine and noticed that the glass was almost empty; she must have been unconsciously drinking all the time that she was talking! No wonder she had given him information about herself that she thought she could never share with anyone.

Luke regarded her through narrowed eyes for a long time and she felt herself colouring up.

'I don't know why I told you all that,' she said weakly. 'It probably isn't much help.'

He leaned forward with elbows on knees and chin cupped in hands, considering. 'What do you think the angel represented?' he asked, finally.

'It depends where you're coming from,' replied Mary. 'The author of one of the books I read says that angels are symbols of the higher self — one's potential — but also a link or doorway between the everyday self and the Divine spark of life within every human. But I imagine that a Christian would think it was a sign from God.' She looked questioningly at him.

Luke shook his head. 'I'm not sure I am a Christian in the usual churchgoers' sense. I know you've seen me going along with the church rituals but that was mainly to keep Mum company. If I have any spirituality, it's more tied up with the music. Anyway, to get back to what I asked about, you seem to be saying that if I meditate and ask whoever or whatever is in the light for help, I will find peace of mind and if I find that I might be able to do without the tranquilisers.'

'Broadly, yes,' agreed Mary. 'Although it probably won't happen immediately, and your way will be different from mine because every person is unique. So don't go looking for my angel! I could send you a book about ways to get into meditation, if you would like to try it.'

He thanked her but said that he never had free time during the day. 'Although I suppose I too could do it if I can't sleep.'

Encouraged by his willingness, Mary told him that she found simply following the breath in and out of the body the easiest way. 'You must be in a comfortable seated position — a chair is fine, but the spine needs to be upright. And a passive approach is essential. When the mind wanders, you just lead it back to the breath. I'll put the book in the post tomorrow.'

He thanked her and glanced at his watch, noticing that it was past midnight. Then it occurred to him that she was supposed to be getting a taxi home, so he asked if she'd booked one.

'No, but there should be some in the marketplace,' responded Mary.

'I'd rather you didn't risk that at this time of night. You could end up in one with a dodgy driver,' argued Luke.

So, they googled taxi firms in Norwich and tried ringing a few that looked well established and big enough to be reliable and safe. While they were doing this, without success, the night porter came in saying that he had to lock up in five minutes and would the young lady be staying the night? Luke looked at Mary and suggested that it did make more sense for her to do that, as she could get a bus or train in the morning.

'In a room of your own, of course!' he continued, noticing her alarmed expression.

She agreed that perhaps it was the best option as it was so late, and the night porter went off to find a key. While he was gone, she spoke impulsively.

'I hope you don't think I'm making myself out to be some sort of guru? I'm still learning myself so I often make mistakes and get sucked into old thought patterns. I don't know why I told you all that stuff about self-realisation. You're probably already much further along that route than I am.'

'I doubt it,' he replied. 'You have much more self-control than I have.'

'But it must take enormous self-control to conduct in somewhere like the Festival Hall in front of so many people! And you are gifted. You write the most amazing music and inspire other musicians to perform it well. And to perform established works, too, in an incredibly moving way!'

Mary stopped in embarrassment as she hadn't meant to give away how much she admired him. Luke looked surprised but whatever he might have said in reply to this outburst was lost, because the porter came back holding up a room key and asking Mary to follow him. As she moved away and wished him goodnight, Luke caught her arm and kissed her cheek with a muttered 'Goodnight — and thank you.'

Chapter 15

The following morning, Luke was woken by his alarm, which he'd set very early in order to make sure he'd left enough time to negotiate London traffic and reach the rehearsal hall on time. Before setting out, he dashed off a quick note to Mary and pushed it under her door. As he drove, he pondered all that she'd said the previous night and felt a surge of admiration. He wasn't sure what he'd expected — perhaps some handy mental device for coping with stress and, in a way, that was what she'd given him by recommending meditation, but she'd also revealed a lot about her innermost self. Another surge swept over him — one that he couldn't identify at first. Then he realised that it could only be love. He'd glimpsed her soul and he loved it. He also loved every bone in her slender body and every corner of her intriguing mind. He'd recognised physical attraction on their first meeting and fascination with her personality had grown over the last few months — he'd poured that into the music that he was writing — but now he realised that, for the first time in his life, he was deeply in love. He'd thought that he felt that for Lily but could now see that the pain he'd felt when she left was mainly about wounded pride and loss of stability. He was certainly fond of her but that paled into insignificance against what he was now feeling for Mary.

He pulled into a lay-by, grappling with an urge to turn the car around, track her down and pour out his feelings there and then. But what would be the probable outcome? Last night she'd said that she admired his musicality, but he had no idea whether she harboured any feelings for anything else about him. She often blushed when they were together but that could just be the result of her innate shyness. She responded to his emails, but he was usually the instigator. Luke kept on driving towards London. He suspected that he'd have to proceed carefully if he wanted to get anywhere with Mary. Besides, he could not let a whole orchestra down.

The traffic was heavy and he arrived at the hall only just in time to dive for the gents before beginning the rehearsal. The only breakfast he'd eaten was an elderly chocolate bar from the glove box. He held the prized position of Assistant Conductor for this well-known orchestra and wanted to get everything right, as he was hoping to be considered for Principal Conductor when the incumbent retired. Fortunately, he was very familiar with the symphony that they were working on, but he still made a few embarrassing slips; bringing instruments in too early or not at all. He didn't miss the eye-rolling that went on between the players.

By the time he got back to his flat, he was beyond exhausted and fell straight on to the bed; asleep as soon as he hit the mattress. On rising, two hours later, he almost fell over the bag containing the dress suit he had carried back to the hotel after last night's concert, having changed before meeting Mary. He groaned on registering that he would have to find time to get the suit to the cleaners, on top of everything else that he had to fit in. He took out the score for the work rehearsed that morning and went over the parts that had given him trouble, then started to familiarise himself with something he was due to rehearse and perform, as guest conductor with a Baroque orchestra in Birmingham, the following week. After about half an hour on this, he realised that nothing was sinking in — hardly surprising as he'd eaten only a chocolate bar and a couple of biscuits all day. Nearly everything in the fridge was past its use-by date, so he would have to go shopping. He decided to get the suit out of the way at the same time.

An hour later, he was back, armed with several microwavable meals, a filled roll from a nearby delicatessen, a coffee and a dry-cleaning slip. (He'd apologised to the shop staff for the smelliness of the perspiration-soaked suit and shirt and hoped Mary hadn't detected an unpleasant odour.)

He bolted the roll and coffee and went back to the Baroque music for a couple of hours. Then he tried to work on Sunburst, but inspiration wouldn't come and he just became frustrated with it. He tried to meditate in the way that Mary had described, but the effect of the food and coffee had worn off, causing his blood sugar to plummet and he developed a headache. He looked at his schedule over the next few months and marked all the things he really wanted to do and all those that he would ditch if he didn't have to earn enough to support his mother. He thought about trying to get funding assistance from adult social care but didn't know how to go about it and didn't have time to find out. Besides, his mother would hate the idea of talking to a social worker. Then he thought about equity release as a possibility. Cadence was a substantial house in a prime location, handy for both town centre and sea front and must be worth a lot of money. Unfortunately, it would take time to explore that option fully and time was exactly what he was short of.

Thinking about this made the headache worse and it was now ten p.m., so he took some paracetamol and a tranquilliser, then wondered if you were supposed to take those together, but of course it was too late. He shrugged and went to bed. By two a.m. he was awake again with unresolved questions about Delia's finances and his own workload in his head. He had a meeting with Steve at nine in the morning and needed to be clear about what he was going to say about cutting back on engagements. The overseas jobs were the ones he'd like to ditch because of time and environmental considerations, but they were well paid. After an hour or so of getting nowhere with this, he got up and ate a bowl of cereal, which sometimes helped him to get back to sleep. Then he sat and pondered Mary's way of coping with stress. Could meditation be the way forward for him, if he learned to do it properly? Last night, as she was speaking of her inner experiences, he had felt as though a door was opening to reveal a hidden room — a room inside himself that was vaguely familiar; one that he'd glimpsed when conducting particularly moving works. Sometimes, it felt as though he and the orchestra were one and that the music was playing them, rather than the other way around. Suddenly, he wanted very badly to solve his problems by getting into that room and he opened his laptop and typed.

Dear Mary

I very much enjoyed our conversation after the concert and have been thinking about some of the things you said. I'm especially interested in what you said about the Higher Self being a doorway to Divinity and it reminded me of the text used by Gustav Holst in his *Hymn of Jesus*, which he paraphrased from the apocryphal Acts of John. At one point, Jesus says:

> To you who gaze, a lamp am I,
> To you who know, a mirror,
> To you who knock, a door am I,
> To you who fare, the way.

I have only conducted this work once, but it was an emotive experience. Perhaps you could listen to it sometime (if you don't already know it) and let me know what you think of it? The above quotation implies that for Christians, Jesus is the doorway to Divinity, and I wonder if this is the same as what you describe as an access point to the Higher Self? I think you said that the Higher Self was a doorway to God, as well as one's own unrealised potential.'

He went on to talk at some length about parallels between the orthodox gospels and Mary's spirituality and when he'd finished, he read through what he'd written and wondered what on earth she'd make of it. He had never shared his passion for the Hymn of Jesus with anyone else and hadn't realised that he was even interested in spirituality. He decided to wait until morning before sending it, because she might think it just too weird if she saw a message written in the middle of the night. He went back to bed and slept fitfully until the alarm went off.

The meeting with Steve was upon him before he'd had a chance to reach any firm conclusions, so he settled for a general chat, discussing possibilities. Steve pointed out that Luke might lose his current popularity if he stopped doing the overseas concerts. Another charismatic conductor would have to be found to step into his place and he or she might elbow in on the UK bookings as well — Luke could be left with very little work. It could also jeopardise his chance of getting the coveted Principal Conductor position. Luke said that all he really wanted to do was compose and conduct his own work but Steve thought this was a pipe dream.

'I wish you luck with it. I really do hope it succeeds, but as a friend I must warn you that I've seen others go under in similar circumstances. No one has asked you to conduct a live performance of Requiem of Life, have they?' Luke shook his head. 'What will you do for money?'

'Sell my London flat, which is worth a small fortune; buy a much cheaper property in East Anglia and survive on the rest of the capital and whatever UK work I can get until the compositions take off,' replied Luke.

Steve, suspecting that there was another dimension to this radical plan, regarded him through narrowed eyes and asked if he would be living alone in the new location.

'Not if I can persuade a certain someone to risk it with me.'

'Ah — anyone I know?'

'Your paths have crossed in a minor way. You won't remember.'

Steve knew Luke well enough to work out that a liaison making him want to settle down to a quiet rural life was highly significant.

'Well, I can't pretend I'm over the moon to lose your overseas work because it's been lucrative for both of us, but I'm pleased for you as a friend, it's time you had some luck with your love life. How about reducing those jobs gradually, so that you have time for your partner and time to compose? I'll do what I can to promote anything you come up with.'

Luke didn't correct Steve about the assumption that Mary was already his partner because, during the course of their conversation, it had suddenly become vital that he should turn the idea into reality; a permanent one, at that. He thanked Steve for helping and said that he'd also like to have his usual two weeks off as soon as it was feasible to create a gap. The meeting ended and Luke went back to the flat, where he put in more work in preparation for forthcoming events, ate one of the ready meals, re-read the drafted email to Mary and feeling a bit embarrassed, clicked send.

***

When Mary awoke in the hotel, the morning after meeting Luke, she found a note on the floor, which read:

Sorry that I had to leave too early to see you this morning. Thank you for speaking so openly about yourself last night — it was a huge help. See you next month.
    Luke x

She looked at her diary and saw that she would be at Cadence from 29th April to 20th May, so a visit "next month" would probably coincide with that. From what she remembered of his schedule, there wasn't much space in May, so he must be quite keen to come. To see her? She remembered the peck on the cheek and looked again at his note, which did sound quite friendly and ended with another kiss.

She thought back over the previous evening and again felt embarrassed about revealing her inner life. (*Look what you've done now!* wailed Mary Mouse. *You've given him our most intimate secrets!*) However, he did seem to value the information and hadn't laughed at her unusual ideas and experiences. Then she remembered the strong physical reaction she'd experienced on seeing him in evening dress, and thinking about that broke an erotic dream that she'd had last night. That was most definitely embarrassing! She could see why he had so many ardent female followers in the concert-going world; now she was no better! She had been nervous when he'd taken her into that cosy lounge, thinking he might make a pass at her but that hadn't happened. A peck on the cheek didn't count because it was a common way of saying goodbye but it had stayed with her all night, replaying itself whenever she awoke from fitful sleep, along with the treasured words of encouragement, "You are the sanest person I know." She put her head in her hands and acknowledged that she was in the grip of an acute infatuation. Perhaps he even thought he felt the same, but the overwhelming probability was that he was attracted by the fact that she was a carer, at a time when he was desperately in need of TLC.

She freshened up and went to find some breakfast, throughout which she allowed herself to think what it might be like to be in a relationship with Luke. Unpredictable, exhilarating, interesting, frustrating (because he would often be absent), and wonderful when he was around. What would their sex life be like? Oh no, not that again. She thought again of the erotic dream but then shied away from dwelling on it, as the mere thought of getting into bed with him, in reality, was alarming in the extreme. So, here she was again, up against the hang-up about sex that she had acquired through the long years of abstinence. This was annoying because Mary knew that most women of her age would not think twice about engaging in an affair with someone they found attractive. She would like to talk it over with Deidre — her usual port of call when emotional issues loomed — but it would be difficult to explain yesterday evening without divulging Luke's state of mind and she felt that confidentiality must be maintained because of his high profile. Deidre wasn't a gossip but would probably talk it over with Tom and either of them might let something slip in the wrong place. It wasn't very likely, but she decided not to risk it.

Mary tried to pay for her room but found that Luke had already done that, so she left the hotel and walked to the bus stop for Cromer. As she rode home, she thought about ways to help herself over her phobia of sex. She thought that even if she had the nerve to encourage anything with Luke, it would be a seriously bad idea because they lived in such different worlds. It could only ever be a brief "fling" and she wanted any relationship she embarked on to be lifelong. She was forty and felt it was time to resign herself to living alone or seriously look for a permanent partner. The latter would have the advantage of pushing Luke out of her thoughts, but how to go about it? Her unusual working pattern made it impossible to join anything new that involved regular meetings. She had the choir but had already exhausted the possibilities there. Perhaps Deidre was right and she should try internet dating; something she had resisted so far because people could lie about themselves, and she had heard tales of hideously embarrassing meetings after seemingly promising email exchanges. Still, she was getting desperate, so she resolved to investigate before she went back to work.

The following day, however, Luke was back on the agenda, as she received his email about Holst's Hymn of Jesus. It was a long message and she wondered how such a busy person had found time to write it. She was at a loss over the best way to respond to such a highly personal communication and went for a walk in the hope of inspiration, allowing the stiff, salty breeze to clear her head. She took the clifftop path up to the lighthouse and sat down on one of the benches that looked out over a bracken-clad valley towards Cromer. She had found, in the past, that this was a good thinking place and also excellent for meditation, so she closed her eyes and just focused on her breathing for a while. Before long, thoughts of Luke intruded and she decided to look the issue in the eye. She was alarmed to find that discussing her own spirituality had resulted in an exploration of his and considered sending back a polite but discouraging reply, explaining that she did not feel equal to the task of spiritual advisor, but in her heart, she believed that anyone seeking advice should receive it. Surely, she could engage with him on that subject without becoming romantically involved and it would be nice to have someone to share her ideas with. No one else had ever shown the slightest interest. On the strength of this thought, she went home and, ignoring the whining objections from Mary Mouse, quickly wrote a reply with more ideas of her own and a promise to listen to the Hymn of Jesus.

After this, the internet Scrabble games were forgotten and a regular exchange of emails, covering a wide range of subjects, continued until they next met.

Chapter 16

Despite the increasingly personal email correspondence with Luke, Mary still felt that there must be some truth in the tales of womanising in his blog — whoever wrote it. Would there be smoke without fire? Therefore, she went ahead with enrolling on a dating site, still hoping to find a more suitable and reliable long-term partner. For her profile, she asked a neighbour to take some photographs but wasn't very happy with the result so made an appointment to have her hair lightened, thinking that this might make her look more attractive and also discourage her father from calling her Mary Mouse.

She also put a lot of work into an article about food and health that she hoped to get published in a magazine, so one way or another, she was very busy for the rest of her time at home. Shortly before going back to Cadence, the dating site came up with a bewildering number of possible matches. Mary read a few but then decided that she could use some help with sorting them out, so rang Deidre, who was pleased that her sister was making an effort to start another relationship and suggested that she went for a meal the next evening;

they could have fun making a shortlist after the children were in bed.

They began by looking at the profiles of musicians (one of her main criteria) and threw out those who weren't involved in classical music. That left only three, but they all sounded a bit weird and unsuitable for one reason or another. Then they looked at gardeners, but there were only two of those and both were much older than Mary. Next, they tried people who were mainly spiritually compatible. Buddhists and Hindus were possibilities because of Mary's interest in yoga. Four people looked promising in that department but then Mary said that she thought she'd prefer a Christian because she'd been to church a few times with Delia and was fascinated by Christ's teaching. Deidre, who didn't have the slightest interest in religion, pulled a face and asked if Mary was serious. Mary was nettled and said she'd had some very interesting conversations about it with both Delia and Luke. Deidre pounced on that straight away and asked if he was a Christian.

'He came to church with us when he was here, but says he isn't a conventional church-going Christian. He does seem to understand where I'm coming from, though.'

As far as Deidre knew, her sister had seen Luke only once since the Requiem of Life recording, because Mary had kept quiet about meeting him after the Norwich concert.

'He's only been home for one weekend! How on earth did you get into a subject so deep in that time? You said he didn't pay much attention to you!'

That was true. Mary had played down the conversations they'd had during the first weekend and omitted to mention the Scrabble games, apart from the one at Christmas.

'We've exchanged a few emails,' she offered.

'Just let me look at your profile again,' said Deidre, grabbing Mary's tablet. 'Right, so you want a man who is a religious musician who likes playing Scrabble, and cares about the environment.'

'And likes gardening,' put in Mary.

'And does Luke like gardening?'

Mary said she didn't know, but a picture of the beautiful garden at Cadence sprang to mind. She must ask him if he'd had anything to do with that.

'And what is Requiem of Life about?' persisted Deirdre.

'The extinction of species, including man.'

'So, its composer cares about the environment, is a Christian of sorts, obviously likes classical music, and plays Scrabble. On top of all that, where do you think you'll ever find another person who actually likes listening to Radio Three? Why are we wasting time looking at these (indicating the tablet screen) when the perfect candidate is already paying attention to you?'

'There are several reasons why Luke isn't in the running,' said Mary. 'He lives a hundred and forty miles away in a totally different world to anything I'm used to, is much more intelligent than I am, has a temper, and — as if all that isn't enough — just look at this!' She brought up Luke's blog and handed her tablet to Deidre, who read in silence for a while, with widening eyes.

'Oh! I see what you mean. It's probably exaggerated — these things usually are — but I suppose it is possible that he's just looking for another notch on his bedpost.'

'Yes — and I won't be one of those!' said Mary, indignantly. 'Actually though, I think he's more interested in me as a shoulder to cry on, but whatever the truth of the matter, I want someone I can trust and someone who won't blow up at me if I accidentally say the wrong thing.' She went on to describe the defecting horn-player episode at Christmas and the way he harangued the orchestra and choir in the Requiem of Life rehearsal.

'I think Mad Maestros are meant to behave like that,' said Deidre, who didn't have the slightest idea of how a conductor should behave. 'When is he coming again?'

Mary gave the date, two weeks hence, that Luke had now provided.

'You have gone bright red,' observed Deidre, with sisterly candour. 'I get the feeling that you like him, despite his shortcomings.'

Mary confessed that she found him physically attractive — alarmingly so — but she was sure it was just a silly infatuation, so she was ignoring it. Before Deirdre could dig any deeper, she swiftly moved on to asking if anything had been arranged about her father's visit. It hadn't, but they decided to make it in Mary's next downtime and spent the rest of the evening discussing her feelings about being abandoned by Leonard and the likelihood of reconciliation.

Chapter 17

When Mary got back to Cadence, she shared a coffee with Chris who asked how the second half of the concert went. She, too, had noticed that Luke looked as though he would struggle to get through it. Mary didn't mention meeting him afterwards but did say that he had emailed about coming again the weekend after next, and this prompted Chris's remark.

'Oh well, at least *I'm* avoiding him. But I have to say, Mary, he doesn't usually come home so often! I hope you're not ignoring my advice.'

'No, but I can't control when he decides to come!' countered Mary.

Chris remarked that she was obviously not putting him off, gathered up her things and left soon afterwards.

The first week or so passed uneventfully in pleasant companionship between client and carer. Church on Sundays and bridge on Fridays were now part of Delia's routine and she decided to go to prayer meetings on a Tuesday morning, as well, leaving Mary to do some shopping alone (having left her mobile number with one of the group, in case she was needed).

Luke didn't get there until late on the Friday evening in Mary's second week. She had given up waiting and was preparing for bed when she heard him come in. She was in her dressing gown but thought she should go down to see if he needed anything as he would have noticed that her light was still on. He was foraging in the kitchen, so she showed him the sandwich she had made earlier and made him a drink. He looked very tired and didn't seem inclined to talk, so she left him to it.

Saturday passed pleasantly, in a similar way to his previous visit, and everything went smoothly until the evening meal, when Luke brought up the subject of replacing the windows and insulating the loft at Cadence in order to save money on heating and at the same time, making it warmer in winter and helping the environment. It became obvious that this subject had cropped up before.

'Oh no. Not this again,' Delia said. 'I've told you, I'm too old to be disturbed like that. I don't feel cold and I hate mess and noise. Can't you just leave me to die in peace?'

'You wouldn't be disturbed very much. We could do the loft without you even knowing it was happening,' responded Luke.

'I would!' shouted Delia. 'That loft is full of my life, and I don't want it all pulling out. Do it when I'm dead!'

Mary was taken aback by her normally calm employer's sudden eruption and wondered if Luke's temper was inherited from her.

'You could live for years!' he shouted in turn. 'And while you're doing that, the world is going to pot! Don't you care about the younger generation?'

'The younger generation will be fine, because all this talk about climate change is exaggerated!' countered his mother.

Delia was clearly agitated and now struggling for breath, so Mary thought she had better intervene.

'I can see both sides of this,' she said quickly, in a firm and reasonable voice. 'But Delia, wouldn't it be nice to see some of your old treasures? We could talk about times past.'

'It's none of your business!' Delia interrupted. 'And I might have known you'd side with him. It's perfectly obvious that you think the sun shines out of him! You work for me, so you're supposed to be on my side!'

Mary tried to reiterate that she could see both sides, but Luke was shaking his head, so she began gathering up the used dishes, quietly commenting that it was indeed none of her business and suggesting that a family discussion took place when both had calmed down and she was out of the way.

Luke also stood up and marched out. The music room door slammed soon afterwards.

Mary put the dishes down again and focused on calming Delia, who was now crying. She found some tissues and took her to her reclining chair, apologising on the way for having spoken out of turn. She found a favourite television programme and went to make a soothing drink. She was upset to find that her relationship with Delia wasn't as good as she thought, but knew that she shouldn't take the attack personally. She had encountered similar outbursts in the care home, and they were usually an expression of frustration and suffering caused by failing health, rather than justified complaints.

Luke didn't reappear until Delia was in bed, when he sought Mary out in the kitchen and apologised for having involved her in a family row.

'I know I shouldn't have shouted,' he said, 'but there is no reasoning with her, and the denial of climate change was the last straw. She never used to be so selfish! It's all about her and she never considers my point of view at all.'

He sat down at the kitchen table, so Mary gave up on tidying the kitchen and sat down opposite.

'I'm afraid that older people who are suffering *can* be very selfish. It's natural to feel hurt and angry about it, especially when it's your mother, who used to be the one to look out for you. I was angry when my Mum became so ill with cancer and chemotherapy that she was unable to be the person I was still very dependent on. I was only fifteen and I'm afraid I behaved very badly. She must have been desperately in need of sympathy, but I was angry with her for abandoning me and was just rude and uncooperative. My older sister did much better, but it still makes me cringe to think of my behaviour.'

'I can't imagine you being like that,' remarked Luke, temporarily diverted from his own problem and looking at her with amazement. Then he sighed and continued, 'I'm afraid I have often been rude and uncooperative with Mum and I haven't even got the excuse of being fifteen!'

'Well, when my mother died I was even more angry but I had a very good grief counsellor, who reassured me that it's a normal reaction when we feel that someone we love has given up on us. I was told the same thing after Sam died. I was angry with him for wasting all the time I'd spent teaching him to read in the face of various "experts" telling me it wasn't possible. A great chunk of my life had disappeared and what was it all for?'

'Your life hasn't been a bed of roses, has it?' remarked Luke. 'You make me feel as though I'm behaving like a spoilt brat. My mother isn't even dead!'

'No, but she has changed, so you're probably grieving for the person you used to know. I think people often overlook the pain of seeing a loved one decline. It happens a lot in families when one person succumbs to dementia. I know that isn't Delia's problem, but older people often become less inhibited about speaking their mind — and I hope you don't mind me saying this — but she does wind you up!'

Luke considered this and nodded in agreement. They sat in silence for a minute or so. 'I suppose I'm also wound up because she's bleeding me financially,' he continued. 'I'm desperate to reduce my workload, so I've been thinking about ways to make her independent again. Equity release is one possibility.'

Mary wasn't sure whether it was wise to become involved with Delia's finances. 'Does your mother know that you're supporting her financially?' she ventured. Luke shook his head. 'Well, do you think it might help if you told her? It might make her more inclined to cut household costs.'

He considered this. 'I suppose I'll have to if I'm ever going to have an authentic life of my own. I need to create a lot more time to compose.'

'If her capital is gone, apart from her house, then she might get help from adult social care,' commented Mary.

'Can you see her talking to a social worker?' asked Luke. 'Anyway, her income is probably too high for her to qualify. It doesn't go very far towards care costs because she spends a lot on expensive clothes and other luxuries.'

Mary knew that and wanted to increase her efforts to persuade him to tell his mother the truth about her financial situation but decided that it was definitely beyond her role as an employee.

The conversation seemed to have petered out, so Mary got up and went back to setting the kitchen to rights, acutely aware that Luke was watching her. He seemed to be wrestling with something internal.

'I'm sorry she attacked *you,*' he suddenly continued. 'You didn't deserve that.'

'It's okay. I got used to people taking their feelings out on me in the care home.'

'But you must have felt angry about the injustice of it. How did you deal with that?'

'I followed the advice I was given when Mum died: recognise my own anger, understand it, accept it and forgive myself for it. Then it's easier to understand and forgive the person who caused the anger. I had to go through those steps every time anger overwhelmed me and gradually it lessened its hold. When the same thing cropped up on losing Sam, I did the same but also meditated and visualised holding him in the light.'

'Will you meditate with me?' asked Luke. 'I have tried but with little success and you said that it took a group meditation to get you started.'

Mary knew that meditation opened up the psyche and tended to bring up buried issues. She wasn't sure that doing it with Luke was a good idea. Anything could happen. His energy was strong — perhaps too strong for her — and he was intuitive and might pick up that she had a thing about him, assuming he hadn't deduced that already from his mother's embarrassing remark about the sun shining out of him and her frequent blushes. Her hesitation caused him to look at her curiously and he asked if there was a problem.

'No,' she said, hurriedly, because she couldn't think of a kind way to refuse. 'Do you want to do it now?'

'Why not?' was the reply. 'Shall we go to the music room?'

Mary pointed out that upright chairs were best, so their seats at the kitchen table were fine.

She set her mobile phone to give a quiet reminder when twenty minutes were up, explaining that she often lost track of time and then spoke about posture and relaxation to get them started. This was as much for her own benefit as his because she was feeling rather tense but surprisingly, she quickly moved into a meditative state of consciousness and the mobile phone alarm seemed to go off in no time at all. She made some remarks about deepening the breath and becoming aware of their surroundings, then opened her eyes, but Luke was nowhere to be seen.

'Oh well, I needn't have worried about that!' she thought. Then, just as she was getting up, she heard the piano playing softly. She was a bit offended that he'd found it too difficult to manage twenty minutes, so knocked on the music room door.

'Sorry,' said Luke sheepishly when she entered, 'Inspiration struck, and I just had to get it down.'

'Are you still angry?' asked Mary.

Initially, he looked as though he hadn't a clue what she meant but then his face broke into a grin.

'No, I'm not. So it worked!'

His face then took on a distant look and he went back to playing chords on the piano with one hand, while writing on manuscript paper with the other, as though Mary wasn't there, so she said goodnight and backed out of the room. He did not reply. She was now amused rather than offended. If he could receive Divine inspiration to compose after such a short period of meditation, then he didn't need her help!

In the morning he announced that he must get on with his composition so would not go to church. Delia was disappointed, as she enjoyed being seen there with her son and commented sadly, on the way, that she was used to him letting her down. Mary tried to console her.

'At least you know he's being creative,' she offered but this fell flat.

'I suspect this composition obsession will end in tears,' responded Delia, glumly. 'Requiem of Life isn't doing very well.'

Luke turned up for lunch but brought his manuscript pad to the table, didn't eat much and jotted things down throughout the meal. Then he wandered back into the music room while Delia and Mary were still eating pudding. Delia sighed a lot then asked to be taken for her nap.

After washing up, Mary also slept, as the previous late night had caught up with her.

Luke continued to work through the afternoon and Mary played card games with Delia when she woke up, in order to make his absence less noticeable.

At dinner he announced that he had to leave very early the next morning. Delia hopefully suggested a game of Scrabble, but Luke wanted to get back to his composition.

'I've been thinking,' his mother said, very loudly, as he left the room. He came back and sat down with a sigh of impatience.

'Yes mother?' he responded, in a resigned manner.

'I think it *would* be a good idea to get a few things out of the loft. I'm not agreeing to anything being done up there, I just want to see what there is. Just a few, mind, but Mary can't do it by herself, so will you help her before you go?'

Both Luke and Mary were somewhat taken aback by this sudden change of heart and Luke wrestled with the desire to get back to the composition, but suddenly capitulated.

'Come on, Mary. Let's do it now.'

Delia wanted to be taken to her sitting room first, so Mary quickly settled her in front of the television and followed Luke upstairs. He had already pulled the loft ladder down and looked rather strange, wearing a headband with a light attached. He told Mary to stay on the landing while he looked round and, after much rummaging and scuffling, started to pass a strange assortment of items and boxes down. They put them in the guest bedroom so that Mary could take a few things at a time to Delia.

'What did you say to make her change her mind?' asked Luke.

'Nothing,' replied Mary. 'I thought it best to let the subject drop. She probably just likes the idea of reminiscing. Older people often do.'

'Well, there's still a hell of a lot up there. If we do some more every time I come and you can get her to stick at it, who knows? We might get some insulation in, after all.'

'I hope there aren't any guests for a long time!' remarked Mary.

Luke smiled and put the loft ladder away, before disappearing back into the music room. He was still there at nine p.m., so Mary plucked up the courage to interrupt his creativity for the second time that day.

'Will you spend a few minutes with your mother before I put her to bed? She won't be awake when you leave in the morning.'

He looked irritated and glanced at his watch, clearly surprised at the time.

'Okay. And I need to speak with you when she's in bed, if that's all right?'

Mary agreed to find him when Delia was settled and then hovered just inside the kitchen until he was safely behind the sitting room door. Then she crept back into the music room and sneaked a look at the manuscript on the piano. It was impossible to tell what it was about from the page that he'd left on top, so she carefully turned back to the first sheet, where he had written the title "Sunburst" and underneath that, "Kaleidoscope", which was presumably the name of the first section of the work. It sounded vaguely familiar but she couldn't think why. She would have liked to explore further and get an idea of the musical themes but, terrified of being found out, carefully put everything back as she'd found it and tiptoed out.

Later, with her charge tucked up in bed, Mary went back to the music room and this time Luke gave her his full attention, joining her when she sat on the sofa.

He explained that he took two weeks off every year and usually spent it in a holiday cottage somewhere remote, catching up on sleep and composing when he felt like it. Most of this period would fall during Mary's next spell of work, the last few days being after Chris took over. (It didn't escape Mary that he seemed well informed about her work dates.)

'Would you mind if I came here this year? It will save money and I'd like to use the Steinway. You won't know I'm here most of the time because, as I'm sure you've noticed this weekend, I tend to become engrossed in the music. I'll try to turn up for meals but can't promise.'

Mary warmly assured him that it wouldn't be a problem for her and added that it was his home and he could be there whenever he liked as far as she was concerned.

'I'll do my best to keep quiet,' she continued, 'but I'll have to use the vacuum cleaner the day before Chris gets here. As for meals, I'll keep putting something out for you and if you don't come to the table, you can re-heat it when you're ready.'

Luke thanked her and added that Cadence had a lovely ambience when she was there, and he would find that helpful.

It crossed Mary's mind that he could be quite charming when he wanted to be, but she wasn't going to be flattered out of saying what was bothering her, so after thanking him, asked if he might find time to take his mother to church on his next visit, as she had been so disappointed that morning. This did not go down well. Judging by his face, he hated taking instructions or even suggestions from anyone else and Mary felt she had cancelled out the compliment he had just delivered.

'Didn't you hear what I just said about needing time to compose?'

'Yes, but Delia is my client and I'm supposed to look out for her!' responded Mary.

Luke leant back, considered for a moment and then gave a somewhat crafty smile.

'Okay. Here's the deal. I will be here for at least two weekends, maybe three, so I promise to take her to church on the Sundays if you come too and promise to have dinner with me one evening when you've finished your spell of work.'

Mary was a bit startled by this sudden twisting of the situation to his advantage, but she had come a long way towards overcoming her shyness with him and was now enjoying their conversations. If he tried anything physical, she would just tell him that she valued her job too much to risk an affair. So, she agreed but added that she might be in the throes of moving house by then.

He looked unduly perturbed by this news and wanted to know the details, so Mary explained the situation.

'Damn,' he said. 'That could be awkward.'

Mary frowned and asked why. Luke appeared to be having difficulty answering this but eventually came up with, 'It's too complicated to explain now, but will you let me know if you're offered a different property before I get back?'

'Okay,' she said slowly, regarding him curiously and wondering why her change of address could have anything to do with him.

'Right,' he said, briskly. 'I'd better sort out my belongings and get to sleep. I need to be away by six a.m.'

Mary assumed she was dismissed, bade him goodnight, still feeling puzzled, and left the room.

***

Luke drove back to London feeling that he'd neglected to do something important. He replayed the weekend in his head.

Mary had come into the kitchen looking soft and accessible in her nightclothes. He had turned away to conceal a sudden surge of sexual desire that got the better of him, despite his tiredness. She had supplied him with food, thoughtfully prepared in advance, and made him a drink. Had he thanked her properly? He wasn't sure. He'd felt shy, which was unusual for him. Social clumsiness had long been his norm, but this was different — he actually felt nervous. It had been easy to pour himself into emails but somehow, Mary in the flesh rendered him tongue tied. She'd asked routine questions about his day, but he had answered briefly and gruffly, and she soon gave up, leaving him to eat alone, wishing he could get her back, hold her close and rest his weary head on her shoulder.

He came up to a traffic queue that stretched far into the distance and resignedly switched off the engine, resuming his replay of the weekend.

He had joined the two women for their morning walk on Saturday, as on the previous visit home, but this time there was a cold north-easterly wind blowing off the sea. He'd set a brisk pace in order to keep himself and Mary warm, but his mother had complained that he was about to tip her out of her wheelchair. He'd slowed down and by the time they reached the fish restaurant, they were all shivering. Luke was relieved to see that the table by the window was already taken, and they ended up in a private corner near the back, which had the advantage of keeping him out of the public eye, but the downside was that he couldn't engage Mary in one-to-one conversation because his mother had nothing to distract her. She wanted him to talk about rehearsals with a pianist she admired. Mary looked interested in what he was saying but contributed little to the conversation. Luke surreptitiously watched her eating her fish with care and respect for the creature that had given its life for her. She obviously believed in what she'd said on the subject the last time they were there. He'd noticed that she did everything very efficiently with total concentration. He'd also noticed that her hair was paler than on previous occasions — almost blonde, in fact. It suited her.

He'd decided to spend the afternoon composing but it didn't go very well, and he was cold in the draught from the large bay window behind the piano stool. It was particularly bad when the wind was in the north-east. Some of the windows at Cadence were double glazed but not the large bays, and the loft insulation was totally inadequate. He'd discussed it with his mother several times before and she'd always dismissed the idea as "unnecessary expense when I won't live much longer, anyway" but perhaps it was time to broach the subject again. Maybe he could get her to see that spending money now — even if it meant borrowing some — would lead to big savings later, and if she wasn't around to see that, it would still benefit the rest of the world. According to her emails, Mary was an environmentally responsible person, so perhaps she would back him up on that front. He'd brought the subject up at dinner with disastrous results, as his mother turned on Mary, as well as him, and then he'd let himself down by losing his temper.

Then there was that awkward time at the kitchen table, with him desperately wanting to tell Mary how he felt about her but deciding to finish Sunburst first. When she heard that and understood what he'd poured into it, she'd surely admit that she felt the same. He sensed that she did, and his mother seemed to think so with her remark about Mary thinking the sun shone out of him, but there was something holding Mary back. Fear? She had been afraid of him at the start of their acquaintance, but he thought she was over it by now. They'd ended up talking about anger management; useful but falling short of what he really wanted to be saying and doing.

He moved on to thinking about the meditation. For the first time in his life, he'd experienced profound peace. Then, after a while, the music came flooding into his mind — inspiration for an additional section to Sunburst. He decided to call it 'Angelus' and felt compelled to get it down on paper as quickly as possible. After that, the music took over the rest of the weekend. He knew that he was missing out on time with Mary and probably appeared rude and unfriendly but launching this composition may well be the key to his future. Hopefully, *their* futures and he knew that he'd lose the ideas that were coursing through his mind if he divided his attention. For him, composition was all consuming. Would Mary understand that well enough to live with him?

Finally, he went over his attempt to make up for ignoring her for most of Sunday. Had she even heard him describe the wonderful atmosphere she created at Cadence? His efforts to deliver a compliment had been met by a lecture on paying more attention to his mother!

At last, the traffic began to move. As he restarted the engine and began to inch forward, he reflected that at least he'd arranged to have most of his two weeks off with Mary, as well as securing the promise of dinner one evening after she'd finished work. Perhaps he could use the first week of his holiday to finish Sunburst and then tell her how he felt? It occurred to him that being in love was a large part of the reason he was feeling so jittery. He wasn't sleeping well because she was on his mind; he wasn't socialising with other women or even noticing them; his work was suffering because his concentration wasn't as good as usual; he was thinking about the things they discussed when he should have been thinking about music; his appetite was poor... the list was endless. Perhaps he was not on the verge of a nervous breakdown, as the doctor thought, but simply besotted. He decided to stop taking the tranquilisers.

At last, the road opened up before him and he put his foot down.

Chapter 18

A week later, Deidre rang Mary to say that Leonard and Kathleen were coming to stay in three days' time. She was a bit worried about coping with the extra work, so Mary offered to go over there for a day with home-cooked food. She was surprised at the depth of feeling that welled up, now that the prospect of being reunited with her father was a reality, but did her best with the food and set out early on the chosen day.

Leonard looked shorter than she remembered, and his skin was heavily lined — presumably the effect of working in a hot climate for years. She calculated that he was seventy-four, so it was hardly surprising that he looked very different from the tall, handsome hero of her youth. He hugged her but she was unable to stop herself from tensing up at the physical contact.

'Mary Mouse!' he said, using the unflattering nickname from long ago. 'Why didn't you come and see us in France? It's been a year since Sam died. I know it was hard before that, but we thought you'd make the effort more recently.'

Mary wanted to say bitter things about how he had ignored her for much longer than a year, but she swallowed them because Kathleen was coughing loudly, signifying that she hadn't been introduced. After that, conversation was not a problem as her stepmother kept up a constant flow of chatter. Sometimes she asked Mary a question, which Mary began to answer but she never got to the end of what she was saying because Kathleen kept interrupting with comments of her own and further questions.

When Leonard finally got a word in, he asked Mary why she was burying herself by looking after an old woman. Why didn't she find a wealthy young man to have a good time with?

'I think a middle-aged man would be more my cup of tea, don't you? I am forty, Dad!' responded Mary.

'That's nothing! Kathleen and I are in our seventies and we're living the life of Riley, aren't we, sweetheart?' The girls' father gave his new wife a smacking kiss and Deidre's two older children looked at each other, pretending to be sick and attracting parental reproof.

Kathleen piped up again saying Deidre had told her that Luke Braithwaite was part of the household where Mary worked. Was he eligible?

'He's not married, if that's what you mean, but I don't see much of him,' said Mary. 'He was there last weekend, but spent most of the time locked in the music room, composing.'

'Well, you ought to get in there and distract him!' said her father. 'He must be worth a penny or two.'

Deidre told him about Mary's part in the Requiem of Life and this prompted Kathleen to ask all about the recording session. She knew quite a lot about music, had seen Luke conducting in Paris and said she'd love to meet him.

'He's really not very sociable,' said Mary, 'and I'm not in a position to arrange introductions — I'm just his mother's carer.'

She was aware that this sounded unfriendly and unhelpful, so quickly changed the subject and suggested a day out with them both, while Tom and Deidre were at work. This was arranged for the near future and they all settled down to play Monopoly — a game enjoyed by the Shuttleworth family many years ago, but the children liked it, too, and became very excited about amassing property. Everyone was happy until Mai lost all her money and her temper. Kathleen jollied her out of it and took the children upstairs to get ready for bed, leaving the sisters alone with their father. He seemed very relaxed and happy, so it looked as though his late second marriage was a good thing. Deidre carried the conversation because Mary was still tense and resentful. These feelings weren't part of the persona she had built up over the years and she was quite shocked to find that so much baggage still lurked below her surface mind. Whatever had possessed her to offer a day out with them?

As she drove home, Mary reflected that her stepmother may be a non-stop talker, but she seemed intelligent, kind and helpful and her easy conversation might help to ease a second day with Leonard. It was arranged now, anyway, so she resolved to make the best of it.

When the day came, they drove down into Suffolk, exploring the quaint villages and seaside towns. Kathleen loved the shops in Woodbridge and spent a long time looking at antiques and clothes. While her attention was taken up with those, Leonard took the opportunity to try and mend things with his youngest daughter. He was no fool and understood why she was angry with him.

'Mary Mouse,' he began.

'Don't call me that!' she snapped quietly, so as not to attract Kathleen's attention. 'I know I was a shy child, but do you really think I could have coped with everything I've been through if I hadn't grown up and learned to assert myself as an adult?'

Leonard checked that Kathleen was still out of earshot and saw that she was in a queue at a till, so he took Mary by the shoulders and asked her to listen to what he had to say.

'I know I wasn't the father you needed as a teenager. I kept it from you girls, but I had a bit of a breakdown after your mother died. The only way I could cope was to throw myself into work — meaningful work. I tried to do that at home but there were too many memories so, as soon as I could, I went to where there was a desperate need for doctors. It was easy to shut off from my previous life because so much needed doing. The hours were long and resources meagre. I know I should have kept in touch but cutting loose was the only way to preserve my own sanity.'

Mary sighed and said that it was water under the bridge now, anyway.

'Do you think we can make a fresh start?' continued Leonard.

Mary nodded silently because Kathleen was bearing down on them, happily holding open a large carrier bag so that they could inspect the garments she had purchased.

After that they ate lunch in a luxurious hotel. Money did not seem to be an object for this couple. When Kathleen went to the ladies, Leonard said that he was well aware of the difficulties involved in caring for a child with special needs and was sorry he had not helped; could he and Mary have a heart-to-heart about it some time? Mary replied that it was too late, and she just wanted to move on from all that. She knew that she was repeating his pattern of avoiding grief by focusing on other things and she knew that she should forgive him, but could not summon up the willpower or the energy to deal with either issue.

They returned to Deidre's house via the inherited property, which was a large and beautiful but neglected thatched house set in an enormous overgrown garden. As they explored, Kathleen explained they were in the throes of deciding whether to renovate it and live there or sell it and buy something smaller and more manageable. Discussion about the pros and cons of this kept them going for most of the journey back.

Despite refusing to engage with her father about Sam, by the end of the day Mary found herself interacting more easily with him on other topics. Perhaps, she thought, in time, they might recapture some of their lost affection.

***

The next day, Luke emailed to say that Radio Three was going to transmit the Requiem of Life recording and wanted to follow it by an interview with him about the motivation for composing such a work, his feelings and beliefs about climate change and extinction of species, and the way in which these had inspired the music. It would put even more pressure on time, but he thought it would help to get the work recognised and give him a chance to be himself. He wrote about all this at some length, which was not consistent with being short of time! Mary was touched that he wanted to share it with her, so replied as warmly and encouragingly as she could and asked to be told when it would be on the air. She didn't hear anything more for a week but then he emailed that the interview was recorded and gave her the broadcasting date, which was shortly before she was due back at Cadence. He did not feel that he had expressed himself very clearly at the interview and was embarrassed about it being heard by a lot of people. Mary wasn't sure how to respond to that, suspecting that platitudes would not go down well. In the end she asked him if they'd given him the opportunity to listen to it. They had, so she couldn't say it might be better than he thought but, after seeking inspiration, she emailed back that the music would speak for itself, regardless of the interview. He messaged back a simple, 'Thank you, Mary' and then went quiet for several days.

When the broadcasting date arrived, she gave her full attention to the programme, then messaged Luke.

I have to admit, you're not likely to ever have a career in radio! However, I thought you got the main points across and that's what really matters. Are you still coming on the 21st? Mary x

He replied, Yes. Looking forward to seeing you. Luke x

Mary spent another day with her father at Deidre's house and this felt easier than the previous occasion. An outing to the inherited cottage for the whole family was planned for the Sunday before Mary went back to Cadence.

The day was a great success. The cottage was packed with original features, fireplaces and exposed beams in every room and an ancient front door. There were two staircases and many nooks and crannies for the children to hide in. The adults all helped with identifying the many and varied renovations that would be needed to make the place habitable and Mary began to feel as though she was part of a family again.

Chapter 19

When she was back at Cadence, Mary quickly settled into the routine that she and Delia had established. The weather was warm and sunny, and the two women enjoyed meals in the garden and picnic lunches on the seafront, as well as continuing the bridge sessions and attendance at church. Mary became interested in the bible readings and found many parallels with the spiritual path she followed. She wished she could discuss this with Luke, but his messages had dried up and she was nervous about initiating a fresh series of emails as he was probably very busy, and she was wary of giving him the idea that she was chasing him. She frequently checked her inbox because she missed their internet chats and was rather annoyed with herself for feeling bitterly disappointed at failing to find anything from him. When it got to two days before his planned visit, she gave in and sent a brief message asking when he would be arriving, to which he replied:

Saturday afternoon, damn it. Essential meeting with the orchestra committee on Saturday morning. Should be there for evening meal. L x

Mary wasn't sure whether he was swearing at her for bothering him, or the orchestra for calling a meeting when he wanted to get away. Then it occurred to her that he might have stopped messaging because he was offended by her flippant remark about him not qualifying for a career in radio. This bothered her greatly, even though she knew that anyone who could be that touchy was probably not worth worrying about. She had to work quite hard at getting him into an imaginary box that night, and he got out again when she remembered that he had put a kiss at the end of his last message and wouldn't have done that if he was cross with her — so sleep came at last.

The day of Luke's arrival was very hot, and Mary decided to serve the evening meal in an outdoor shady spot. Fortunately, it was salad because he did not arrive in time to eat with them, so Mary left his share in the fridge. Delia fell asleep in her wheelchair after they had eaten, and Mary left a bell push within easy reach and cleared the table. Then she remembered that she hadn't opened the front gate and only just managed it in time, because Luke swept his car into the drive at considerable speed and Mary had to flatten herself against the gate in order to avoid being squashed. He parked quickly and leapt out apologising profusely, dismayed at having nearly run over the object of his affection. He was wearing shorts and Mary noted that he had very nice legs, before hastily removing her surprised gaze from them. She felt hot and dishevelled and suspected that her face was like beetroot — not altogether because of the sun — and she cursed herself for reverting to reacting like a silly teenager with a crush. When Luke had finished detailing the horrors of the temperature in the capital and the dreadful journey he'd just endured, she offered him a cold drink and suggested he join his mother in the garden after freshening up. They urged Mary to keep them company, and she felt herself unwind as they chatted about music that Luke had recently conducted. After a while, he said that he would love a stroll on the seafront to cool off and, surprisingly, asked Delia if she would like to go with him. Delia looked non-plussed because she wasn't used to such thoughtfulness, nor going out in the evening, but she agreed after seeking reassurance that she would be back home by nine o'clock.

'And Mary — will you come too?' he asked.

'Yes, of course. It's a perfect evening for sea air,' she agreed and hastily whisked Delia indoors to get her ready.

It really was perfect on the sea front, the kind of evening not experienced very often on the north Norfolk coast; warm and balmy with only the gentlest of breezes to keep it comfortable for walking. Conversation was relaxed, if spasmodic.

'Are you two still going to church on Sundays?' Luke asked.

'Yes. Are you coming with us?' replied Delia, hopefully.

'I certainly am,' Luke answered, managing to sound enthusiastic. 'And next week, as well.' He shot a sideways glance at Mary, who smiled beatifically and inwardly vowed to keep her half of the bargain with good grace.

'But I'm here to work really, so apart from those occasions, I'm afraid you won't see much of me,' continued Luke.

'You'll be ill if you never stop!' exclaimed Delia. 'Why can't you work for a week then give yourself a holiday, for once?'

This put Luke in an awkward position because he was planning to do just that — but was hoping to spend most of the second week with Mary rather than his mother. He placated her with a half-truth.

'Well, if I can get the composition to keyboard stage by the end of the first week, I can do scoring in the second.[2] That doesn't need quite so much concentration, so perhaps we could have some of our meals together.'

Delia looked satisfied with that and asked if they could stop and look out to sea for a while. They sat on a bench and exchanged comments about the idyllic surroundings, it was just past mid-summer's day, so children were still playing on the pebbly beach in the evening sunshine and a few people were swimming in the improbably calm sea. Luke pointed out areas of water that were pale in colour, indicating sandbanks

---

[2] Arranging the orchestration of a piece of music.

below the surface, and went on to describe a reef that stretched for miles, parallel to the coast. He said that it was made of consolidated sand tubes made by ross worms and described some of the fascinating sea creatures that could be found there. His face was alive with enthusiasm for the natural world and Mary was assailed by a wave of love so strong that it snatched her breath away. She quickly got up to adjust Delia's blanket in order to conceal her agitation.

'Whatever's the matter?' asked Luke.

'Nothing, I'm fine' she replied, more sharply than she intended and taking much longer than was necessary to tuck the blanket in.

Oblivious to this exchange, Delia stopped Luke from further probing by announcing incongruously, 'I think I would like to be buried at sea.' Mary assured her that she was in good health, apart from the osteoporosis, so it was much too soon to be thinking of such things, but Luke responded unsympathetically.

'I'd rather you didn't choose that, mother, it would be too much trouble and hideously expensive!'

With a shake of her head, Mary tried to convey that Delia would be upset by his remark and Luke relented.

'Sorry Mum, I was only joking'.

'That's a first then!' exclaimed Delia.

As they moved on, Mary reflected that her feelings for Luke must run deeper than she thought, and she vowed to displace him by communicating with some of the men showing an interest on the dating site.

At the pathway that led to Beeston Bump, Luke announced that he would like to climb it, so Mary, taking the opportunity to get away from him, said that the exercise and fresh air would help him to get London and the traffic out of his system and offered to take Delia home by herself. He was obviously torn between gallantry and what he really wanted to do, so Mary persuaded him that she was quite capable of pushing the wheelchair the short distance to Cadence and went back without him, with Delia chuntering, all the way home, that she knew his manners were too good to last.

**

Luke breathed deeply as he climbed the Bump, enjoying the fresh air and exercise. It was June and the wildflowers were at their best, brilliant red poppies competing for attention with masses of deep-pink flowers which should have clashed but looked perfect in this setting. The breeze was more noticeable as he climbed higher and it created pale green waves in the long grass. He made a mental note to come back with a book one day so that he could identify the many different types of grass and flowers and allowed himself a daydream, in which he had a garden with a much smaller but similar wild area. There would be a pond, as well, stocked with fish and plenty of water-loving plants around the edge.

The house would have a music room similar to that at Cadence and the kitchen would have Mary in it. He stopped. He could hardly expect Mary to spend her life looking after his domestic needs! His father had done that with Delia and as a young man, Luke used to feel outraged that she did all the cooking, washing, cleaning and decorating with the occasional perk of singing in a concert, while Eric Braithwaite enjoyed a rewarding career. Guiltily, he realised that he had probably repeated the pattern with Lily and that it may well have contributed to the breakdown of their relationship.

It would be different with Mary (assuming that he could persuade her to live with him in the first place!) Perhaps she'd be writing articles about healthy eating, while he was at the piano, composing. And maybe she'd want to be involved in planning and maintaining the garden, so they could do that together. He would have to help out with the chores. Well, that would be okay; a lot less stressful than conducting a South Bank concert. *But wouldn't it get boring?* said a little niggly voice in his mind. He was at the top of the hill now and sat down on one of the benches. It all depended on the success of his compositions and getting opportunities to conduct them. If that happened, he could cope with the boring bits of domesticity — even enjoy them. Of course, Mary might be shocked to find that he hoped to make her a permanent fixture in his life. Their lengthy emails showed that they had a lot in common, but it didn't necessarily follow that she'd want a long-term relationship. He rehearsed various ways of broaching the subject and decided that playing a keyboard version of the finished Sunburst to her was still probably the best option. The music was for her and about her and would speak far more eloquently than a rehearsed speech. So, the next few days would have to be dedicated to composition.

Chapter 20

Over breakfast the next morning, Delia asked Luke what he was composing. He said it was an orchestral suite but wouldn't be drawn on the theme of it, saying bluntly that he wasn't ready to disclose that.[3]

'Hmph,' said Delia. 'I can't see how it could be important enough to be top secret!'

'Well, it's important to me,' was all he would say on the subject.

There had been a storm in the night and it was still raining, so the walk to church was a soggy affair with Delia covered by an enormous waterproof cape that had to be removed and shaken in the church porch; a tricky exercise that left Luke feeling damp throughout the service.

Mary wasn't singing and he asked her why, frowning with scepticism when she pleaded a sore throat.

On the way home, she asked about the meaning of the parable in one of the readings because she felt that it resonated well with her personal form of spirituality. This sparked off a lively discussion about themes that

---

[3] A set of musical pieces, often with a common theme.

were common to Christianity and so-called "New Age" thought. Delia was doubtful as to whether there really was a similarity, but Luke was still very interested in Mary's ideas and continued the discussion over lunch. Afterwards, however, he shut himself away in the music room in order to get to grips with Sunburst. From now on, he would have to stick with it until it was finished, no matter how many hours that took.

**

Mary didn't see Luke again until she was tidying up the kitchen when Delia was in bed. He fished his meal out of the fridge, stuck it into the microwave oven and asked if they could meditate together each evening.

'Yes — if you really want to, but you abandoned me when we tried that before!' she responded.

'Well — it did help me a lot with the music I'm working on,' he explained, 'and if such a big surge of inspiration strikes again, I'll have to go with it. But even if that doesn't happen, I'm hoping it will help me to sleep well while I'm here. You did say that it helped you with that. Perhaps we'll both sleep better — except you have to get up to Mum, of course, so perhaps it's not a good idea from your point of view. I don't want to keep you up late and make life harder, so please say if it's too much.'

'It'll be late tonight because you're only just having your meal, so we won't get started until ten at the earliest. I'll cope with that once, but I'd appreciate an earlier start on other evenings, if that's all right with you. Could we start as soon as Delia's in bed — about nine thirty?'

He agreed and so, for the next few days, they sat together for half an hour each evening.

Luke stayed until the end every time but, on the first few occasions, merely said thank you and goodnight before going straight to bed. This felt strange to Mary because he wasn't communicating much during the day either, but after a couple of sessions she found that a profound sense of peace permeated the meditations and lasted through the night. Even though her sleep was still broken by Delia, she always dropped off again as soon as she got back into bed. Also, as the week progressed, although she was working hard to get the house ready for Chris, as well as looking after Delia, she felt increasingly serene and able to cope with anything. Having Luke around began to feel natural and Mary was strangely content to provide domestic back-up while he produced beautiful music.

This continued until Friday afternoon, when Mary settled Delia for her nap and decided to use the time to catch up with her emails. She was now corresponding with two possible candidates on the internet dating site and one of them sounded especially promising. The weather was still fine, so she took the bell sounder and headed for her favourite bench in the garden, only to find it already occupied by Luke, who was leaning forward with his chin cupped in his hands staring unhappily at a lawned area of the garden. Mary was hesitant about disturbing him, in case he had music running through his head, but he instantly registered her presence and asked her to join him. She sat beside him, saying that she loved the garden and asking who designed it.

'I did — with the help of a landscape gardener. But some of my ideas were vetoed by my mother; for instance, the lawn over there was supposed to be the location of ground-source heating pipes.'

'That's a shame,' said Mary, remembering how keen he was on saving energy. 'I'm afraid Delia is set in concrete when it comes to anything green, but you've made a great job of the rest, it's perfect for someone with mobility problems. You must have given it a lot of thought.'

'Thank you. I did, but sometimes, just sometimes, it would be nice to do what's right for me, and I'm never going to manage it in my mother's house or in London.' He told her about his plans for reducing conducting work and relocating to East Anglia. Then he described in detail the kind of property he would like and how he would aim to make it carbon neutral.

'My sister and brother-in-law have managed it with their home in Suffolk,' said Mary. 'Come to think of it, they have ground-source heating. Tom is an engineer for a water company, so he knows a lot about these things. It seems to work well.'

'I'd like to see their home,' said Luke, 'and your sister. Is she like you?'

'Not at all! She's gregarious and extravert; a teacher.'

'Does she look like you?'

'No. She's darker and much more attractive but a bit heavier than me. She has had three children, after all,' said Mary, wondering about the relevance of Deidre's appearance. 'I'm sure they'd be happy for you to visit but wouldn't it interfere with your composing?'

'I hope to finish Sunburst by Monday,' he reminded her, 'so I'll be free for several days.'

Mary was surprised to hear him name the suite as he had so far resisted telling her, or Delia, anything about it. Of course, she already knew the title from her snooping session and remembering this threw her, so she failed to make a definite arrangement to take him to visit Tom and Deidre and lapsed into silence. Luke prompted a response.

'Mary? Could we visit your sister next week?'

'Oh — well, if you're sure you want to, I'll ask when it would be convenient. Tom loves to show people what he's done, but the children are very boisterous,' warned Mary.

'If I can control a symphony orchestra, I can probably manage three children,' remarked Luke airily, turning to look at her. 'Why are you smirking?'

Mary tried to straighten her face. She asked if he actually knew any children and he admitted that it was a long time since any had crossed his path. 'Perhaps you and Deidre could deal with them while Tom and I are busy?' he suggested. 'That's if you don't mind spending your downtime visiting with me?'

She shook her head and said that she would phone Deidre to arrange it. Since the episode on the seafront, she had tried to avoid meeting his gaze but for some reason she forgot on this occasion and was shocked to see an unmistakeable look of desire in his eyes. He was very close already and made a slight movement towards her. For a moment, she thought he would try to kiss her. She panicked and stood up quickly, saying she had just remembered something needing attention in the kitchen.

She walked quickly back to the house (where nothing needed attention), wondering if, in that brief moment when their eyes had locked, she had revealed as much as he had. She felt embarrassed and confused. How could he practically ignore her for a week and then look at her like that? What would he make of the abrupt manner of her leaving? Only one thing was certain, she had suddenly lost all interest in the dating agency. It now felt utterly pointless, so she sat at the kitchen table and wrote brief emails thanking the remaining candidates for their interest and explaining that she would not continue the correspondence because she'd found a partner. It wasn't true but she thought that it was the kindest way to sever the contacts. Then she sat for a while longer, wondering what to say to Deidre, who would no doubt be delighted about the proposed visit, assuming Luke still wanted to do it after her childish behaviour. And would he still want to take her to dinner? Did she want that to happen? Her thoughts were broken by Delia's bell and then she was busy for the rest of the day, so didn't get round to ringing her sister.

Luke did not come to the evening meal and Delia grumbled about his bad manners. Mary worried that she may have offended him but when nine thirty came, he was seated at the kitchen table, ready to meditate as usual. When Mary's phone alarm signalled the end, he stretched his limbs.

'I can't tell you how much these sessions have helped me. I have never in my life felt so peaceful or slept so soundly. And because I'm well rested, I haven't been short of inspiration for the composition. Thank you so much. However do you do it?'

'I don't do anything,' explained Mary. 'I just put my everyday self to one side so that the stillness within can come through. You are responsible for it as much as I am. We're reinforcing each other.'

'But I don't feel anything at all if I practise it alone!' he protested.

'Well, *I* don't feel much on my own,' she confessed. 'It works best with at least two people. Didn't Jesus say something about prayer being most effective when two or three are gathered together? My initial profound experience was in a group of eight or nine. I do usually feel peaceful when I'm by myself but nothing so deep as that first time with other people, or what I've experienced this week.'

Luke stared into the distance and tapped his fingers on the table.

'I think Jesus actually said, "Whenever two or three are gathered in my name, I will be in their midst." He also recommended going into a quiet place to pray. I wonder if he meant a quiet place within ourselves, rather than a place without noise?'

Mary pointed out that she wasn't doing it in anyone's name, but the inner stillness she experienced could be described as Divine. Then she suggested that Luke might find a group to practise with in London.

'No,' he said, unequivocally. 'It wouldn't be the same as it is with you. When we meditate together, I feel comforted, soothed — cherished, even. Where do you suppose that comes from?'

'I'm not sure. I feel that, too.'

Luke looked at her sharply and Mary Mouse shrieked *Way too much information!* so she quickly swept on. 'The primary influence of the Divine core on the human psyche is wholeness, harmony, balance — I think a Christian would interpret that as "God is Love" so we could be feeling that.'

'But that book you lent me said that meditation can open up dormant abilities such as telepathy, so does that mean we could, alternatively, be picking up those feelings from each other?'

'It's possible,' said Mary carefully. 'Or it could be a bit of both. But anything picked up from each other would be greatly increased on the principle that we've just discussed. I mean, it would be magnified just because there are two of us.' She had kept her eyes down throughout this attempt to diminish what he was implying, but here she risked a glance at Luke. He was regarding her intently, so she quickly cast her eyes down again. 'But I am not a guru and I'm not really sure what is going on.' She risked another glance at him and this time he was the one to quickly look away. There followed a slightly awkward silence and it occurred to Mary that she wasn't the only one feeling shy.

'Okay,' he said, slowly. 'Anyway, this may seem strange after saying how beneficial meditation is, but I would like to do something different tomorrow night, if it's all right with you.' She looked at him questioningly. 'Sunburst is almost at the stage when I can play it on the piano,' he continued, 'and I should have it ready by tomorrow evening. Would you like to hear it?'

'I'd love to!' said Mary, 'but shouldn't we do that with your mother? I'm sure she'd like to hear it, too.'

'No — it definitely has to be you first.' Luke noted Mary's perplexed expression, 'For reasons that will become clear when you hear it.'

This was intriguing and she found herself agreeing to join him in the music room the next evening as soon as Delia was settled. She didn't sleep so well that night because of wondering what the Man of Mystery was up to.

The next day, he appeared at the table just as Mary was serving the evening meal.

'Oh hello,' said Delia, sarcastically. 'I thought you'd gone back to London! You might as well have for all we've seen of you.'

'I apologise for being so uncommunicative,' said Luke, with remarkable forbearance. 'I was desperate to get the suite up to the scoring stage and I'm almost there now — thanks to you both — and Mother, if I'd taken my down time in a remote cottage as usual, you wouldn't be seeing me at all! We can go to church together again in the morning, if you'd like that.'

This was a considerable improvement on the door-slamming and shouting that Delia's needling usually provoked and Mary was impressed. Perhaps the inner peace was having a wider-ranging effect than sound sleep!

Delia ploughed on.

'What I would really like is for you to listen to my wishes for when I die and to take it seriously this time. I'm getting chest pains and I think my heart is packing up.'

This was the first Mary had heard about chest pains and she reacted with concern, questions and a promise to mention it to Chris, who would no doubt make a doctor's appointment to get it checked out.

Luke, still in patient mode, promised to have the requested conversation with his mother after dinner and the meal progressed with Delia frowning as she ate in silence, the other two doing their best to have a normal conversation.

Luke joined Mary in the kitchen later, as she was clearing out the fridge, having spoken to his mother and left her watching a favourite travel programme.

'Did you know she was afraid of dying?' he asked, sitting down at the kitchen table.

'No — but most people are. Or, at least, afraid of pain leading up to it.'

'Well, she's in pain now and has been for a long time, but she's *really* frightened of death. Terrified, by the sound of it. She asked what I think about it, but I've never given it much thought. I'm usually too busy keeping pace with living! What are your thoughts?'

What was actually going through Mary's head was that living with Luke had an unnerving side, he either ignored you completely or asked intensely personal questions when you least expected them. She joined him at the table as such a conversation could take some time.

'I'll tell you what I think happens, if you really want to know, but I'm not sure that it will help your mum.'

He said that he was always fascinated by what Mary thought and waited expectantly, so she took a deep breath and began.

'There's a part of the brain that enables us to perceive time. As death approaches and the brain shuts down, it stops functioning and I think that a state of consciousness without a sense of time must be experienced as eternity. I suspect that we are suspended in that timeless place, in whatever state we have reached in life, so a person who has achieved peace of mind will remain for ever at peace. Yogis aim for union with God while still living, so that they can pass seamlessly into a state of pure, blissful consciousness at the moment of death.'

Luke looked horrified and asked how her theory worked for the overwhelming majority of human beings — himself included — who had *not* achieved peace of mind. Were they all in Hell?

'I think that there are probably varying degrees and levels of unease that are shown in a final, dreamlike state and I don't know how they are dealt with. Hindus would say that it's through reincarnation, but I don't think a personality can stay intact to move from one body to another. It's probably more a case of everything going into the universal mind and the unsatisfactory traits in the collective human psyche being worked out in a new birth. Something like that. Perhaps for the worst offenders, the enduring experience *does* stay with the individual and *is* hellish.'

Luke still looked perturbed, so she reminded him that these were only her thoughts, influenced by things she had read, and no one really knew the answer.

'Yes, but what you say makes sense!' persisted Luke. 'Kind and helpful people will spend all eternity in a benign, heavenly state and selfish, angry, cruel people will spend it in Hell. You'll probably be all right but I'll be stuck with my bad temper!'

'I won't be all right because I can't forgive my father!' she objected. Luke wanted to ask her more about that but she continued. 'And you may not be perfect either, but surely there's nothing bad enough to justify eternal torment! Anyway, I'm sure Delia needs to hear something much simpler and Christ-orientated. Perhaps you could just tell her that it's important to have peace of mind when she dies, so she should let go of any old grievances; forgive anyone she's angry with — that sort of thing — and just reach out for God.'

Luke sighed. 'Yes, that sounds about right. I suppose I could ask the vicar to have a word with her, as well.' He smiled at Mary and her heart turned over.

'As for me,' he added, 'I'd better start behaving myself! Anyway, thank you for sharing your thoughts. It must be nearly Mum's bedtime and I've interrupted your work — and I've asked you to spend time with me after she's in bed. Does that mean you'll have to stay up half the night catching up on housework?'

'I'll just have to sort this lot out.' Mary indicated the assortment of food on the worktop. 'I must get the things that are worth keeping back into the fridge tonight.'

He started to tell her how much he appreciated her always making time for him, but Delia's bell rang and she headed for the door. He wasn't sure she'd heard but at the last minute she turned and bestowed a radiant smile that made *his* heart turn over.

Chapter 21

Delia's bedtime routine took more than half an hour and then there was the food to deal with. After that, Mary went to her room to freshen up before going to the music room. With Beryl encouraging her and Mouse looking askance, she took off her work clothes, had a very quick shower and went to her wardrobe for something clean to wear. She decided on a flattering dress that she'd found in a charity shop and planned to wear to dinner with Luke next week. Why not wear it tonight, as well? It was an honour to be the first to hear the new composition so the least she could do was to look nice for the occasion. She put it on and checked her reflection in a full-length mirror. It looked as though it was made for her so, with a brief nod of self-approval, she went downstairs.

Luke was pacing the music room, wondering why Mary was taking so long. Had she changed her mind? He opened the door the instant she knocked and did a double take as she walked in.

'Oh! You do look nice!' he said in a surprised tone. 'Sorry — I didn't mean you usually look a mess but...' He petered out, aware that he was heading for a hole.

Mary helped him out.

'I know what you mean. Everyone thinks that jeans and check shirts are permanently bonded to my skin but occasionally I like to surprise people.'

He smiled in relief and indicated the sofa. Mary sat down, made herself comfortable and willed herself to relax. Luke handed her a piece of paper on which he had written the following:

SUNBURST SUITE

Kaleidoscope

Grief

Courage

Prevarication

Angelus

Clouds and Sunburst

'Do these headings mean anything to you?' he asked.

As Mary registered the title and first word, she tensed up again and looked up at him guiltily.

'Oh dear,' she said, thinking that he must have found out about her sneaking a look at what he was working on. Did he have a hidden camera in here? 'I'm sorry. I know I shouldn't have looked. I was just overcome with curiosity.'

'What on earth are you talking about?' he asked, genuinely at a loss.

Mary opened her mouth to speak but couldn't think of any way to back out of what she had just unnecessarily divulged, so closed it again and blushed.

'Are you saying you've seen these words before?'

She nodded wretchedly. 'Only the title and kaleidoscope.'

'And when was this?'

'Last time you were here. You went to talk to your mother, and I came back in and had a quick look. Only the first couple of pages, and then I lost my nerve. I'm really sorry. I don't usually behave like that.'

Luke sat down alongside her, took a pen out of his top pocket and pulled the slip of paper from her fingers. When he handed it back, the word "Angelus" had been crossed out and was replaced by "Sneakiness and Guilt". Mary stared at it in incomprehension but then a glimmer of light dawned.

'Some of these are personal qualities,' she ventured. 'Three of them could be mine now you've put guilt in.' She threw him a tentative questioning look.

'Only three?'

'I can't own courage or anything angelic — but that's gone now, anyway.'

'I think you have a lot of courage. You sang in Requiem of Life in front of a hall full of professional musicians; you single-handedly took on a severely disabled child; you stand up to me and fight my mother's corner... Need I go on? And you are kind and patient and wise — the qualities of an angel in my book so that will have to stay after all.'

Her eyes widened in surprise:

'Even though you now know I'm sneaky?' she asked, having reached the conclusion that this composition must indeed be about her.

'Looking at two pages of music hardly qualifies as the eighth deadly sin,' he commented in an off-hand manner. 'Okay, I am a bit surprised that you looked at it behind my back. Why was that, by the way?'

'You were being really mysterious about it and I was overwhelmed by curiosity,' she explained. A silence grew between them and she broke it by asking what the Kaleidoscope section was about.

He took a deep breath and decided to risk all.

'Right. Well — I'm not very good at talking about this sort of thing but when you sang in that Christmas concert — the first time I saw you — I was absolutely transfixed by the variety of expressions that crossed your face. It reminded me of the changing patterns in a kaleidoscope, so I put that idea into the music.'

There was a pause while Mary registered this. 'Do you mean you've been writing it ever since the Christmas concert?'

'Not quite. What actually got me started was the first time we played Scrabble. Christmas Eve, wasn't it?'

Mary agreed. She was having trouble breathing.

'Well, apart from when we laughed about your 'whining voice', you were so tense — not at all like the expressive, uninhibited person I'd fallen for — and I made it worse by pressing you for personal details. I began to think I'd imagined what I'd seen in the concert, but then you got a seven-letter word and your face lit up. It was like the sun bursting through clouds and it took my breath away. I started the composition on Christmas Day and "Sunburst" just seemed the right title for it. Initially I wrote Kaleidoscope, Grief, Courage and the last section. Then I added Prevarication and Angelus as I got to know you better.'

While he was making this speech — more of a declaration really — Mary was experiencing the kind of physical sensations that come from going down a sudden drop on a roller coaster. He'd said he had fallen for her and surely writing music about someone meant being obsessed with that person — possibly deeply in love with them. How could that have been going on all this time without her noticing? She knew he liked her enough to seek her company, even to the point of confiding in her, and after the episode in the garden, suspected that he found her physically attractive, but this sounded more serious than anything she had considered. His next words confirmed it.

'I know it must sound crazy, when I've been ignoring you for most of the last week, but I'm hopelessly in love with you. I wanted to finish the music because that's how I express myself best. I didn't know how else to tell you.'

She turned to look at him, opened her mouth to speak but then couldn't find the right words and looked away again.

'Mary — please say something. Even if it's only "get lost." At least I'll know where I stand!'

'I'm sorry,' she managed, in a low voice. 'I had no idea you felt like that. I feel the same... But I've been trying not to dwell on it because I thought it couldn't possibly go anywhere. We're worlds apart in so many ways.'

He gently brushed her cheek with the back of his hand. 'Are we really? We seem to share the same interests and ethical values and, as you now know, I'm planning to move to this area. It seems to me that we're growing closer by the minute. Will you listen to the music and then see what you think?'

She whispered, 'Yes, please.'

He went to the piano and turned to the opening page, apologising for not having practised it for performance and explaining that it was really intended for a small orchestra, so didn't lie easily under the fingers. He then proceeded to deliver what was, to Mary, an exquisite and totally accurate performance. The music made her feel like a long-neglected harp whose silent strings were being stirred into life by deft and loving fingers; it resonated with her on every level. "Kaleidoscope" was a fast-changing series of themes that meshed seamlessly, one with another. "Grief" had a simple, haunting melody accompanied by ever-changing harmonies. "Courage" had a strong core theme that persisted throughout the section, with other themes weaving in and out. "Prevarication" made her smile because it was made up of fragments of melody that kept going off in unexpected directions. "Angelus" was serene, beautiful and uplifting, and "Clouds and Sunburst" began with a faint melody obscured by heavy chords, which gradually lightened until the theme suddenly burst through in all its triumphant glory.

When it finished, Mary sat in stunned silence for a minute or so. Sadly, because it was the most beautiful part, she couldn't identify with the angel section, but she felt that he had captured her in the rest of the piece. How could he read her so well? Then, abruptly, she got up and made for the door, trying to explain that she needed tissues and would come back, but it didn't come out very well because she was in floods of tears. She ran to the bathroom where she washed her face and blew her nose and eventually got herself sufficiently under control to go back to the music room.

Luke stayed at the piano, unsure of what to make of Mary's running away for the second time that day. He wasn't used to being the pursuer, as women in his past had tended to throw themselves into his arms. But Mary was different and he didn't know what to do next. He realised that he'd put all his eggs into one basket by playing Sunburst to her. If they broke, he'd be devastated.

When Mary returned, she paused just inside the door and registered that he hadn't moved and looked anxious and uncertain. Beryl stepped in and propelled her across the room where she joined him on the double piano stool, put her hand on his shoulder and kissed his cheek.

'Thank you,' she said simply. 'It's beautiful. Too beautiful for words. It really got to me.'

'I thought it had upset you,' he stated, tentatively putting an arm around her.

'It was just that it stirred up long-buried emotions,' she explained. 'It made me cry, but in a good way.'

He was still wary of going too far, too fast, so asked if he could kiss her properly. Mary hesitated.

'You did say you felt the same,' prompted Luke.

'I do,' she admitted. 'It's just that I'm out of practice. There wasn't much time for that sort of thing when I was looking after Sam. I'll probably be hopeless.'

Luke was amused.

'It isn't something you get marks out of ten for,' he reassured her, while gently cupping her chin and raising her face to his.

The kiss went on for a long time and Mary had another roller-coaster moment as she surrendered to it. As he felt her relax, he gathered her up as closely as sitting side by side on a piano stool would allow. Then he buried his face in her hair and asked her to marry him.

This sent her down the longest plunge yet and she stiffened and almost stopped breathing. Luke detected the change and released his hold enough to look at her.

'I didn't mean to say that yet. It's too soon, isn't it? Sorry — it just slipped out.'

Mary was overwhelmed and had no idea what to say in response.

'I'm in shock,' she finally managed. 'Can you give me time to catch up with you, please? It sounds as though you've been thinking about me a lot while I've been trying not to think about you at all! At least, not romantically. I need to adjust — and I'm not ready for such a big question.'

'Of course,' he said. 'As long as you need.'

After a pause, he suggested they move to the sofa to talk. He told her what he'd done about reducing conducting commitments and described some of the things Steve was doing to help him to create composition time. He talked about the pros and cons of keeping his chance of the principal conductor position open. He confessed that he was entering a period of financial uncertainty and said he was sorry that he couldn't offer her security in that way. Mary said that she was used to financial insecurity so it wouldn't be a major issue for her. Encouraged by her willingness to discuss a possible future together, Luke asked whether she had any career plans and, conscious of the glaring gap between his aspirations and hers, she told him about the magazine articles she was writing. Then he asked what her ideal house would be like. A bit reluctantly, because it was another leap in his direction and Mary Mouse was getting edgy, she said it was the eco-friendly house that he had described when they met in the garden.

'There — you see. It seems as though we're a perfect fit,' exclaimed Luke.

Mary smiled and said it did look promising, but there was a lot to take in. She needed to sleep on it then come back to him with a few questions. The next day would be busy so could they get together on Monday?

'Yes, of course. You've promised to have dinner with me,' Luke reminded her. But it can't be anywhere too public because we'll be discussing personal things.'

Mary took the plunge after a deep breath. 'Come to my place then. In the evening, so I have a chance to recover after work. Mouse was now screeching in terror but Luke was already agreeing and offering to bring takeaway food so there was no way out. He extracted a goodnight kiss before she finally left the room.

I don't know how you think you're going to sleep after what you've done, muttered Mary Mouse as she mounted the stairs. *Did you really have to throw yourself at him like that? You do know he'll never give up now until you say yes, don't you? And he's probably unreliable. You haven't even asked him about his blog!* But Beryl the Peril was ecstatic and exhilarated with the joy of being loved enough to inspire a piece of music and was already planning the wedding.

Chapter 22

Mary tossed and turned all night, replaying bits of conversation and reliving the kisses and the sensation of Luke's beautiful, artistic hands on her body. She couldn't quite believe that it had all happened. She tried to recall the musical themes from Sunburst but all she could bring back was the feeling that he had got right under her skin, read every aspect of her personality and translated it into music. On reflection, she even recognised Angelus, it was the calmness, joy and serenity that sometimes came when she was in a deep meditative state. He had experienced that with her and then expressed it perfectly in his composition.

At one point she got up and put together a list of questions for Luke, desperately hoping that the answers wouldn't throw up anything that would stop the relationship from progressing. She just had to be as sure as anyone ever was that he'd be faithful — and, if they were to be together, there would have to be a good understanding of how they would live their everyday lives. It was lovely to have a soulmate but many a relationship broke down over much more ordinary things, such as who did the washing up! Of course, he had been quite helpful with chores at Cadence — except when he was composing. Then he turned right in on himself and she knew that that would always be the case. Perhaps they could just live together for a while and see how they got on.

In the middle of all this thinking, Delia needed help twice, and Mary only managed one short spell of sleep before it was time to get up. She dressed quickly and did as many jobs as possible before the others arose. Delia rang at eight thirty and then it was a challenge to help her to wash and dress and serve breakfast in time for church. Luke joined them to eat and Delia mentioned that she had heard him playing the piano late last night. Did that mean he had finished The Great Work? Fortunately, Luke had anticipated this question and he replied that, on playing it through, he'd found one or two things he needed to change, but it should be ready to play to her in a couple of days. Mary was grateful for his foresight because it protected her thinking time but rather sad that it meant they weren't being open with Delia. She would have to be told about the subject matter of Sunburst soon.

Mary didn't really have time to go to church but remembered that she had promised to accompany them and felt that it was important to stick to her part of the bargain. The upside was that it made her sit down and relax — so much so that she almost fell asleep in the sermon but then Luke surreptitiously took her hand and the joy of that kept her awake. She recalled one of the words he had used when describing the cumulative effect of several days of joint meditation. He'd said that he felt cherished. Now, the firm but gentle and reassuring pressure of his hand meant that *she* felt cherished — something she hadn't experienced since her mother died.

The rest of the day was hectic and hard work. Luke asked her to sit with him for a while during Delia's rest but she explained about the bad night, and said she needed to cat-nap in order to keep going. They compromised and sat on the sofa in the music room on the understanding that they didn't have to talk, and Mary could nod off if she needed to. She thought it unlikely that she could relax with him enough do that, but he was considerate, and read a book with his arm around her. She put her head on his shoulder and went out like a light. When Delia's bell went off, she nearly jumped out of her skin and then felt groggy and disorientated. Luke said his mother could wait for a few minutes while she woke up properly and used the time to deliver the kiss that he'd been thinking about while she slept. Mary wondered how she was ever going to resist anything he asked of her in the face of the intense physical reaction he could stir up.

In the evening, Luke went back to scoring Sunburst and Mary attended to Delia and cleaned the oven. She worked late into the night, partly because she wanted to leave the house as pristine as Chris did, but also because she thought it best to keep Luke's increasingly passionate embraces at bay until she'd had a chance to talk to him properly.

Chris arrived at ten the next morning and was amused to find Mary ironing Luke's clothes. Was she thinking of applying for a permanent position as his housekeeper? This was, of course, very near the truth, but Mary decided not to tell her anything about recent developments on that front in case something went wrong when she posed her questions. Chris thought that Mary looked tired yet at the same time radiated what could only be described as inner joy. As she'd been with Luke for over a week, she suspected that he might be the cause. She feared for Mary but thought it best to keep out of it.

***

Luke accepted that Mary had to work and applied himself to scoring for the rest of Sunday. On Monday morning, the two carers spent ages doing what they called a handover. He had never witnessed this before and was amazed at the time and effort that went into making sure that the incoming carer was well informed. Having got so far with Mary, this delay was frustrating on every level, but he made the best of it and got through a lot more work on Sunburst, continuing after she left until it was time to go to Cromer.

He wanted to take some flowers from the Bump but decided that they should be left where they grew for others to enjoy, so instead, gathered a small mixed bunch of fragrant blooms from the garden at Cadence. He then waited until Chris was elsewhere and located a pretty glass to use as a vase. He sensed that he wasn't quite home and dry with Mary — one minute she seemed to respond to his embraces but the next it was as though she had put the brakes on. She said she felt the same as he did but there was something not quite right. He gazed at his floral offering and ruefully surmised that if his music hadn't won her over, it was unlikely that a bunch of flowers would do it.

***

In the bungalow, Mary unpacked and ate a light lunch, after which she quickly fell into an exhausted sleep. Sometime later, she began to surface and hovered between sleep and full awareness in a deliciously relaxed state until suddenly, a startlingly clear picture of a giant Mary Mouse flashed across her mind's eye.

I suppose you do realise that he'll expect you to dance to his tune? said the Mouse.

Mary sat up and looked around the room in amazement — half expecting to see this figure because the impression of it was so real. Of course, there was nothing there and she shook her head, but then, after a moment's thought, got up and went to her bedroom where she retrieved a box from the back of the wardrobe. It contained a few of her mother's things that she hadn't looked through for a long time but now she carefully and reverently took everything out. There were photographs; one of herself and Deidre at school-age with both parents, in which they all looked radiantly happy. Then there was her mother's favourite scarf, some jewellery, a bottle of perfume, a diary and — right at the bottom — a small book, clearly intended for a child. This must have been one of her mother's childhood books. The cover was predominantly yellow and on it was an illustration of the red, black and white Mary Mouse figure that she had just seen.

'Right,' she thought. 'I've got you now, Mary Mouse. Now I know exactly where you came from. I must have identified with you when I was very small and you're the one who has given me so much trouble over the years, making me lose out on interesting and rewarding experiences through fear of something going wrong. Please listen to me carefully, I think you have been protecting me because you know how much I've been hurt, but it's time to stop now. I know that Luke will try to conduct me as if I'm a member of his orchestra, but I can give as good as I get — and I won't let him walk all over me. If I marry him, it will be based on mutual love and respect. I'll make sure of that.' However, the Mouse wasn't so easily displaced and quickly pointed out that he might not be faithful.

Beryl the Peril seemed to be jumping up and down.

Marry him! You're crazy about him. It doesn't matter what he's done before. You'll never get another chance like this!

Was Beryl just an extreme reaction to Mouse? Mary flopped down on to the bed with a sigh and spoke aloud.

'I'm fed up with both of you and your arguments!'

She could see that Mary Mouse was her anxious side and Beryl the Peril her reckless side. What did she need to do to integrate them into something worthwhile? The answer eluded her so she ran a bath, needing to freshen up before Luke came and thinking that a relaxing soak might help her to resolve the problem. She closed her eyes and let her mind drift, soothed by the warm water and enjoying the absence of Delia's bell. She must have started to doze again because another voice suddenly rang out in her mind.

The only way out is up! This time it was her mother's voice, accompanied by a vivid sense of her presence. Mary was reluctant to open her eyes because she thought that if she could just postpone the moment, her mother might stay. Even after so many years, she still missed her qualities of calmness, wisdom and discernment. The world seemed to stop turning for a moment as in a sudden burst of certainty, she realised that these were the very qualities she needed to reconcile the Mouse with Beryl. Calmness, Wisdom and Discernment. They rose above anxiety and recklessness and would surely dispel the need for either. Mary opened her eyes at last, feeling that she would always keep her mother close by if she could realise those qualities in her own life. As this idea took root, she felt as though something uncomfortable had at long last been resolved.

By the time Luke arrived, she was well groomed and feeling calmer. When he gave her the flowers, she was touched and immediately felt inclined to forgive him anything. He had judged correctly that a small mixed, fragrant bunch would mean more to her than a lavish bouquet. Tears sprang to her eyes because it had been so long since anyone brought her flowers and she forgot about keeping her distance until she'd asked him about his blog, and tried for a peck on his cheek. He somehow managed to turn it into a bear hug and she felt herself dissolving. It was not going to be easy to hang on to her new qualities!

They were soon seated either side of her tiny table and Mary remarked that it felt odd to be eating without Delia.

'I hope that doesn't mean that you want her to be present at every meal we ever have!' he replied. 'Assuming we are going to have lots of them. Have you decided yet?'

'Can I ask you a few questions before we get into that?' she asked.

'Of course. Anything you like.'

'Well — you know all about my pathetic and limited love life, but I don't know anything at all about yours.'

'Ah — well, I will tell you about it but I'm warning you — I haven't been a saint.'

Luke proceeded to describe his college love affair and the time spent living with Lily. Then, with some trepidation, he said he wasn't proud of the next phase and admitted that he had taken advantage of success in his early conducting years and had short-term affairs with many women. He concluded by saying that he'd seen why the relationships weren't working and had given all that up. He hadn't had a partner of any description for the last year or so. It was a long story and by the time it ended they had finished eating. Mary cleared the dishes to give herself time to think. She still wanted to know if he was involved in writing the blog, because that made it sound as though he was still seeing a lot of women.

'Do you write your own blog?' she asked, aloud.

'My what? Don't tell me you've been reading that rubbish! Why, for heaven's sake, when you can speak to me about anything you like? Okay, most of it has been by email but I thought we had shared deep and meaningful information about each other. Why would you want to read social media rubbish?'

'I've only looked at it twice,' said Mary, quickly. 'The first time was before the emails began, just after the Requiem of Life recording. It implied that you had affairs with many women, most of them professional musicians. I was pretty sure you hadn't written it yourself because Requiem of Life wasn't even mentioned, and I knew how important it was to you. I wanted to ask you about it but—' She paused, biting her lip.

'Well?' he prompted.

She sat down and confessed that she didn't want him to know that she was interested in his love life and behaving like one of his fans.

He looked quite pleased as he digested this information and then asked what the second occasion was.

'A few hours ago, I looked at it again because I wanted to say yes to everything you're suggesting, but in view of the frequent change of partners, I thought you might quickly get tired of me. The blog still suggests that you're having a high old time with several different women.'

After an ominous pause, Luke took out his mobile and found the offending blog. He looked angrier by the minute as he read.

'I'll wring his scrawny neck!' he eventually burst out. He started to scroll through his mobile phone contacts, searching for the unfortunate culprit and Mary realised that other women were perhaps less of a threat to their future happiness than was his quick temper. It suddenly felt very important to find a way to calm him down. She needed to be sure she could do that before committing to a long-term relationship. What would a wise person do?

'Look, please don't spoil our evening with that. Surely it can be sorted out later?' She put her hands around his and gently removed the phone, then drew him over to the sofa.

'You don't understand,' he persisted. 'This affects my reputation and my career. The sooner I put a stop to it, the better.'

'Yes, but it sounds as though you haven't been monitoring it properly,' she pointed out. 'Some of the blame must lie with you!'

'I don't have time for that sort of thing!' he protested and retrieving his phone from the table, rang Steve and accused him of not keeping an eye on the blog.

Steve's voice came over loud and clear so Mary could hear every word of his response:

'Come on, mate. Don't try that on me! I clearly remember warning you of the pitfalls of out-sourcing that and I said you must keep an eye on it. You need to write a statement distancing yourself from the content immediately. As soon as you let me have it, I'll have your page taken down.'

Luke ended the call and threw the mobile on to the settee where it fortunately met with a soft landing.

Mary put her arms around him in an attempt to calm him down, but he felt rigid and unresponsive, so she removed them again.

'Who wrote the blog?' she asked

'Declan — a cousin of some sort. I can never remember exactly what the relationship is. He was out of work, so I paid him to do it, thinking I was doing him a favour.'

'Is he younger than you?'

'Yes, by about twenty years.'

Mary observed that Declan was probably too young to convincingly sound like the real Luke — and he might envy his cousin's success both in the music world and with women. Perhaps he had strayed into the realms of fiction because he was seeing himself in that role.

She received a sceptical frown for this, although, on reflection, Luke thought she might have a point. He didn't want to spoil the evening either, so he sighed and said he would ring Declan but confine himself to saying that the blog appeared to have lost touch with reality, and he'd decided not to keep it going. He'd pay him a modest severance fee, but Declan must stop writing it forthwith. He couldn't get a reply as it turned out, so he put it into a text message.

Mary breathed a sigh of relief and relaxed.

Luke took her hand and apologised for getting cross. Had he jeopardised their budding relationship? Mary hedged and said that they should talk about it because she was bound to do something to upset him, sooner or later, and then he would lose his temper with *her*.

'I can't imagine doing that!' he protested.

Mary argued that all couples sometimes got on each other's nerves but he had a tendency to overreact.

'Are you saying it's a deal-breaker?'

'Only if you start using me as a punch bag.'

Mary was only half joking about this, physical abuse had to start somewhere, and he was so passionate and unpredictable. Could he turn violent?

Luke was deeply wounded. 'So — basically, you're saying that you can't trust me to be faithful or to control my temper.'

'It's not that I believe either of those things will go wrong. I just don't know. That's why we need to spend more time together!'

An uncomfortable silence grew between them. After a while, Mary broke it.

'I think lack of trust is a problem for me because of the way I've been treated in the past.' She described the feeling of abandonment caused by Leonard leaving soon after her mother's death and how that feeling was reinforced by Adrian's departure. Luke could see where she was coming from and tried to say so but Mary swept on.

'But I'm still worried about your temper. Do you know why you lose it so easily?'

'Not really. Of course, my mother flares up totally without warning and has done for as long as I can remember. It was mostly directed at my father until he died and then I found myself in the firing line. Unfortunately, you got caught up in it, as well, when she sounded off about the insulation I was suggesting. She does tend to lash out in all directions once she gets going! But I don't know why she can't control her temper and I'm afraid I've been shouting and slamming doors for as long as I can remember. But it doesn't mean I'll turn violent. I've never hit anyone in my life. At school I was accused of being "lily-livered" and I was the punch bag. As for hurting you — well, that's just absurd. You're by far the most precious person ever to enter my life and I've spent all those hours composing for you. How could you think that?'

Mary apologised and asked him to forget she'd ever said it, but Luke wouldn't let it go.

'Actually, now I come to think of it, there is just one thing you could do that might drive me to violence and that's what you're worried about *me* doing — being unfaithful.'

'That will never happen,' said Mary, unequivocally. I'll never want anyone else.'

'Neither will I,' he responded instantly. 'No one else has ever come close to the way I feel about you. Look, I know on the face of it I'm not the sort of person you could rely on but you have my solemn promise that I will always be faithful to you, always love you and look after you — even if you're ill — and I'll share everything I have with you. I'll be honest and open with you and respect you. We'll be equal partners and we'll discuss everything that affects us both. I want to live in the wonderful atmosphere that surrounds you and breathe the same air. I want to hold you at night and wake up beside you every morning and I want it to be for the rest of our lives.'

Mary was totally disarmed by Luke's unflinching gaze and his spontaneous outpouring of promises. In essence, he had stated the marriage vows and in the face of this, her resistance began to crumble. She made a few false starts before forming a response.

'Those promises will be hard to keep, especially the one about being equal. You might forget I'm not a member of one of your orchestras!'

Luke smiled and admitted that he might unconsciously lapse into that from time to time because he'd been directing musicians for so long.

'But you'll only have to remind me that we're equal partners,' he pledged, 'and I'll stop.'

A silence followed as Mary digested everything he'd said. It all seemed to be happening very fast but he was obviously sincere and the mere thought of a future without him was too horrible to contemplate. In the end, she looked him in the eye and said that she very much hoped to be his wife one day but, for now, could they try living together? He could stay at her bungalow for the rest of the week if he didn't mind the spartan conditions. He took her face between his hands and thanked her several times before kissing her soundly. She kissed him back and melted into his embrace and everything suddenly felt natural and right — until the zip of her dress somehow came undone and he tried to carry her into the bedroom.

'Stop!' she protested. 'There are some things we need to talk about first!'

'We've been talking for ages! You can't prevaricate now!'

'You're going too fast and I'm nervous!' she cried.

'Oh — sorry, I should have thought about that.' He put her back on to the sofa and apologised for getting carried away.

'I haven't so much as kissed anyone since Adrian left,' she explained. 'And that was about fourteen years ago.'

Luke was stunned. He had taken on board that she was 'out of practice', but not that it meant total abstinence for so many years.

'How on earth have you escaped everyone's clutches for all that time?'

She reminded him that her social life had been severely restricted by the demands of her caring role.

'But still, people could come here,' he said.

She described her disastrous attempt to start something up with a choir member and said she'd given up after that. 'And another thing, because it's been so long, I don't have any contraception in place!'

Luke felt out of his depth. In his experience, people just got on with it if they felt like having sex and had condoms to hand as a matter of course but Mary was unlike any other woman he'd ever slept with and obviously required a very different approach. After a short silence, he responded.

'Okay, I can take care of the second thing. As for being nervous—'

'I'm sorry,' Mary cut in. 'Perhaps the best way is just to get on with it,' and she began to rise. 'I'll pray for courage. That's always worked before.'

Luke gave a slight chuckle.

'Now you sound as though you're facing a trip to the dentist! Listen, I have a better plan. Why don't we pretend we've been together for several months and are just spending a normal evening together?' He looked at his watch and saw that it was only eight p.m. 'We'll do whatever you like doing to relax in the evening then go to bed — together — at a more normal time and just let things happen naturally. That might mean we just curl up together and go to sleep if you don't feel like making love. We'll get around to it when you're ready.'

As he delivered this speech he was wondering if he had the self-control to carry out what he'd just described, but Mary was already gratefully agreeing to the plan. He established that she liked to be out of doors in the long summer evenings, either pottering in the garden or walking near the sea and they agreed on the latter.

They wandered through the town to the sea front and eventually ended up on a bench beneath an old-fashioned shelter on the pier. There was a cool breeze so Mary was happy to snuggle up against Luke and he put his arm around her and felt her body relax against his. They watched some surfers who were displaying considerable skill in negotiating the robust waves, and periodically exchanged comments and observations about their possible future together. Mary described the articles she was writing about eating for health and her hopes for getting them published.

'I know it won't bring much money in and it's a million miles from your glittering career, but I'd like to carry on with it. I would feel I was contributing something.'

'Absolutely. I don't expect you to spend all your time cooking and cleaning for me. I'll help with all that — well, maybe not the cooking! Re-heating readymade meals from the supermarket is all I'm good for! It won't be like the last week at Cadence with me locked in the music room and you slaving away at all the domestic stuff. I want a partner, not a slave.' And he described his father's treatment of Delia and promised to never be like that.

The light was beginning to fade and lights were coming on in the town. Mary realised that they had both slipped into talking as though their relationship was permanent. It was obviously what they both wanted, so why waste time on a trial week? When Luke went back to London, his career and practical matters such as property transactions would intrude. The next few days might be the best chance of a honeymoon period they would ever get. She took a deep breath before speaking.

'You made some wonderful promises earlier and I want to make it equal. I'm afraid it won't be as eloquent as yours but I do want to try.'

Luke was overjoyed to hear this and said that it was the intention that mattered. He was also gratified to have the word 'eloquent' applied to him for the first time ever.

Mary spoke carefully, with frequent pauses.

'I love you very much and always have, although I've tried to hide it from myself. Now I don't have to hide any more and I feel as though I've been let out of prison. I promise to be faithful to you and to look after you "in sickness and in health". I don't have much money but will share anything I ever have with you. I will nourish you in every way I can think of and support you in your work, and will also forgive you if you get cross sometimes and hope you'll forgive me when I annoy you — because I'm bound to do that from time to time.'

She ground to a halt at this point.

'Thank you, Mary.' Luke said. 'That means more to me than you'll ever know.'

After that it just seemed natural to kiss and move into a more intimate embrace, until Luke pointed out that they had both omitted to mention, 'With my body I thee worship'. Was it time for that yet?

Mary simply took his hand, then got up and pulled him to his feet.

Chapter 23

The following morning, Mary woke up with a man alongside her for the first time in many years. She lay on her back and listened to his breathing, while mentally replaying the previous evening. In spite of his impulsive nature, Luke had been incredibly sensitive about her fears over sex — and wise to suggest a more measured approach. She had asked for wisdom and it had come through him! For all that, she was still too nervous to enjoy their first attempt much and had clung to him as though she were drowning. He had responded by stroking her hair and murmuring soothing endearments and later in the night made love to her again — slowly and tenderly — and this time she was able to reach a climax.

Remembering that event caused electric shock sensations to shoot down through her body from her solar plexus to her genitals and she felt close to experiencing another one. She hugged her knees to her chest and smiled at her ability to morph from nervousness to unleashed sexuality in the space of a few hours. Luke showed no sign of waking, so she got up, drank her usual morning glass of water and armed with a bowl of cereal, picked up her tablet. Luke had mentioned equity release as a way of making Delia independent, so she did some research on the subject, wryly observing that this was much more effective than a cold shower for damping down excess sexual energy.

By the time Luke appeared, Mary had plenty of information, so they spent the rest of that morning discussing the possibilities. Equity release seemed to be the best option but Mary thought that an adult social-care assessment would also be sensible just in case they could help. Although this made sense to both of them, they were still faced with the tricky problem of how to present it to Delia, who didn't even know she was no longer self-supporting. They decided that Luke should tell her about the money situation, as she'd reacted badly to Mary being present when they talked about environmental improvements to the house and this was even more personal. He would also have to reveal his plans for reducing conducting commitments, moving to East Anglia, and setting up home with Mary. The last item would be a stumbling block because his mother was old-fashioned about people living together out of wedlock.

'Would it help if you told her we're engaged and plan to marry in the church she attends?' asked Mary. There was a pause as Luke registered her U-turn on the subject of marriage.

'Absolutely!' he finally exclaimed. That would turn it into something she can look forward to. Are you sure? I know I'm rushing you.'

'I'm sure,' replied Mary. We've made solemn commitments to each other and I for one won't be backing out. I can't see any reason why we shouldn't legalise it. Can you?'

He shook his head then kissed her. He wanted to delay going to Cadence so they could celebrate more thoroughly but Mary pushed him out of the door, saying the longer he left it, the harder it would be to broach the list of things to tell Delia.

While Luke was out, Mary caught up with emails and text messages. Chris had messaged.

'Has Luke got a girlfriend (or boyfriend!). His car has been missing since yesterday afternoon!'

Mary replied, enigmatically.

'All will become clear soon. He is on his way to talk to his mum now. He'll probably have dinner with her if she's still speaking to him by then.'

Having deduced that Luke must have just left Mary, Chris texted back. 'It sounds as though you haven't been taking my advice!'

Mary resisted the temptation to keep that conversation going because she thought it best if Delia knew about the engagement before it was discussed with Chris. She dealt with a few routine emails and then phoned Deidre to ask whether she could bring Luke to see their eco-friendly house. Unfortunately, the only free time that Deidre had before Luke went back to London was Saturday and it was already arranged for

Leonard and Kathleen (who were now living among the rubble in the inherited cottage) to visit on that day.

Mary had mixed feelings about being there at the same time, on the one hand it would be useful to announce the engagement when everyone was together but on the other, Kathleen might monopolise Luke. She said she'd speak to him and get back to Deidre to confirm the visit. Then she decided on the spur of the moment to forewarn her sister about the engagement.

'I was just thinking that your relationship with him had come on apace if you were bringing him to visit, but marriage? Are you sure about this, Pipsqueak?' was Deidre's surprised response.

Mary winced. That name (a throwback to childhood) was even worse than Mary Mouse and it screamed of big-sisterly superiority! She wanted to break away from being the little sister looking to Deidre for approval, so replied very firmly.

'Yes, I am. Surer than I've ever been of anything in my life. All my doubts have been laid to rest. I know it won't be a bed of roses; what relationship ever is? But we have spent a lot of time talking about the aspects of life that really matter and we're on the same page. He is impulsive and unpredictable (actually, that is quite exciting!) and he loses his temper with his mum and with musicians who can't or won't dance to his tune. One day, he will probably shout at me — but I can deal with that. The main thing is that we have a good, solid core of love and respect and he is sensitive and caring about the things that matter most.'

Deidre, surprised at her sister's sudden confidence, backed off on hearing this and moved to asking questions that Mary couldn't yet answer about wedding plans. Then she wanted to know all about the proposal, and had they slept together yet? Mary confirmed the latter (minus the 'juicy details' that Deidre was asking for) and told her about Sunburst.

***

Meanwhile, Luke was having a difficult time with his mother.

'What happened to all the scoring you were going to do?' asked Delia as soon as she saw him.

'There was something else I had to sort out first,' he replied, mildly.

'There's only one kind of "something else" that takes all night!' she snapped back, with her voice rising.

Luke abandoned the idea of breaking his news gently and went for the direct approach.

'I was with Mary,' he explained. He tried to follow this with the news that they were engaged but Delia shouted over him.

'What! You're messing with my carer?'

'No! Not messing! She has agreed to be my wife!' he shouted back.

Chris — nearby in the kitchen — heard every word and sent a 'Congratulations! (Are you mad?)' text to Mary.

'But you hardly know each other!' continued Delia at the top of her voice.

'She isn't taking it very well,' Chris informed Mary.

Luke sighed and explained about the emails and late-night conversations. 'I promise you Mother, there hasn't been any hanky-panky going on under your roof — or anywhere else for that matter until last night — but we have got to know each other really well in ways that matter a lot more.'

This took the wind out of Delia's sails and she gave his response a moment's thought.

'She's a lovely girl — there's no denying that — and I think you have chosen well, but can you make her happy? How will it work? Is she going to fly around the world hanging on to your coat tails?'

This gave Luke the perfect opportunity to explain about his plans to change career direction and move to East Anglia. He could tell by his mother's pursed lips that she was less than happy about his reducing the number of concerts, but she remained silent as he went on to talk about the financial situation.

Chris texted Mary again. 'It has gone very quiet. Either he has murdered her or talked her round.'

When Delia finally spoke, it was merely to say that she felt overwhelmed by everything Luke had told her and would think about it all. However, over dinner she asked for more details and pleaded with him not to throw away a perfectly good career. Luke said he wasn't planning to throw anything away — just to change direction and explained that he felt most truly at home in his own skin when he was composing. There would still be some conducting but he hoped that it would mainly be performances of his own work. His mother shook her head sorrowfully and he could see that she was disappointed in him. The meal progressed in an uncomfortable silence after that and as soon as they'd finished eating, she asked Chris to take her to the sitting room because she was tired and needed to rest.

Luke texted Mary.

Mum is thinking about it all but I'm afraid too much news at once has worn her out. I'll do some scoring while she rests but want to see her again briefly before she goes to bed so won't get back until nine-ish. Sorry. ILY xxxxx.

No problem, replied Mary. ILY2 xxxxxxxxxxxx.

She used the time to phone Chris and fill in some details. It was a difficult conversation because Chris was genuinely worried about her, even after Mary told her about the fabricated blog and it ended on an uncomfortable note with Chris saying that it was Mary's funeral, an unfortunate phrase to use about a forthcoming wedding!

Luke did see his mother again before bed, but she was not ready to discuss the way that the proposed changes would affect her. Instead, she asked him to bring Mary and a bottle of champagne to dinner the following evening, signifying that she did approve of the engagement. She even asked Luke to look out some antique family rings in case Mary would like to have one. He breathed a sigh of relief. He knew he shouldn't let it affect him so much, but he hated to be in his mother's bad books.

***

The next morning, it occurred to Mary that Chris would have to wait on her at dinner, so she offered to help with meal preparation and washing up, thinking that she could perhaps talk Chris round in the informal setting of the kitchen. Chris texted her reply.

'No worries. I'll have to get used to your changed status! You'll be my boss soon.'

Mary didn't want her relationship with Chris to change. She enjoyed it just the way it was, so messaged back.

'*Delia* is *our* boss! I hope to carry on being your job-share partner for the foreseeable future and will always be your friend.'

Luke tentatively showed Mary the rings, explaining that she could have a new one if she'd prefer that. He needn't have worried because she loved antiques and spent a long time deciding which to have. She chose a small red ruby surrounded by tiny diamonds but it was too big and would have to be altered. The sight of it on her finger was quite a shock, bringing home the reality of what she'd agreed to. Mary Mouse resurfaced with a lecture about *Marry in haste and repent at leisure*, but Beryl quickly squashed her with reminders about ecstatic nights and sublime music. The new wise Mary thought that after the sensitive way he'd dealt with her nervousness about sex, she could surely trust him. What did the occasional burst of temper matter in the face of that? It was just the way he was. Perhaps Deidre was right about the 'Mad Maestro' syndrome. She loved him, anyway.

Luke worked on Sunburst until it was time to go to Cadence and Mary gathered more information from the internet, then meditated for a while. They arrived in time for a drink with Delia before dinner and Chris joined them for a toast. She was pleasant enough but still refused help from Mary and quickly went back to the kitchen. When she had gone, Delia announced that she was determined to avoid social workers so would sell the house and go into a care home, where she wouldn't be any trouble to anyone. Mary and Luke exchanged glances; judging by Delia's tone of voice and choice of words, this was not what she really wanted to do.

'There's no rush to decide anything,' Mary urged. 'Luke still has a lot on, and it will be a long time before we can start planning a wedding. I can carry on job-sharing with Chris for now.'

'But if I sell the house now, I can use the money to pay care-home fees, so you won't have to complicate things with equity release,' persisted Delia.

Luke and Mary were pleased that she had understood the problem, but both noticed that she looked far from happy about the solution she had come up with.

'I think you need to take a bit longer over such a big decision,' Luke put in. 'This house is worth a lot, so equity release plus your income should pay for live-in carers for a long time. Mary will probably have to stop eventually but you'll still see plenty of her and we'll find someone else to job-share with Chris.'

Chris chose that moment to come and tell them that dinner was ready. Mary felt that it was a good thing that she had heard Luke upholding her continued employment; perhaps it would soften Chris's view of him. There wasn't any point in pretending that they hadn't been discussing her, so — ever the diplomat — Mary spoke.

'As you've just heard, we'll have to make some changes eventually about my work here, but we hope yours will continue. Shall we just enjoy the meal tonight? I hope you're eating with us, Chris.'

'Oh, I think this should just be a family meal,' protested Chris.

'Rubbish!' said Delia robustly. 'You've been here so long you're as good as family. I insist that you join us!'

Chris gave in and they enjoyed the meal together, chatting about the best location for Luke and Mary's house. Delia thought that finding a suitable property at the foot of Beeston Bump would be problematic as the gardens were small and parking space was very limited. Chris wanted to know why Beeston Bump was so important.

'Because anything feels possible up there,' explained Luke. 'It's where I get many of my ideas for new compositions and working out tricky bits in work in progress.'

Delia seemed to have accepted his passion for composing and asked if they could hear the suite that he had worked so hard on so, after the meal, they all went into the music room to hear Sunburst. At the end, Delia said that she liked it more than Requiem of Life, which was too sad, but this was beautiful, and she congratulated her son on his accomplishment. These remarks may have been encouraged by champagne but Luke's face lit up and leaping to his feet, he kissed his mother enthusiastically.

Chris finally accepted help with the washing up, giving Mary the opportunity to chat and get back on to a friendly footing.

'Well, you've obviously worked some magic on him,' observed Chris at the end of their conversation. 'He seems much kinder to his mum and as for having music written about you — that's the most romantic thing I've ever heard!' She hugged Mary and wished her every happiness.

Later, as they drove back, Mary suggested parking the car and walking up to the lighthouse, as she'd like to share one of her favourite places with him. The evening was warm and still and the sun was only just starting to go down, so they settled on a bench at the top of the climb and admired the view. After sitting in companiable silence for a while, Luke spoke, with a sense of wonder.

'I feel content. I don't think that's ever happened before!'

'Me too. I can't remember when I last felt like this.'

'We must be good for each other,' continued Luke.

Mary wrapped her arms around him by way of agreement.

After a while Luke asked her if she'd ever thought about having any more children. Mary had stopped thinking about that a long time ago and couldn't believe her ears.

'Not recently,' she admitted. 'Are you seriously saying that's what *you* want?'

'Plenty of couples do,' he pointed out mildly.

Mary moved away from him slightly to let this unexpected development sink in.

'As far as I know, there's no reason why I can't have more children,' she said, carefully. 'After Sam was diagnosed, I was told that his condition was not genetic and I have as good a chance as anyone of having healthy babies. But what about your composition plans? Children of all ages are demanding and intrusive. You'll experience that when we visit Deidre.'

'I don't think that will put me off. Look, I know there'd be times when I couldn't help out; when I was in the grip of inspiration or just before a concert, for instance, but I'd want to be involved as much as possible. I would help.'

Mary didn't answer immediately. She needed more thinking time as this was an enormous issue for her.

They were bathed in a surreal golden glow as the sun set over the town, so set off back down the hill while they could still see the path.

'What if you were preparing for a concert and I was ill?' asked Mary, as they carefully picked their way through bumps and hollows. 'I hardly ever am but it could happen!'

'I'd remember the "in sickness and in health" promise, of course, and put you and the child first,' he answered instantly.

They continued to discuss the implications as they made their way down to where they'd parked the car.

Chapter 24

The next day, Luke received a phone call from a publisher who was impressed by Requiem of Life and wanted to know if there were any more compositions in the pipeline. Luke described Sunburst and was asked to send a recording of it as soon as he had one ready. While he was delighted at the interest in his work, this put pressure on his remaining time with Mary as he now had to finish scoring the work, get parts printed and find players for an orchestra to record it, on top of the rehearsals and performances already scheduled for the coming weeks. He said he would stick to visiting Deidre in Suffolk but wanted to stay in a hotel afterwards so that he could continue down to London on Sunday morning and get organised.

'Will you come with me?' he asked Mary.

'To London? Won't I be in the way? You'll be very busy.'

'I've been thinking. You could bring work of your own to do and perhaps arrange for some valuations of the flat, I'll struggle to fit that in on my own. We'll be able to sleep together and share most meals and you could come to the prom rehearsal, or even the concert if you can stay until the twentieth.'

Mary swallowed. She felt as though she was being plunged into the role of Mrs Braithwaite in a very short space of time and it was disconcerting. 'Can I think about it? There's nothing to keep me here really; it's just that I'm only starting to get used to our being together and that would be very intense.'

'No, it wouldn't! I'd be out a lot of the time.'

'I mean it would be like becoming your wife overnight.'

Luke was disappointed that this was a problem for her. He wanted instant, full-on commitment from both sides but said he'd make some calls and leave her to think it over.

She went to work in the garden, which was a good thinking place, and imagined what living in his flat would be like. This was difficult because she hadn't seen it and he rarely mentioned it, so she went inside when she heard him ending a call and asked him to describe it.

He looked sceptical and said he couldn't see how that would help.

'It will help me to adjust if I can visualise it,' she said.

He fought to control his impatience to get on with arrangements for the Sunburst recording.

'It's about the same size as this, overall, on the top floor of six, so the views are good. Air-conditioned and totally soulless. Okay?'

Mary wasn't much the wiser, but she thanked him and went back to gardening, telling herself that it was more important to think about how she would use her time. Then it occurred to her that it would be useful to be thrown in at the deep end. If she always stayed in East Anglia while he was in London, she would have a very distorted view of what married life would be really like, so next time she went in, she said she'd love to come with him. This got her a hug and instructions to get her belongings organised.

Luke spent most of Friday working on Sunburst at Cadence while Mary got their washing up to date, bought some more charity shop clothes and packed. In the evening, they ate with Delia and Chris again, explaining that this was farewell because the next day, they had to head south after visiting Tom and Deidre.

They arrived there in good time for lunch on Saturday and Mary introduced Luke to everyone. As expected, Kathleen questioned him about everything musical that he'd ever done, which he tolerated with good grace until Mary intervened by suggesting he went with Tom to look at the ground source heating system. This went down very well and the two men arrived at the table still discussing various environmentally friendly possibilities for Luke and Mary's future home. Kathleen looked bemused as engineering projects didn't fit with her idea of what famous conductors did.

During the meal, Jack announced (to his parents' surprise) that he wanted to be a conductor when he grew up and asked Luke how to go about it.

'You have to go to a music college, and to get into one of those you have to be very good at all sorts of musical things, such as playing at least one instrument and passing exams,' explained Luke.

'I can play the keyboard,' offered Jack.

Deidre grimaced and pointed out that he hadn't had proper lessons and his keyboard was a child's instrument. She thought Mr Braithwaite meant much more serious skills.

'They can call me Luke. And Jack, can I see your keyboard when we've finished eating? Have you any other instruments?'

Jack listed a variety of percussion instruments while his mother shook her head in attempted discouragement. It was a waste of time because Luke was absolutely determined to prove to Mary that he was father material and as soon as they finished eating, he motioned to the children.

'Right, you three. We've got enough for a band so show me where all these instruments are.'

'It's a bit of a mess up there!' protested Deidre feebly but Luke was half-way upstairs by then, on the heels of three stampeding children.

'Do something!' cried Kathleen. 'You can't expect a musician of his calibre to play with their toys!'

'Leave them,' laughed Mary. 'He says he wants us to have children and I want him to be thrown in at the deep end to see if he really means it!' she explained. She caught her father's eye and saw that he, too, was highly amused.

'Well! You have been keeping a lot of secrets!' exclaimed Deidre. 'Is there anything else we should know?'

With some censoring, Mary filled them in on everything she could think of until they were interrupted by a loud cacophony from upstairs and they all dissolved into laughter.

'I think he's passed the father test!' said Leonard, with tears running down his cheeks, and Mary remembered from her childhood how he couldn't stop laughing once he'd started and usually ended up in tears. It was good to see him like that again.

They more-or-less had themselves under control by the time Luke came back downstairs, but he still suspected mockery. Mary said he'd done a great job, but it wasn't quite his best and he said he'd deal with her later. He turned to Tom and Deidre.

'Jack does have some keyboard aptitude, but he'll need a better instrument in order to develop it. They're all quite musical and Rohan, in particular, has an excellent sense of rhythm.'

'Really?' said Tom. 'We'd better change our tactics then. We've been shouting at him for making too much noise on that infernal drum of his!'

All in all, the visit went very well. The only misgiving Mary had was that her father didn't get a chance to talk to Luke because everyone else was clamouring for his attention.

The engaged couple drove down to their hotel in Ipswich in the late afternoon. They looked at Luke's work schedule over the evening meal so that Mary would be prepared for his various comings and goings.

'There's no denying it will be hectic,' he said, 'but just remember that it's temporary. Our married life won't be like that.'

'I think you'll always be in demand,' was Mary's comment. 'But at least it won't be in London. I don't think I could live there permanently.'

They went to bed early and lay with their arms around each other, talking softly about their plans. Then Luke asked if he had done well with the children that afternoon.

'You were amazing!' Mary answered.

'Good. So, can we do away with these now?' he smiled, reaching for the packet of condoms and waving them in her face.

Once again, Luke was several steps ahead of Mary, who was still wondering if she could see herself with a baby after so many years since giving birth to Sam.

'Er — if we hit the jackpot first time, it will really pile the pressure on!' she pointed out, hoping to buy some time.

'True, but we're not in the first flush of youth, are we? I think the sooner we start trying the better — and I want us to be natural and spontaneous.'

By now he was exploring her body with his hands and lips and making it very hard for her to deny him anything — Wisdom flew out of the window. Sex had been wonderful all week for Mary as she was extremely sensitive to his touch. Now, as he entered her, unsheathed, she was transported to new heights — as was he — and they reached orgasm at precisely the same moment.

The release of energy was like nothing Mary had ever experienced before. Initially, she lost awareness of where she ended and he began and then suddenly, she seemed to be floating near the ceiling — looking down on their entwined bodies. Then there was another sudden shift and she seemed to be zooming high into the air above the hotel until she could see the building, the town and the surrounding patchwork of fields, as though she were in an aeroplane. Then it seemed as though she were in space, and after a brief glimpse of the earth as a globe, she lost consciousness. It probably only lasted for a minute or so, but it seemed like an age to Luke as he called her name repeatedly.

'What happened?' he asked, when she finally came to.

Groggily, she did her best to describe the episode and he said that he, too, had felt the dissolving of boundaries between them. To him, this was hugely significant. 'But as for the rest, I think you must have experienced an expansion of consciousness. I didn't get that; I soon came back to earth. The question is, are you all right now?'

Mary smiled and stroked his face, saying that she was. She thanked him for giving her an awe-inspiring experience of togetherness.

'Do you think conception is more likely if orgasm happens like that? We were exactly together, weren't we?'

'Yes, I think we were. I don't know if that makes conception more likely, but the fact that I'm mid-cycle almost certainly does! Anyway, I'm sure we'll find a way to cope if I'm pregnant.'

She couldn't remember actually agreeing to a baby, but it didn't seem to matter any more.

Mary dozed for a while but Luke's mind remained active.

'I think we're like baroque counterpoint,' he suddenly announced, waking Mary up. 'In counterpoint, the parts are clearly related but not identical. Each part sounds good by itself but, if you put them together, the whole is far richer and more satisfying. We're like that because our personalities weave together beautifully. When we get a house, we could call it Counterpoint. What do you think?'

Mary sleepily agreed that it would be perfect.

Luke elaborated at length on baroque counterpoint, until at last, he too fell asleep, but in the middle of the night, Mary awoke to find him seated at a small table, scribbling away on manuscript paper by the light of a lamp — presumably inspired with some new musical theme. Perhaps it was a piece of modern counterpoint! She closed her eyes again and reflected that the probable future scenario was that he would throw himself wholeheartedly into each composition and she would be left literally holding the baby. Strangely, this didn't worry her, she knew that it would always be the case that he was the creative one and she the more practical. As long as they remembered to listen to each other's tune as well as their own they would be fine. She went quickly back to sleep, bathed in a warm glow of contentment.

Chapter 25

They arrived in London on Sunday afternoon, having stopped off for lunch and shopping. As soon as Mary saw the flat, she knew that she would find it claustrophobic. The living room was dominated by a grand piano and the walls were lined with bookshelves laden with scores and sheet music, as well as numerous books. The only seating was a small two-seater sofa and two stools at a breakfast bar that divided the kitchen area from the main space. There was a river view of Canary Wharf, but the window was obscured by a large computer monitor, standing on a desk that was covered with heaps of papers and music. She looked around and wondered how this space could ever be made appealing to a prospective buyer. The guided tour revealed one bedroom with an en-suite bathroom and Luke apologised for the lack of hanging space. (The fitted wardrobes along one wall were entirely taken up by dress suits and shirts along with a modest quantity of everyday clothes.)

'I really should throw some of these suits out,' he remarked, apologetically.

Mary said that she didn't mind living out of a case and set about putting food away in the kitchen.

It was obvious that clearing this flat would take some time and she suspected that she would be very much involved in that.

Over the next few days, they settled into a routine of sorts, with Luke dashing out to rehearsals and meetings at intervals and usually coming back tired. Mary shopped, cooked meals and did a bit of her own work, as well as arranging valuations by three estate agents. On the third day, Luke asked if she would mind working out how much they could spend on a house when the flat was sold, and how much money they would need to live on. To this end he provided her with a heap of papers regarding his various sources of income and related expenses. This was time consuming and crowded out her own work, but she gladly got on with it because it was for their future and would probably never get done if it were left to Luke.

The valuations were all similar and Mary was staggered at the value of the flat. She researched the property market in Sheringham and worked out how much they could spend on a house, leaving enough to live on for at least the first year until Luke became established in his new career. She enjoyed reviving her old finance skills in order to do this but was conscious of a slight feeling of resentment at being an unpaid secretary and accountant — not to mention housekeeper. 'Better get used to it,' she told herself. 'Because no matter how much he promises to help, he'll always be too busy!'

To be fair, Luke was appreciative and usually made time to discuss her ideas. The shared meals and shared bed were lovely. Mary decided to go to the prom rehearsal and to stay in London for the concert, thinking that she may as well spend as long as she could there in order to get as far ahead as possible with the planned move. Also, she was keen to go to the Albert Hall; something that she had never done before. It meant arriving back in Cromer on the day before she returned to work, but she'd just have to cope with that.

Each time Luke went out, Mary spent some time playing the piano, so as to give herself a break from all the screen work. She found copies of Bach's *Two-Part Inventions* and Mendelssohn's *Songs without words*, and played the ones she knew, enjoying the lovely instrument. One day, Luke came home early and walked in just as she finished one of the Mendelssohn pieces.

'How much of that did you hear?' she asked, suspiciously.

'All of it. Well done — that three-against-two timing isn't easy to manage.'

Mary over-rode the compliment by accusing him of lurking in the corridor like a common spy. She said that she wouldn't have been able to play if she'd known he was there.

'That's exactly why I crept up on you! Were you planning to avoid being heard for our whole lives?'

'Yes, I was actually. It's embarrassing living with someone who can do it so much better. That was full of wrong notes and you never play any.'

'Well, that's just silly. Of course I play wrong notes and I miss a lot out. I just know which ones I can leave out without anyone noticing. Anyway, accuracy isn't the most important thing. You were right inside the music and that matters more.'

Mary had the good grace to thank him for that and went into the kitchen to check on a casserole.

Later, after they'd eaten, Luke suggested that they tried a piano duet. He thought it would be very apt if they played one at whatever gathering they had after their wedding.

Mary looked horrified at this prospect, but he found some music, brought a chair from the bedroom and carried her bodily to the piano.

She tried to rise from the chair he'd plonked her on but failed because he had his hands firmly on her shoulders.

'Just listen for a minute. It's an easy piece, you can choose which part to play and it doesn't matter if it goes wrong. I *can* distinguish between a professional orchestra rehearsal and a piano lesson!'

'Okay, I'll have a go,' Mary capitulated. 'But I need time to practise it on my own first, when you're out.'

Luke changed his tactics and sat on the piano stool alongside her chair, wrapping his arms around her and pressing his cheek to hers.

'My lovely girl, please humour me and just try a few bars. I can give you some sight-reading tips if you need them and I promise not to shout at you — unless you run away!'

Mary gave in at this point and after looking at the music, chose the top part because it looked easier and she didn't think that she could manage two base clefs.[4] Her sight-reading was not good and she needed all of his tips, but they eventually got going at a painfully slow pace. It was a Brahms waltz, so at least the timing was obvious.

'You see, I can only play the Mendelssohn because I've practised it for hours and hours. If you give me time to practice this, it will be a lot better.'

'Of course it will. Everyone needs to practise, but if we just play through this twice more, I think you'll be surprised at how quickly it improves.'

So, they continued, and it did start to sound much better. Of course, Luke could play the bass line with his eyes closed but he was remarkably patient and when they finished, Mary said that he was a good teacher; perhaps that would be something he could do if they needed money.

---

[4] A clef is a symbol indicating the pitch of music written on the five ruled lines on which music is written.

'Haven't you heard the saying, "Those who can, do; those who can't, teach?" he responded, immediately bristling at the mention of teaching.

'Yes, but I don't agree with it. Deidre had her heart set on teaching from an early age so she's doing it from choice, not because she's failed at something else. She finds it very fulfilling and she's widely admired and respected.'

'Well, I didn't mean to insult your sister but it's not my scene at all. Anyway, I won't need to teach because I intend to make a success of composing.'

Apart from the odd exchange like this, they lived together in harmony in the rather cramped space, but Luke became noticeably stressed in the two days between the last rehearsal and the concert. He was conducting the premiere of a work by a little-known composer and finding it hard going, lacking the degree of rapport with the music that he would have liked. There were also some works by Britten, which were more his cup of tea, but the thing that made him most nervous was the BBC interview that would take place shortly before the performance. He was usually tense before a major concert, anyway, and dealt with this by using certain inner processes and rituals that required privacy and time to himself. On this occasion however, Mary was thrown into the equation and he struggled to cope. The day before the prom, they ate lunch together but then Luke wanted to study scores, followed by a long walk by himself. Mary understood the need for this but asked if he could just spare half an hour to look at some figures that she had prepared. She was worried that the amount of paid work that he planned to retain would not adequately cover their living expenses and wanted to discuss some ideas for bridging the gap. This would be the last opportunity before she went home. He knew she was working hard for them both and felt that he should give her his attention for a short time, so agreed to look at what she'd done, but this was a mistake because he couldn't conceal his impatience to be getting on with his habitual concert preparation. Mary recognised tension but felt that half an hour wasn't much to ask when she'd used her down-time from Cadence to organise his finances, so she batted on, showing him her latest calculations. Then she made a grave error of judgement; she asked if playing the violin in chamber music groups in East Anglia would be a possibility for generating more income. It seemed perfectly logical to her, but Luke reacted badly to the mention of the violin. He hadn't played for years, he'd lost all interest in it, his performing days were over. She shouldn't interfere in what she didn't understand. His voice began to rise as he delivered these statements.

'Oh, I'm sorry,' said Mary. 'You spoke at length about the merits of different instruments recently, so I thought violin playing still meant something to you.'

'Well, it doesn't — and how could you bring that up immediately before a major interview and concert?' He was shouting now. 'You know how difficult I'm finding this one! Can't you just get off my back for two days?'

Mary sat in shocked silence. She'd always known that one day he would shout at her but wasn't prepared for angry accusations that revealed that she'd been getting on his nerves, or for the viciousness of his tone as he delivered the final sentence. How could he be like that after all the loving things he'd said to her recently? How could he go back on his promise to discuss everything as equal partners!' She felt as though he'd struck her physically. He was already on his feet grabbing car keys, a jacket and a large score. Then he abruptly left the flat, slamming the door behind him.

Being on the receiving end of his temper hurt Mary more than she would have believed possible. When she had witnessed it at Cadence, it was directed at other people and she had been in the role of soothing counsellor. Now, the full force of it was directed at her and it made her realise how vulnerable she was. She felt as though a deep chasm had suddenly and unexpectedly appeared in her path. It represented the relationship failing, and she knew that if she fell down it, she would never climb out again. Tearfully, she cleared away the remains of their lunch and wondered what to do for the best. She didn't want to throw away the wonderful sense of togetherness that they had enjoyed but at the same time, she didn't want to appease him because she knew he had reacted out of all proportion to her mistake. Was it even a mistake? Surely, she had the right to come up with ideas about their future. The timing for that one may not have been ideal, but she had to go back to work the day after next and it would be difficult to discuss anything after that. She dwelt on this for a long time before remembering her survival strategies for emotional emergencies. In Cromer, she would have gone to the lighthouse to think, but it was hard to find uplifting places in London, so she went for the solution that she'd used when tied to the house with Sam — a soothing bath with a few drops of lavender oil. Once in it, it was easier to relax and seek the best way forward. She asked her Higher Self for inspiration then closed her eyes and concentrated on letting go more and more each time she breathed out. Her mind began to drift, then she suddenly had a vivid picture of herself and Luke in the kitchen at Cadence. It was the time that they had spoken about managing grief and anger and she could hear her own voice.

'I was told to accept my feelings, understand them and forgive myself, then forgive the other person.'

She got out of the bath and with the towel still wrapped around her body, went to sit on the bed, where she reflected that she wasn't very good at forgiving, judging by the way she still felt about her father. However, she knew that forgiving Luke was vital. It was hard because he had hurt her so much and she was angry, but she went through the motions, anyway. Then she meditated for a few minutes before imagining them both bathed in light. Nothing dramatic happened as a result of this so she dried herself off roughly, then crawled into bed and remembered the love that they had shared there. The thought of losing it made her cry in earnest for a long time.

She slept for a little while but was woken by a message coming through on her mobile, which she grabbed in a surge of hope, only to find that it was just a reminder from her dentist. Presumably, Luke was still angry with her, otherwise he would surely have been in touch by now. At least her mind was clearer, so she made herself a drink and sat in the lounge to form a plan. She thought it best to give Luke the space that he obviously needed, but to avoid doing it in a way that would make him think that she'd gone off in a huff — or worse still, left permanently. Because the flat was so small, the only way to create space between them was for her to move out for the night, so she rang the hotel that she'd stayed at with Delia and Chris and booked a room. Then she sent a message to Luke.

I am moving to a hotel for tonight, to give you time to yourself in the flat before the concert. I'll come back tomorrow night if you want me to. M x

***

Luke drove to a park and walked around until he felt calmer. Then he sat on a bench and thought about what he'd done. He tried to understand where the sudden surge of uncontrollable anger had come from; he'd swiftly moved from mild irritation at having to take another person into account to feelings of intolerable pressure and rage. Perhaps it had built up in his subconscious. He wasn't used to anyone trying to influence his behaviour; the only person who had lived with him closely enough for that to happen was Lily, and it was many years since they'd split up. She had a weaker personality than Mary, anyway, and he suspected that he'd been able to manipulate her into doing what *he* wanted. Mary appeared timid at times but there was no doubt that she knew her own mind and she could call on a formidable bastion of inner resources to bolster herself up when she needed to. He truly wanted them to be equal partners, but it would take time to get used to that. Ultimately, he would have to take responsibility for his outburst because he'd asked Mary to do the work and she was only making suggestions. When he remembered the things he'd said, he felt ashamed and almost rang her, but then decided to let the dust settle before making contact. He must read through the score for the new work again if he was to be ready for tomorrow evening, so he drove to the nearest library with desk space and installed himself. Immersing himself in music was the one thing guaranteed to drive everything else from his head and he lost track of time, so it was early evening before he emerged. He wasn't very hungry but made himself eat at a restaurant to keep his strength up and while he was there, Mary's message came through.

He felt very guilty as he read it, realising that he should have contacted her long before this, so sent back the following.

Thank you. I know it's hard to understand but I do love you very much. So sorry I shouted at you. We will talk about what happened after the prom but please come to it as planned and then come back to the flat with me. L xxx

Okay. Good luck, was all that came back.

Luke returned to the flat and spent the night missing her.

Chapter 26

Mary had a problem the next day because she had to check out of the hotel by ten and didn't have anywhere to go before the Albert Hall in the evening. After some thought, she left her luggage in a locker at the nearest station and went to have a look around Harrods — an establishment that she'd always been curious about. The only thing she bought was a pregnancy-test kit. In view of the rift with Luke, she was reluctant to confront the fact that her period was several days late but felt that she shouldn't put it off any longer. The kit was probably the most expensive one in London, she reflected ruefully. After that she went to the Victoria and Albert Museum, stopping to buy and eat a sandwich on the way but she didn't stay in the museum for long because her feet were getting sore and she wasn't really in the mood. She saw from her map that Hyde Park was within walking distance so headed that way, passing the huge bulk of the Albert Hall en route. It was warm and sunny, so she contemplated staying in the park until it was time for the concert; she couldn't easily get back to her luggage to change and, if she had done, didn't have anywhere to freshen up so would have to go in her jeans, shirt and sandals, but she suspected that plenty of people did that for the Proms, anyway, and was past caring. She ate an ice-cream — not her usual fare but thought she might as well fit in with the other tourists — and lay down on the grass, where she instantly fell into a deep sleep. Her phone rang sometime later and it took her a while to surface well enough to answer. It was Luke.

'Hello darling. Sorry I've left it so long before speaking to you; sorry for everything. Where are you?'

She told him that she was in Hyde Park.

'Oh — that's handy. What are you doing there?'

'Being a tourist. I had to leave the hotel at ten.'

'Oh God! I should have thought of that. I've really messed up, haven't I?' he exclaimed, as he realised the full extent of his selfishness. After an awkward pause, he asked if she was anywhere near the Albert Hall.

'Just a few minutes away.'

'Is there any chance of your coming to my dressing room? I'm here early to get settled in before that blasted interview. I know we need to talk and it's a bad time for that, but I'd really like to see you.'

Mary pressed her lips together and briefly contemplated saying that he didn't deserve it but found herself agreeing instead. He told her how to access the building and where to find his room and she dusted herself down and set off across the grass.

He opened the door as soon as she knocked, saying thank goodness it was her, because several of the wrong people had bothered him since they spoke.

'I've only got twenty minutes before the interview and I'm not in a good place. Can you help?'

He did look very stressed, so she put her wounded feelings to one side and encouraged him to sit down. Bringing up another chair, she sat down opposite, with her knees close to his.

'Do you know what they'll ask you?'

He didn't, so she suggested that he talked to her generally about the works that he would be conducting — just as though they were conversing in the flat, in order to prepare his mind. This worked quite well because, although hesitant at the start, he was soon off on one of his musical monologues. At last, he paused for breath.

'That all sounds great,' said Mary. 'Just pretend you're talking to me instead of the interviewer.'

'Thank you. I know I've survived interviews before but, as you know, I'm not all that comfortable with the new piece. What if they ask me if I like it? I can't be honest because the composer will be there, as well!'

'I can see that could be awkward, but can't you do what politicians do? Talk about things that are slightly off at a tangent? How interesting the music is; how much you've enjoyed the challenge of getting to grips with something a bit different; things like that.'

Before Mary could come up with any more suggestions, the phone in the room buzzed and he had to go. She hurriedly kissed him, wished him luck and said she'd wait there until he returned. There really didn't seem to be any point in undermining him at such a crucial time just because she felt badly treated.

'I might know you'd be good with ideas for going off at a tangent!' he joked as he left.

Mary sat down again with a sigh of relief. She had no intention of letting him off the hook for the horrible way he'd spoken to her yesterday, but that could come later. At least they were back together.

Half an hour later he returned, looking much better and saying that the composer had been keen to do most of the talking. He would tell Mary about the rest later but the audience had been allowed in now so she could take her seat. She gave him a quick hug and left him to make final preparations for going on stage.

The auditorium was almost full, and Mary was pleased to have a seat with a good view, instead of a standing place. Now that she was inside the Albert Hall, she was amazed at the number of people it could accommodate. For the first time, she had a real sense of the enormity of what Luke did on a regular basis. What would happen if he messed everything up or succumbed to uncontrollable stage fright in front of all these people and all those watching the broadcast? She began to feel ashamed; of course he needed uninterrupted time in which to prepare. How could she insist on him looking at her boring spreadsheet when he needed to stay focused? She looked at her engagement ring, which now fitted perfectly, and thought that she was going to have to get *her* act together if she wanted to make a good job of being Mrs Braithwaite.

Fortunately, Luke gave no sign of his earlier nervousness and the concert went well. Mary was impressed by the performance of the new work, which was complex and required absolute concentration from conductor and players. It wasn't the kind of music that she usually enjoyed, but she was fascinated to see how efficiently and sensitively Luke handled it. The Britten pieces in the second half were more to her taste; she hadn't heard Sinfonia da Requiem before but was deeply affected by it and made a mental note to find a recording. The applause at the end of the concert was thunderous and there were many shouts and whistles as Luke took his bows then indicated the orchestra so that they, too, could receive their share of appreciation.

Returning to the dressing room afterwards, she found Luke slumped over the worktop in front of the mirror. She put a hand on his shoulder.

'It was brilliant,' she whispered. 'I'll wait over there until you're ready to move.'

After a few minutes he sat up, stretched, then arose and gathered his things together.

'Come on. The taxi should be waiting,' was all he said as he made for the door.

Mary offered to carry one of the scores, which was gratefully handed over and they were soon out of the stage door, where several people were waiting to see Luke. Mary put everything they were carrying into the taxi so that he could easily deal with autographs and shake hands with admirers, and then got in herself because she realised that she was attracting curious stares. She thought she must look incongruous in her jeans, alongside his beautifully cut velvet jacket. Many of the well-wishers were middle-aged women, no doubt attracted by his appearance and what they believed to be single status, as well as his musicianship. Mary kept her ring hidden as they had not yet made their engagement public and now did not seem to be a good time to do it. Eventually they were on their way, but it took a long time to get back to the flat because they had to go via the station where Mary had left her luggage. Luke held her hand tightly and apologised profusely for shouting at her and then leaving her to her own devices for so long.

'It was partly my fault,' she confessed. 'I didn't think! I was so pleased to find that I could still do that finance stuff that I wanted to show it off. It was unforgivable to try and do that while you were preparing for what you've just done.'

'Of course, it's forgivable, you silly thing,' he said. 'I asked you to do all that work. It was just a timing problem and we'll work that out next time we're together before a concert.' He put his arm around her but then apologised for his sweat-soaked state and tried to take it away again.

'You were quite vicious with me,' she couldn't resist saying, as she hung on to his arm. 'It hurt. Perhaps if I get anything else wrong you could tell me a bit earlier, before you explode?'

He kissed the top of her head and promised to remember that. Mary wanted to ask why the violin was such a sore point but kept quiet because she was afraid of spoiling the benign atmosphere.

Once inside the flat, Luke made for the shower and Mary got ready for bed as well as she could while waiting for the only bathroom. At last, they were both lying down.

'Sorry,' he muttered, 'but I'm exhausted. I'll probably fall asleep quickly.'

'No worries,' she said as she kissed his cheek and settled down with a hand on his chest. Their breathing fell into time and soon she was asleep herself.

At first light, Mary woke up and became aware of pressure in her bladder. She usually lasted all night without any problem so this was unusual. She had also felt a bit nauseous on and off over the last few days and, come to think of it, she felt sick now. She made a mental note to use the pregnancy test kit as soon as she got home and slipping out of bed as quietly as she could, went to the bathroom. When she got back into bed, Luke asked if they could talk. She agreed and apologised for waking him.

'You didn't. I've been awake for a while, thinking about why I explode. You see, I don't know that it's about to happen. I think I'm in control and then suddenly this... this storm of feelings comes out of nowhere and I can't stop it. I thought you'd made a reasonable request for my attention and I was coping with mild irritation at having my routine disturbed but then it suddenly all seemed unbearable.'

Mary asked what his usual pre-concert routine was.

'Well, in the first place, I'm usually alone; when I've been in a relationship before I've discouraged the other party from being in the flat with me at all, choosing instead to spend time at their place. For a couple of days before a big concert, I would move back here by myself. I wanted you to share that time with me because we both need to get used to it — and I thought I was handling it really well.'

He went on to describe some of the rituals that he had developed, reading through the score, a long walk with the music running through his head and sitting with his forehead resting on the score immediately before going on stage.

'I've never told anyone else about that one. You must think I'm crazy!

Mary smiled. 'No, I don't, because it makes sense to me. In some thought systems, the part of the brain behind the centre of the forehead is believed to influence one's powers of intuition. So, you work hard at learning the work and prepare as well as you can using the thinking, reasoning part of the brain and then you mingle that with an intuitive feeling for the music. No wonder you end up with such fantastic results. The audience loved you tonight. Are you absolutely sure you want to reduce the conducting?'

'Yes, because it gets more stressful as I get older. I have to work much harder than most to pull it off because I'm not naturally talented. I put in a great deal of time and effort to be able to handle the sort of thing you've heard tonight. That will never work well in a domestic situation and I don't want it to come between us. Also, I don't thrive on adulation as some do, and my success, if it can be called that, is because I'm popular with middle-aged women who think I look good. What they don't know is that I'm starting to lose my hair and I'm already spoken for! At least I hope I still am.'

'Of course,' Mary reassured him. 'Look, I've been thinking, too. What you do is enormously stressful. How do other conductors handle that?'

Luke said he'd never heard anyone mention having a problem.

'I bet they do *something* to prevent stress building up too much. It's probably just too private to discuss. Your rituals are probably not unusual. Anyway, now I know what you need at that time I'll simply keep out of your way. It will be easier when we have our own house.'

Mary was thinking, even as she said this, that a baby would complicate things considerably, but she wanted to be sure she was pregnant before introducing that subject. Instead, she just reminded Luke that she had an early train to catch in the morning so must get some more sleep.

Chapter 27

It was hard to get moving when the alarm went off because of the late night and interrupted sleep. On top of that, the nausea had progressed to actual vomiting, so she felt weak and light-headed. Luke was unaware of this as he was still sleeping soundly when she was sick, but he surfaced a little later as she was fumbling around trying to pack. As he was climbing out of the bed, her handbag slipped off it and landed upside down, spilling the contents all over the floor. Prominent among the heap of belongings was the brightly coloured pregnancy test packet, and Luke immediately pounced on it asking if there was something she needed to tell him.

Mary sat on the edge of the bed with a little sigh of resignation and said she was only a few days late, which might not mean anything. She was planning to do the test at home and ring him if the result was positive.

'You can't do that!' he protested. 'We have to be together to find out. Do it now!' waving the packet towards her.

Mary gave a slight laugh and said that she didn't think she could produce any urine just now, and in any case, the taxi was due soon and if she didn't get into it straight away, she'd miss her train.

Luke walked through to the kitchen and came back bearing a pint glass filled with water, which he ordered her to drink, adding that he would drive her home if she missed the train.

'I can't,' she said, weakly. 'I won't be able to keep it down.'

'You're sick as well?' he exclaimed. 'Well, that's it then. Well done!' and he joined her on the bed and smothered her in kisses. 'What's the number for the taxi? We'll cancel it because I'm definitely taking you home.'

'This is supposed to be your time for preparing for the next big thing,' she argued.

He thought for a moment, then said he could take the music for the Monday rehearsal with him, go through it at hers, then drive back early the following morning.

She hesitated and he asked her again for the taxi number, at the same time thrusting the glass of water into her hand. She took a tentative sip and handed him her phone with the relevant contact displayed.

While he made the call, she slipped into the kitchen and found some dry biscuits to nibble on, remembering that they'd helped to settle her stomach when she was expecting Sam. A little later she was able to drink and a little later still, the pregnancy test was done. It was positive.

Luke was ecstatic and immediately began to talk about ways to incorporate the baby into their plans.

'Steady on!' said Mary. 'A lot of pregnancies don't progress beyond the early stages, especially for older women.'

'But you're in excellent health. You'll be fine, I just know it,' he replied, optimistically.

Mary gave up and made final preparations to leave the flat. Luke's elevated mood accompanied them all the way out of London and down the M11, so she risked asking him why he was so sensitive about the violin. Luke didn't know. He hadn't thought about it for years. His violin, which was valuable, was kept in a security vault.

'Did you stop because it was something you associated with Lily?' she asked.

Luke winced at this invasion of his past personal life but knew that he should answer her questions. She was to be his wife and they should share everything, so he said that he'd carried on playing for about two years after breaking up with Lily. He didn't think there was a connection. Mary let the matter drop but Luke continued to think about it as he drove. The mention of violin playing had definitely contributed to the stress levels that led to him losing his temper.

'I think that the breakup might have influenced the way I felt about the violin,' he said, carefully. 'I know I didn't enjoy those two years of going freelance before I stopped completely. It's possible that I've continued to blot the idea of playing out of my mind even though I no longer feel anything for Lily.'

Mary was pleased that he was giving the matter more thought and even more pleased that he no longer had feelings for Lily. She didn't know what to say, so just snuggled up against him to signify gratitude. A few more miles went by.

'I suppose I could get it out of the vault,' Luke said, 'and see if I can still play well enough to think about joining an East Anglian chamber group.'

Mary kept her head down so that he couldn't see her self-satisfied smile.

A little later, Luke suggested going to Sheringham before Cromer, to see if Delia had reached a decision about equity release. It would reduce their time alone together but it did make sense, so Mary agreed and alerted Chris to their flying visit. Mindful of how busy she'd be before changeover, Mary offered to make the sandwich that they would need when they arrived. Then she fell asleep and didn't wake up until they were pulling into the drive at Cadence.

'Sorry about this,' she said to Chris, giving her a quick hug. 'If there's anything you don't get done, I'll sort it tomorrow.'

'Is there any chance of letting me know if I have a future here?' asked Chris, and Luke replied that they hoped to pin Delia down about that and apologised for keeping her up in the air. Mary felt bad about the uncertainty they'd left her in; she'd been too preoccupied with sorting out Luke's finances to give her much thought.

As efficient as ever, Chris had already made sandwiches and they ate with Delia, who was delighted to see them. When lunch was over, Luke asked if she had decided about equity release.

'Oh — I thought you were doing that already,' she replied. Chris was in the room and she, Mary and Luke exchanged surprised glances.

'Er — I was just checking that it was still all right. I wanted to give you time to make sure it was what you wanted,' said Luke, thinking on his feet and deciding it was best not to mention the care-home option, as his mother had clearly forgotten it. 'I'll sort it out as soon as I can.' Delia sniffed and said perhaps it would be better if Mary did it.

'She doesn't have Power of Attorney but I'm sure we can manage it together.'

'Yes, yes,' said Delia, wearily. 'Will you take me for my rest now, Chris?'

Luke confirmed that Chris's job was safe when she came back after settling Delia but did not mention complications that would be caused by Mary's pregnancy, because it was at such an early stage.

They took their leave and spent the rest of the day working; Luke preparing for his rehearsal and complaining about Mary's out-of-tune piano, and Mary washing and repacking clothes in readiness for her next stint at Cadence.

When they were in bed, they cautiously made love — conscious of the precious new life inside Mary —

then exchanged sentiments about how much they'd miss each other in the forthcoming month. Mary was to search the internet for a suitable house while she was at work, then arrange viewings in her first week back at home. Luke would join her in the second week, when he had a few days free and they would look at shortlisted properties together. He would have to do all the legal things associated with selling his flat and arranging his mother's equity release. He hated that sort of thing but would just have to bite the bullet in order to make the desired life-changes. He still had a fair amount of musical work scheduled, so Mary suspected that he would enlist her help when they finally got back together.

'And when can we have our wedding?' Luke asked, once these practical matters were out of the way.

Mary hesitated. 'I thought it would be best to wait until the baby was born before planning that,' she eventually answered. 'There's a lot involved in arranging a wedding, and we already have plenty to do.' (Mary Mouse had reappeared, saying that they also had to be sure Luke's temper was not going to cause any more problems.)

'Do you want the full works then? Church, lots of guests and a big reception?' Luke sounded alarmed at this prospect.

'No — absolutely not,' she said quickly. 'Neither of us are in touch with many relatives and because of the strange lives we've lived, we don't have many friends either. I'd only want Deidre's family and my dad and Kathleen to be there. Perhaps Fran from the choir.'

'And I only want Mum and Chris — and Steve, because I'd have to have a best man, but I would like it to be in church — Sheringham, ideally — then Matthew could play the organ. So, what's to stop us doing it now, or as soon as we can get a date at the church?' As Mary didn't answer immediately, he pressed on. 'And Mum will want it to be instant when we tell her you're pregnant. She's very old fashioned about babies appearing out of wedlock!'

Mary was in a quandary. She didn't want to be rushed by her future mother-in-law and certainly didn't want to disappoint Luke, but there was still that nagging voice in the back of her mind.

Be very sure before you take this final step. Lots of people live together for ages before marriage. Why can't you?

'Please tell me you're not still having doubts!' Luke burst out after a lengthy pause.

Another voice in Mary's head said, very clearly, *Tell him about Mary Mouse.* Was it her mother again?

'I'm not, but I need to tell you something.' He sighed with impatience, so she quickly said, 'I know it might seem like prevarication, but it's important.'

'Okay, I'm listening.'

'Do you remember my telling you that my father annoyed me with the nickname Mary Mouse? Well, I've had trouble with that side of my personality for years. It waits until everything is going well and then interrupts with niggling doubts, stopping me from doing what I really want to do.' She told him about hearing and seeing a cartoon representation of the Mouse, just before she accepted his proposal, and about finding her mother's book. 'Often, Beryl the Peril — my reckless side — jumps in and I find myself saying or doing the opposite to whatever Mary Mouse wants, as a reaction I suppose. Sometimes they argue a lot before I can move forwards. After I found Mum's book, I thought I'd nailed them both and transformed them into Wisdom and Discernment, but I'm afraid the Mouse got back in when you said you wanted our wedding to be soon.'

'What do you think was the reason behind that?' he wanted to know.

'She wants us to live together for at least a year, to be sure you won't get fed up with me and keep losing your temper because you feel bored and restricted, but Beryl wants us to get married right away.'

'I like Beryl best,' he interjected, but Mary ignored the comment and pressed on.

'Then, when you asked me if I was still having doubts, I heard a voice — an actual voice — as if it were coming from a radio, saying that I should tell you about Mary Mouse.' He was silent for a long time and she added in a small voice, 'I suppose you think I'm absolutely crazy.'

'No, it isn't that,' replied Luke at last. 'What I was actually thinking was that I thoroughly messed things up by shouting at you before the Prom. Was Mary Mouse a problem before that? I mean, during the time we've been together.'

Mary pondered. 'I don't think I've heard from her between accepting your proposal and now.'

'So it is my fault that she has come back,' stated Luke. 'I'm not worried about your voices and visions; we've talked about those before and I just think they're your way of expressing inner conflict.' He turned on to his side so that he could look at her directly. 'I *am* worried about the damage I've done so to be perfectly clear, when I exploded at you before the Prom, it wasn't because of anything you'd done — it all came from inside me. Years of stress and anxiety about conducting coming to a head — and I suppose the violin hang-up also played a part. I'm truly sorry that you bore the brunt of it. Can you forgive me so that we can put it behind us?'

'I already have done, and I still think I was equally to blame so you have to forgive me as well. As for Mary Mouse, I think she's just an old anxiety habit resurfacing. I thought I'd dealt with her, but these things tend to get stuck in the brain. Anyway, I'm pleased I told you because I want you to know everything about me. Now you know how insecure I really am.'

'It's easy to forgive you, my darling, because your sins are such little ones. We're all insecure when you get right down to it. Whatever you do, you'll still be my angel,' he said, kissing her. 'Now we're as close as close can be. So, shall we ring the vicar tomorrow?'

'Yes,' she said, decisively. The difficult work of understanding each other was now well under way.

EPILOGUE

Christmas Eve 2020

Luke is pacing the upstairs rooms of Counterpoint with his nine-month-old daughter, Melody, in his arms. She is distraught, missing her mother who is desperately ill in hospital with Coronavirus, and Luke knows that the baby will fall asleep only when she is exhausted. He is exhausted, too, but there is no one to help so he must keep going. This is more stressful and tiring than the most intense period of conducting work that he can remember but giving up is out of the question, so he continues to pace, softly humming every soothing tune that he can think of.

Everywhere he looks, there are signs of Mary's presence, the retro décor, the curtains she'd laboured over, the transfers on Melody's bedroom walls. He wants her to return to a house that is as well cared for as when she was taken away in the ambulance, struggling to breathe, even with the oxygen mask on her face, but he can't tidy away the rising tide of clutter because when he isn't snatching sleep, he is soothing Melody. He has to let her scream while he prepares her meals and then she won't eat much. How did Mary cope with her? Of course, Melody had been much calmer then, because she had both parents and a steady routine that Mary sustained, even when he was too immersed in work to help.

At least their financial future is looking rosier. The BBC is using Requiem of Life as background music for a series about dwindling species and it has become very popular, generating much-needed income. A month ago, they also commissioned him to write music suitable for a series on climate change, but he had to abandon it when Mary became ill. Perhaps they have found another composer by now. He hasn't touched the piano or the violin for weeks and feels disorientated because the music that normally rules his life is gone. Concerts no longer take place because of the infection risk, so opportunities to conduct or perform in chamber groups have vanished.

Thankfully, the garden doesn't need attention at this time of year, it would be awful to see it revert to the tangled jungle that they'd taken over. The house is warm because of the ground source heat pump that Tom helped him to install, and free of draughts thanks to the Victorian-style double-glazed replacement windows that the planning department authorised. Mary was thrilled that they had a home of their own to work on and spent her down-time from Cadence organising belongings and decorating until she grew so big that Luke, worried that she might fall, locked the steps and ladders away so she had to stop. He painted all the ceilings and other high places himself while she was out.

When Mary was seven months pregnant, a replacement carer had been found for Delia and after that, Mary was free to prepare the nursery and go a long way towards turning what had been a very shabby, neglected house into a home. Mercifully, both Chris and the new carer (heavily clad in protective equipment and thoroughly sanitised) continued to work for Delia, keeping her safe throughout the difficult first year of the pandemic. Luke is pleased that his mother has remained free of the horrible disease but can't help wondering why she has been spared while Mary — robust, healthy Mary is lying in hospital at death's door. He was the first to go down with the virus, closely followed by Melody. Neither was seriously affected, and Mary cheerfully looked after them both, but became ill herself just as Luke was getting better. Initially, she followed the same pattern, seeming to recover after a week, but then, one night, he woke up to find her clutching at him, desperate to get enough air into her lungs, and by the following morning she was in hospital. On arrival they put her into an induced coma, and on to a ventilator. He hasn't been allowed to see her since.

At last, Melody cries herself to sleep on his shoulder and he gently lowers her into her cot, hardly daring to breathe in case she senses the change of location and starts all over again. It is ten p.m. and he needs to sleep, himself, but has to wash his daughter's bottles and dishes, so they'll be ready to use when she wakes up again. There is just one more thing to do before turning in. He sits at the kitchen table with his laptop and looks up recordings of *The Owl and the Pussy Cat*. Mary used to sing it at Melody's bedtime when she thought he was out of earshot, and he hopes that it might help his little daughter if he does the same. He finds a similar version, and his acute musical ear helps him to learn it quickly.

'Right, little Miss,' he thinks. 'We'll see what that does for you tomorrow!'

Christmas Morning

Melody wakes at five thirty on Christmas morning — long before first light. Luke sleepily changes her nappy and gives her some milk. At least she is taking a bottle now. Melody was on solids, supplemented by breastmilk when Mary went into hospital, and Luke relied heavily on feeding advice given over the phone by the health visitor. He is very grateful to that lady.

Melody takes only a few mouthfuls of milk on this occasion and then her little body arches as she takes a deep breath in preparation for another howling session, but Luke launches into *The Owl and the Pussy Cat* and Melody quickly peters out in astonishment on registering her favourite song being delivered in her father's rich baritone voice. He can't remember all the words but has the tune off pat and it works like magic, sending her back to sleep within five minutes. Luke puts her back into her cot and creeps back into bed, luxuriating in a further two hours of blissful sleep.

Boxing Day

Today is the day Mary is being brought out of the coma and Luke has been told to ring at four p.m., to see how she is. Well before that, he puts Melody into her pram and walks around an area of good mobile phone reception until the appointed time. He often walks in the afternoon as it sometimes results in his child taking a nap and fortunately it works on this occasion. He finds a bench to sit on because he is shaking as he makes the call — life without Mary doesn't bear thinking about. He is on hold for an age before a doctor tells him that she has regained consciousness and appears to be responding well. A tide of relief sweeps over him, bringing him close to tears as he asks when he can speak to her.

'Not until tomorrow,' he is informed. 'If you ring at the same time, we'll see what we can do.'

Luke babbles his appreciation of all their efforts and his knees continue to feel weak all the way home.

Two weeks later

Mary is in a wheelchair waiting for Luke to arrive at the pickup point outside the hospital. He won't be able to come in because Melody will be with him. Mary has been tested to ensure that she is now virus-free, and a healthcare assistant will wheel her to the car when they arrive.

She and Luke have had several phone conversations when Melody was asleep, so she knows a little about how they've coped without her. Now she can't wait to see them but is worried about two things: will Melody remember her, and will Luke be shocked — or even repelled — when he sees her emaciated body, pasty face and short, unevenly cut hair (it was hacked off when she was in intensive care). She must remember to smile — that always helps. She is very weak, and he will have to look after her as well as Melody, to begin with. Poor Luke, he did promise to stick by her "in sickness and in health" but this must be more than he'd bargained for.

Her mobile pings with a message saying that the car is in position, so with butterflies in her stomach, Mary asks the assistant to take her out. If Luke *is* shocked by her appearance, he makes a good job of disguising it, but he does look a bit taken aback when he is given a walking frame to place in the boot. Mary will need that to get from the bed to the bathroom. He helps her into the car, and she twists round to say hello to Melody who just stares back at her, wide-eyed. Her father is the only person she's seen for the last few weeks and she wonders who this wild-looking person is.

Once they're out of the hospital precincts, Luke puts a hand on her bony knee and asks how it feels to be going home. Mary just bursts into tears because when she first regained consciousness, she thought she would never live to see this day. So much for smiling. She tries to explain, and he pulls into a layby and gives her a hug, as much as the handbrake will allow. Melody doesn't like that and begins to wail so, groaning, Luke releases Mary and sets off again — singing *The Owl and the Pussy Cat*, which has the effect of turning Mary's tears to laughter.

'How did you know she likes that?' she asks.

'I heard you singing it. When she wouldn't settle for me, I looked it up, sang it myself, and it worked like magic.'

'Well good — because I don't think I can sing any longer!'

'You'll get your voice back. You'll get everything back,' he replies, optimistically.

'You do know that it could take a long time?' she asks.

He turns towards her and nods, adding soberly, 'I'm just very grateful to get you back.'

Mary lapses into a light doze after this and the next thing she knows, they are home. Luke straps Melody into a low baby chair in the kitchen, then carries Mary up to bed.

'Can't she just sit with her toys, surrounded by cushions?' asks Mary, because Melody instantly begins to protest loudly, drumming her heels on the footrest.

Luke explains that she can now shuffle around the room and get into every type of danger imaginable if he takes his eyes off her. Mary realises that a lot has changed while she's been absent.

She spends the rest of the day lying in bed, wishing she could help as Luke dashes between her and Melody. She can hear by the tone of his voice and Melody's babyish responses that they have bonded well and that's one good thing to come out of her illness. Before that she was the primary carer, with Luke frequently offering help but always looking to her for advice. Now he is confident and competent; so much so that she is redundant!

When he finally joins her in bed, she tells him how much she admires the way he's coping with childcare, and he tells her that he made a pig's ear of everything until he discovered *The Owl and the Pussy Cat*. After that, Melody decided that he was useful after all and things steadily improved. He is worried about losing the climate change music though, and says he must ring the BBC tomorrow to find out if they'll give him more time.

By the end of the first week, Mary is feeling a bit better and can make it to the bathroom without using the walking frame. Soon afterwards, she finds she can get downstairs on her bottom and back up on her hands and knees. It makes a huge difference as she can take some of the pressure off Luke by helping with light household tasks and playing with Melody, who has now remembered she has two parents. She is saying 'Dada' very clearly now and Mary accuses Luke of teaching her his name before 'Mama'.

'All children learn to say D before M,' he objects. 'I've looked it up.'

'That's as may be, but she's holding out her arms for you to pick her up when she says it, so she knows it means you!' counters Mary.

Luke is trying not to smile but it's obvious that he is delighted because Melody has clearly worked out that he's her best bet for a cuddle and she appears to like him very much.

He is given another month in which to complete the commissioned background music, so has to work until late at night and he and Mary don't get much time alone together, but she doesn't mind. While he is composing, she works on her magazine articles, which were abandoned in the rush to get Counterpoint habitable before Melody arrived and shelved yet again when she was demand-feeding. She wonders if she has any right to share her ideas on eating for health, as hers has just failed dramatically, but remembers that the virus causing the pandemic strikes down people of all ages and health status. Perhaps she could write about eating to strengthen the immune system and share easy recipes for families like theirs, under time pressure to earn money and also having to care for someone. The recipes she is now planning (to replace the endless ready-made soup and oven chips that Luke serves) will fit the bill.

So, she and Luke are sharing the chores and childcare by day and both are being creative in the evenings. It feels balanced and harmonious.

By the end of the next week, Chris is on duty and Mary is Facetiming her every day so that she can hand Delia her mobile and let her see Melody. The social restrictions mean that households cannot mix, so she hasn't seen her granddaughter for months. In the period between lockdowns, they'd met out of doors, but the carers don't risk taking Delia beyond her own garden any more.

Mary has seen her sister and the children only once since the pandemic began and that was also out of doors. Her father and Kathleen are stuck in their French home because of travel restrictions and are worried about the safety of their Suffolk cottage. Tom drove down there to check on it twice but then the latest lockdown started, and now they are all abiding by the "Stay at Home" rules.

One day, Mary tells Luke that she thinks she's fit enough to join him and Melody on one of their afternoon walks. Luke's dream of living near Beeston Bump has been realised and he often climbs to the top with Melody on his back, but that is definitely too much for Mary so they walk a little way along the sea front. She quickly tires but is proud to manage it at all and goes a little further each time they go out. She can now climb the stairs properly.

At the end of the third week, Mary finds that she can lift Melody by herself and after that there is no looking back. She realises that perhaps her efforts to build good health were useful after all. Many virus victims are dying or suffering long-term severe debilitation, but she is getting stronger every day. She does tire more easily than she used to, and her breath control isn't very good when she tries to sing but these seem to be small prices to pay for getting her life back.

Late January 2021

Luke is relieved that Mary is taking on more domestic work because it now looks as though he will meet the new deadline for the climate-change music. He can sense her quietly supportive presence in the background while he's composing. He knows that she meditates before settling down to sleep and is convinced that this helps him to be creative and gives him the energy to work late into the night — but despite all that, he feels their relationship has changed. They spend many hours sharing chores and childcare when Melody is awake but whenever she sleeps, he retires to the lounge (which doubles as the music room) and Mary works on her nutrition articles. When he gets to bed at night, all he sees is his wife's hair above the duvet. When he wakes in the morning, she is already up. He wants them to have time together without Melody, but they can't ask anyone else to look after her because of the social restrictions. The only way for him to achieve what he wants is to sacrifice some composition time, so one evening he works for about two hours after Melody has settled and then goes to find Mary.

She has already gone to the bedroom and he finds her sitting cross-legged on her pillow in meditation. She looks serene and beautiful in her simple nightgown. Her hair has improved because she coloured it herself and, as all the hairdressers were closed, commandeered Luke to trim it to an even length. (It wasn't perfect and they joked about preferring the asymmetric look.) The frail and bony creature who left hospital is still thin but she looks healthy again.

Of course, Mary detects movement and breathes more deeply in order to end the meditation and snuggle down beside him.

'Hello stranger,' she murmurs. 'Don't tell me you've finished already!'

'No, but the end is in sight. I just wanted us to have some time awake and alone together.'

'I have been missing you! I've seen plenty of Daddy recently but nothing of my husband.' Then quickly, in case that makes him feel guilty, Mary adds, 'But I know you're doing it for all of us.'

Hopefully, Luke moves in closer and asks if she feels up to making love yet.

Mary says she thought he'd never ask and proceeds to touch him in a way that he's missed more than he realised. Their sex life has suffered enormously; firstly because of pregnancy and frantic house renovations, then because of childbirth, sleepless nights and demand-feeding, then because of illness. Later, when they are both relaxed and content, Luke tells Mary about a telephone conversation he's had with a BBC executive, while she was bathing Melody:

'He wanted to know if I would like to rehearse the orchestra that will be performing the music and then conduct it at the recording session. I told him that I couldn't possibly go backwards and forwards between here and London, where the infection rate is high and that new deadly variant is spreading like wildfire. He understood of course. Said he also had a family, so they're finding someone who lives in London to do it.'

Mary is silent. She knows that it has always been his dream to conduct his own work and would love to say, 'Go anyway, we'll be fine,' but there is no denying that it would be risky. Some people are getting the virus twice. Children are usually all right but what if she or Luke died in a second bout? Should they risk Melody losing a parent? It does make sense to avoid travelling until they've all been vaccinated.

'Mary? Do you think I said the right thing?' he prompts.

Mary sighs. 'Yes — but I feel awful. Because of Melody and me, you've had to turn down what you always wanted. You'll hate someone else interpreting something you've just composed!'

'The last bit's certainly true but I'll survive, whereas I wouldn't survive losing you. You should have seen the state I was in when I thought you might not pull through! It's a no-brainer as far as I'm concerned, I won't do it. Anyway, when this emergency dies down, I think there'll be other, better opportunities than conducting a socially distanced orchestra in which the players are so far apart there isn't much hope of cohesiveness.'

'Requiem of Life,' stated Mary. 'One day people will want you to conduct live performances of that because it's become so popular. Only I don't think I can sing the whale song any more.'

'Your voice will probably come back if you practise breathing exercises and vocal warm-ups every day,' he encouraged. 'I'll help you.'

'On no! I know what your singing lessons are like! Seriously though — I have something to tell *you*. I checked my emails while you were working and one of my magazine articles has been accepted. They're talking about me writing a whole series. I'll be able to make a modest contribution to the family purse.'

'Oh, well done! That means we both have fulfilling paid work outside the family sphere. We're equally strong in our own right but even stronger when we join together and support each other.'

Mary agrees. 'And one more thing, I realised today that I haven't heard from Mary Mouse or Beryl the Peril for ages now. They must be living in harmony at long last and that's because of you. After years of lurching between over cautiousness and recklessness, I found a middle way when we married.'

Luke was gratified. 'That's good to hear — and speaking of problems resolved, I haven't thrown a temper tantrum since that one before the Prom.'

'Do you know what stopped them?' asks Mary, deciding to overlook the flakes of fallen paint that she keeps finding near the music room door, the result of an occasional slam. At least his outbursts are now only about venting feelings of frustration rather than serious anger.

Luke thinks about this. 'I think it's a combination; partly it's being a parent. I don't want to teach Melody to respond to stress by shouting and throwing things, and I realised when I was looking after her by myself that it would make her distress worse if I lost my temper. But it's also that I feel that life is more natural — more balanced. Even though the performing side of music has been taken away, I live with a beautiful person in a beautiful place and I'm living out my values.'

He can always make Mary melt with statements like that and she kisses him enthusiastically. 'I feel that, too — and I love being part of a team. Thank goodness I met you and thank goodness you persisted in chasing me.'

'Chasing you? I've never chased a woman in my life! I wooed you, to coin an old-fashioned phrase.'

They curl up together and Luke remarks that they are now living in counterpoint. They have a house of that name and a relationship to match. Melody seems happy now so perhaps they can even claim three-part counterpoint. Mary considers this.

'We've had our bumpy moments and there will probably be more to come — especially when Melody is a teenager. But overall, I think you're right.'

They settle down to sleep, happy in the knowledge that they have survived a storm and made their relationship better and more resilient in the process. They can accommodate each other, and their child, without resentment or struggling for dominance. They are truly living in Counterpoint.